The terrorist was candy

Bolan had the Desert Eagle out and cocked before Nidal reached him. At that range, one shot from the .44 Magnum was all that was needed.

The terrorist catapulted to the wall, then slid to the floor. He tipped over, his eyes locked wide, his waste of a life ended at long last.

Bolan scooted to the priest. The man had stopped twitching and a check of his pulse confirmed why. Pulling the body inside, Bolan closed the door so he would not be disturbed. A distraction might prove fatal, not only for himself, but for many thousands besides. His next job was every bit as dangerous as tangling with Nidal had been.

He had to disarm the nuke without it going up in his face.

DON PENDLETON's
MACK BOLAN.
THERMAL STRIKE

A GOLD EAGLE BOOK FROM
WORLDWIDE.

TORONTO • NEW YORK • LONDON
AMSTERDAM • PARIS • SYDNEY • HAMBURG
STOCKHOLM • ATHENS • TOKYO • MILAN
MADRID • WARSAW • BUDAPEST • AUCKLAND

First edition December 1996

ISBN 0-373-61451-9

Special thanks and acknowledgment to
David Robbins for his contribution to this work.

THERMAL STRIKE

He that will not apply new remedies must expect new evils; for time is the greatest innovator.

—Francis Bacon
1561-1626

There can be no compromise with evil. It will always need to consume more and more. The only way to meet it is head-on, and the only innovation I bring to the fight is that kind of uncompromise.

—Mack Bolan

CHAPTER ONE

It should have been a routine training exercise, not a killing ground.

An old warhorse Hercules C-130 cargo plane flew smoothly through the night. Retrofitted with a full array of instrument flight rules avionics and specialized equipment, the aircraft was primarily used to make low-level insertions.

The two three-man teams were busy chuting up and rigging their heavily padded backpacks for the jump they were about to make.

An inspection officer was also aboard. His job was to jump with them, monitor how well they performed and file a report the next day with the general who headed their unique unit.

The seven men were set to go as the transport plane swooped in over a remote corner of the Special Warfare Center at Spartanburg, South Carolina. There, Special Forces, Delta Force and other elite units routinely trained in counterinsurgency, psychological and unconventional warfare courses.

The light over the bay door changed from red to green—the signal from the pilot that they were over the drop site. At a word from the inspection officer, the two teams lined up.

Sergeant Daniel Anderson was third in line. He hid the worry that churned his stomach as he stepped to the edge, then leaped. For five seconds it was like being in a runaway elevator, then his parachute opened. Studying the landmarks below, he steered it toward the insertion point.

Anderson noted the positions of the other chutes. The first team was descending right on target. He didn't know whether the inspection officer would land with SADM-1, as his team was designated, or with SADM-2. It added to his worry. He had a limited amount of time to do what he had to. If he was late, the two people he loved most in the world would pay with their lives.

A knoll covered with brush loomed below. Anderson came down smoothly, rolled to cushion the impact, then got up. In moments he'd shucked the parachute, uncased his M-16, locked the magazine and chambered a round. That was expected of him.

But Anderson's next act wasn't part of the exercise. Taking off the special backpack he wore, he opened a side flap and slid his hand inside. Nestled in a corner, snug against the devastating device few men but him could operate, was a nonmilitary issue Ruger MKII fitted with a Ceiner sound suppressor.

The sergeant took out the pistol and slipped it under his fatigue jacket. He'd barely removed his hand when combat boots sounded on the turf behind him and Captain Wiocek spoke.

"There you are. What the hell is keeping you? And why is your pack off?"

Anderson kept his voice matter-of-fact, saying, "It came loose, sir. I thought one of the straps had busted."

The officer moved to the crest and surveyed the wooded countryside. "All right. Let's get moving. We're under the gun, remember?"

"Don't I know it." Anderson forced a grin as he shrugged into the pack. It never ceased to amaze him that a device capable of killing so many should be so light.

"Clements had better not be late," Wiocek said as they made their way toward the rendezvous point. "If he screws this up, I swear I'll make him do push-ups until his arms fall off."

Anderson didn't reply. Everyone knew Wiocek was a stickler for efficiency. This night, in particular, had to go by the book, or the captain would throw a fit.

Fortunately Corporal Clements was right where he was supposed to be. Without saying a word, he fell into step behind them. He was the spare wheel; while the captain and Anderson assembled the device, he would guard their backs.

The sergeant constantly scoured the area. The inspection officer was out there somewhere, either watching them or spying on SADM-2. It would help immensely if he could pinpoint the IO's location before he committed himself.

The exercise called for their team to run four miles across some of the most rugged terrain east of the Rockies. After they had almost covered the distance, which included navigating a thick forest, Wiocek consulted a compass and the stars. He veered to the southwest, skirting a patch of briars. "We're nearly there, men," he said excitedly.

Once, Anderson would've felt the same. Before his nightmare began, he'd taken great pride in his work. He would've regarded this Pentagon-ordered inspection of their training procedures as a challenge, and he would've celebrated when they passed with flying colors, as SADM-1 did every time.

A minute later the team came to a small clearing on the bank of a creek. Wiocek motioned, and Clements promptly hustled to a willow a dozen yards away and climbed it. The officer sank to one knee to remove his backpack. "What are you waiting for, Sergeant?" he asked impatiently. "Christmas?"

Anderson started. He'd been lost in thought, reviewing his escape route when he should've been focused on the job at hand. Squatting, he took off his backpack and set it next to Wiocek's. As the officer bent to open his pack, Anderson reached under his jacket, palmed the Ruger, pressed the muzzle against Wiocek's temple and stroked the trigger.

The slug cored the captain's brain. He stiffened, tried to rise, then slumped to the ground, the backpacks cushioning him.

Anderson was sweating, and the blood pounded in his veins. Licking his dry lips, he stood.

The shot had been as quiet as a whisper. Yet he couldn't help fearing that Clements would cut him down before he took a step, or that the IO would barrel out of the brush and take him into custody.

Nothing happened, though. The woods remained quiet under the stars.

Clements was perched on a low limb, gazing in the other direction. He didn't even notice Anderson's approach.

"Ted?" the noncom called softly, trying not to think of the times they'd shared before he'd gotten married.

"What is it?" the corporal responded, twisting to see him.

"I'm sorry."

Clements blinked. "What for?"

"This," the sergeant said, and shot his friend through the head. Clements fell like a stone, thudding to the earth. Anderson stared at the hole in the middle of his friend's forehead for a moment. "I'm so sorry," he repeated.

Off in the forest, a twig snapped, reminding Anderson that the IO was still out there, and that his task was only half done.

Moving swiftly, he tucked the Ruger under his jacket again, hoisted his backpack onto his shoulders, slung Wiocek's backpack over his left arm and headed toward the northeast at a brisk jog. He had only five minutes to cover the better part of a mile. Normally that wouldn't pose a problem. The members of the SADM unit could run rings around a typical grunt. But this time he was lugging two thirty-pound backpacks over some of the most rugged terrain anywhere.

He tried not to dwell on the consequences should he fail. No matter what, he wouldn't let his wife and son die. They were more important to him than life itself—his, and everyone else's. "I won't let you down, Azadeh," he vowed aloud.

Appalled by his lapse in caution, Anderson scoured the vegetation. The IO was nowhere to be seen. He prayed the man was with SADM-2. If the inspection officer realized what was going down and sounded the alarm, Azadeh and little Thomas would end up dead and Anderson would spend the rest of his days rotting in prison, branded a traitor to his country. If not the entire human race.

Pulling a lensatic compass from a pocket, Anderson double-checked his bearings on the fly. He raised the eyepiece and aligned the slit in it with the slit in the cover, then both with a distant hill, his destination. The azimuth was correctly at sixty degrees.

Anderson paced himself. He was careful to avoid ruts and other obstacles, but after covering half a mile, he came to a large log. He elected to scramble up and over it, rather than go around. Just as he reached the top, the backpack he'd slung over his arm slipped off.

Frantically, he lunged for it, and his hand caught one of the straps. The pack thumped against the log, and he prayed that the heavy padding had protected both parts of the bomb.

For a moment, Anderson's resolve weakened. He told himself that he shouldn't have given in, that he should've gone to his superiors at the outset.

Before SADM, Anderson had been on SEAL Team Six—the best of the best. No tougher guys anywhere. Yet the moment the lives of his loved ones had been put on the line, he'd caved in, and agreed to do whatever the enemies of his country wanted.

Anderson shook himself. There was no time for regret. He'd made the only choice he could and he'd have to live with it.

Rising, he slung on the second pack once more and moved on. He probed under his fatigue jacket to ensure the Ruger was still there. If he dropped it, he'd lose the element of stealth so crucial to the success of the Golden Jihad's plan.

Lights were visible far to the south. That would be the Special Warfare Center's main compound, Anderson knew. There were bound to be dozens of Special Forces soldiers there, as well as military police. To avert the catastrophes to come, all he had to do was turn around and alert them. But he couldn't bring himself to do it.

Shutting his thoughts to everything except the hill in front of him, he forged on. He had maybe three hundred yards to go when he saw a lanky figure coming up on him. He drew up short, his hand darting toward his pistol.

It was the IO, Major Bullock, carrying a clipboard. He reacted with surprise at seeing the noncom. "Sergeant Anderson?" he said. "Is that you?"

"Yes, sir," Anderson answered.

"What's going on?" Bullock demanded, drawing closer. "Don't tell me that your team assembled its unit so fast, you had enough time to get way over here? SADM-2 just got their little beauty put together. They were going through the arming and disarming sequence when I left them."

"No, sir," Anderson replied. He had his part down pat. "It's the captain. I'm afraid he missed the LZ and is caught up in a tree. I think his leg's broken, sir."

"Damn!" Bullock swore. "General Wilson wanted to impress the Pentagon brass with a top efficiency rating." The major lowered a hand to the radio clipped to his belt. "I'll put in a call and get a chopper out here." His eyes narrowed. "Wait a minute. What are you doing with both packs? Don't you know that's against protocol?"

"Most definitely, sir," Anderson said, then shot him. In his haste he aimed at the man's chest instead of his head.

Bullock staggered but didn't go down. He turned, opening his mouth to yell a warning.

Anderson put two slugs into the officer's back. Bullock collapsed onto his knees and knelt there, swaying, blood dribbling from the corner of his mouth and his nose. He looked up at Anderson.

"I wish I had the time to explain, sir, but I don't."

The sergeant touched the suppressor to the major's temple. A single round and the job was done. Three down, three to go.

He still had five rounds in the Ruger's magazine, but he knew that he had to account for a margin of error. Popping it out, he replaced the spent rounds.

Starlight bathed the hill. As Anderson recalled, SADM-2 was supposed to assemble their unit at the top of it. He climbed slowly, deliberately making noise so their spare wheel would hear him coming. Private Thompson was notorious for having an itchy trigger finger.

The precaution paid off. A voice challenged him just shy of the crest. "Halt! Identify yourself immediately!"

"It's Sergeant Anderson, Private. Captain Wiocek sent me with a message for your captain."

Thompson materialized out of the vegetation. He'd stuck leaves and twigs into the mesh covering his helmet as added camouflage. "Come right ahead, Sarge."

A dozen yards beyond, Captain Stanford and Staff Sergeant Baker were huddled beside their unit. Both men looked up at Anderson's approach.

"Anderson?" Stanford said. "What in blazes are you doing here?"

"Just this, sir," the noncom replied, and killed Thompson with a round to the heart. The captain and Baker went for their side arms, but their attacker had enough of an edge to drop them both before they could unlimber their hardware.

It took less than two minutes for Anderson to take the device from his backpack, separate it into its two primary components and place them in the backpacks belonging to the SADM-2 team.

It took him almost twenty minutes to carry the four packs to the northwest perimeter, and he was exhausted by the time he got there. The Golden Jihad had already rigged a bypass on the electrified outer fence and cut through it and the inner fence. Silently four swarthy men claimed the packs and ushered Anderson through the holes.

Within moments, the night had swallowed them.

CHAPTER TWO

Mack Bolan was honing his skills. He had to, in order to survive.

The man known as the Executioner lived on the razor's edge, going up against any of the thousand and one kinds of two-legged predators who clawed at the soft underbelly of the human race. The nature of the enemy hardly mattered. All that counted was staying alive to carry on the good fight.

To that end, Bolan practiced every chance he got. Whenever new ordnance came along, Bolan made a point of familiarizing himself with it. He never knew when he might need to use it in the field, or when those he hunted might use it against him.

On this afternoon, Bolan was at Stony Man Farm. Situated in the Blue Ridge Mountains of Virginia, the U.S. government's most top-secret facility boasted one of the finest indoor firing ranges anywhere. But when possible, Bolan liked to test new hardware under simulated field conditions. This often meant that he could be found prowling the hardwoods and conifers covering most of Stony Man Mountain.

Bolan lay on his stomach in a dense thicket. A half hour earlier, he'd snaked into the heart of the growth. Since then, he'd hardly moved a muscle.

His line of work often required him to pick off enemies from long range. The latest distance weapon to arouse his interest was known as the Knight Revolver Rifle, which was special in several respects.

The revolver used was a Ruger .44 Magnum Super Redhawk. A man couldn't ask for more stopping power. With the proper load, such as a 240-grain hollowpoint, the Redhawk had a muzzle velocity of 1760 feet per second, more than enough to lift the average bad man off his feet. At one hundred yards, the velocity of the slug was still a respectable 1372 fps. At two hundred yards, over 1100.

The Redhawk had a black-oxide finish, as did the other components, which included an eighteen-inch suppressor, a detachable buttstock, a scope, a Harris bipod and a state-of-the-art image intensifier.

Bolan had already tried the Revolver Rifle on the indoor range. At one hundred yards, he'd consistently had one-inch groups, so there was no denying the gun was accurate. Now he needed to test another aspect of it.

Many assignments called for him to get in, make his kill and get out again—all without being detected. A silenced revolver that didn't live up to its name could get him killed.

On the indoor range, the chug of the suppressor had been no louder than a low cough. By any standard, that was superb. But Bolan hadn't been satisfied. He had to see how it would do out in the open.

He remained motionless. A small flock of sparrows had settled above him. Nearby, a gray squirrel foraged for acorns. These creatures would be the final measure of whether the revolver passed muster. A silenced weapon that spooked birds into flight or animals into fleeing was bound to give away the person who fired it, and would be useless to the Executioner.

He pressed his eye to the scope. Earlier, he'd picked a knot on a pine eighty yards away as his target. Settling the cross hairs on it, he held his breath to steady his aim, mentally counted to three and stroked the trigger. Wood slivers went flying as a hole blossomed in the tree knot.

None of the sparrows flew away, nor did the squirrel take fright. Bolan fired again, then a third time. After each, the small birds went on chirping and the squirrel went on nosing the ground.

Bolan cracked a smile. The Revolver Rifle had passed with flying colors. He might even take it with him on his next assignment. Pushing to his knees, he startled the sparrows into flight. The squirrel took to its heels as well, scrambling up a maple tree.

Crawling into the open, Bolan cradled the weapon and hiked down the mountain to the main building. He wasn't expecting a welcoming committee, so he was surprised to see two men and a woman waiting for him outside the coded access steel door on the north side of the farmhouse.

The larger of the men was Hal Brognola, director of the Justice Department's Sensitive Operations Group. Beside Brognola stood John Kissinger, Stony Man's weapons expert. The woman was Barbara Price, mission controller. All three of them looked serious.

"If I had to go by your expressions," Bolan said, "I'd say the world was about to come to an end."

"You don't know how close you are to the truth, Mack," Brognola responded. A big bear of a man, he was one of the few people in the country who had direct access to the President at any time of the day or night.

"Cowboy" Kissinger, as everyone called him, nodded. "This was bound to happen, sooner or later."

"Let's get to the War Room so we can fill Mack in," Price suggested. "Every second we waste is a second closer to disaster."

Bolan had known these people for a long time. The constant pressure and stress of the jobs took a toll on all of them at one time or another. Yet never before had he seen them as troubled as they were at that moment.

Bolan remained silent until they were seated around the conference table in the War Room. "Okay," he said, "what's going on?"

Brognola pulled a cigar from his jacket pocket and wedged it between his lips. "What's the worst-case terrorist scenario you can imagine?"

Bolan shrugged. "I suppose the very worst would be hearing that one of the more rabid groups had gotten its hands on a nuc—" He broke off. Intuition told him that he'd hit the nail on the head. The look in their eyes confirmed it.

Brognola nodded. "You've kept up with our latest intel on the Golden Jihad."

It was a statement, not a question. Bolan routinely had access to top-secret briefing papers on all terrorist organizations.

"They've been active for about five years," Bolan said, sorting through his mental file on them. "Their leader is an Iranian named Ahmed Tufayli."

The big Fed nodded. "They're made up of the dregs from other groups that have gone by the wayside. To call them fanatics doesn't begin to describe them."

"Just seven months ago," Price interjected, "they were responsible for that business at a NATO banquet in Naples. Dozens of top-ranking NATO officials and their families were there. I think the final tally was thirty-one dead and seventy-two wounded."

Bolan had seen the images on the news. They would stay with him as further reminders of why he waged his personal war against the forces of evil and depravity. "And this group has a nuclear weapon?"

"We're afraid so," Kissinger replied, "and not a crude homemade job, either."

As he often did when he needed to think, Brognola got up and began to pace the room. "I know you're familiar with the SADM program, Striker."

Bolan was privy to not only the latest Intelligence reports, but also to pertinent news on hardware developments, so he guessed right away why

Brognola had asked. "SADM is an acronym for Small Atomic Demolitions Munitions. They're more commonly known as backpack nukes. We had them as far back as Vietnam, but we've never used them."

"Not for lack of trying," Brognola said. "The Pentagon wanted to use one on the Ho Chi Minh Trail but the politicos wouldn't go for it." He paused. "What concerns us is that the Golden Jihad now have two SADMs in their possession."

"Two? How?"

The big Fed leaned on the table. "We're still sorting out all the facts. What we do know is that the SADM unit was conducting a routine training exercise at the Special Warfare Center at Spartanburg, South Carolina, last night. The unit is composed of two three-man teams. Five of the team members were found dead. The sixth man is missing. So are two of our latest model backpack nukes."

"How do we know the Golden Jihad is involved?"

Brognola scowled. "Because they couldn't resist phoning the Associated Press and boasting that they now have the means to hit us where it'll hurt the most. The AP called Spartanburg for confirmation. We've been able to clamp a lid on the whole affair in the interests of national security."

"It's a stopgap measure at most," Price said. "Sooner or later word is going to leak out. We could wind up with a wholesale panic on our hands."

"Which is why the President wants our recovery efforts to be low profile," Brognola said. "Can you imagine what would happen if word leaked out that a nuclear device was going to be detonated in, say, Washington, D.C.?"

It wasn't hard for Bolan to picture. It would be a scene straight out of a Hollywood B-movie. The highways would be jammed with motorists frantically trying to flee. Bus terminals and airports would be mobbed. It would be every person for himself. Panic would escalate, violence would spread. The overtaxed police would be unable to cope, prompting a call for the National Guard.

"The President asked me to put my best man on the job," Brognola went on, "and that would be you, Striker. Will you take it?"

"Where do I begin?" Bolan asked.

The big Fed consulted his watch. "I'm expecting word along that line at any moment. Cowboy can fill you in on the SADMs while I hustle up to Communications and see what the delay is."

Kissinger wasted no time. "Technology has come a long way in the past twenty-odd years. A typical SADM used to be a bulky affair, compared to current models. It was designed to be broken into three parts and had a yield of .2 kilotons, or about 400,000 pounds of TNT."

Price whistled. "That much?"

"You think that's a lot?" Kissinger warmed to his topic. "The new models have a yield of .4 kilotons even though they're a lot smaller. They break down into only two parts, thanks to the wonders of microchip circuitry. They're also very dirty, fallout-wise. They cause twice as much as earlier versions. If one were to be set off in the heart of a big city, the radioactive particles would wind up killing more people than the explosion itself."

"Give me the essentials," Bolan said.

"Okay. The two stolen nukes are officially designated T-type devices. Most people just call them the Gun models."

"The Gun?"

Kissinger drew an imaginary circle on the table, about eighteen inches in diameter, saying, "The base is doughnut shaped. There's a long cylinder, or barrel, made of steel and titanium, that fits into the hole in the middle. Ergo, the Gun."

"How high are they?"

"Twenty-four inches from the bottom of the base to the master detonator rod at the top. They're black. Each weighs just under eighty pounds when fully assembled. They come packed in special rigid black containers padded with foam. They also come fitted with a built-in destruct mechanism, but you don't want to be anywhere near one when it self-destructs. The blast is equal to that of ten grenades going off at once."

"I'll keep that in mind," Bolan said dryly.

MACK BOLAN DROVE through the Pocono Mountains of northeast Pennsylvania, flicking on his Jeep's headlights as he passed one of the dark cabins that dotted the area. Twilight shrouded the mountains, and he hadn't set eyes on another soul in hours.

On the back seat rested a duffel bag crammed with tools of his trade; an M-16, a .44 Desert Eagle, spare magazines and ammo for both, as well as for the 9 mm Beretta 93-R leathered in a shoulder holster under his left arm, and assorted lethal odds and ends. It also contained a combat blacksuit.

Bolan always liked to plan ahead, to have every contingency covered. Being prepared was half the war.

A break in the vegetation appeared on the left. He slowed, but it was only a narrow gap where a tree had fallen, not the turnoff. He went on.

Less than two hours had gone by since Brognola had burst back into the War Room, waving a report he'd just received on the missing member of the SADM unit.

Sergeant Daniel T. Anderson was twenty-eight years old. He'd enlisted at eighteen, and been a qualified Special Forces demolitionist by the time he turned twenty-four. He had served with distinction, earning a commendation for his part in a covert Middle East operation.

While on R and R, the noncom had met a young Kuwaiti woman by the name of Azadeh Dursak, whom he'd married. They had a one-year-old son, Thomas.

Shortly after his son's birth, Anderson had been tapped for the SADM unit. He'd signed on, and his performance to date had been outstanding.

Now Anderson and two Gun nukes were missing. So were his wife and son. Brognola's people believed that the Golden Jihad had gotten to her and the boy and were using them as leverage to get the sergeant to do their bidding.

It was the only scenario that made sense. None of the psych boys could see Anderson going over to the Jihad of his own free will, nor was he the type to sell out for money.

Bolan tended to agree. A patriot like Anderson would die before he'd betray his country. But the noncom had an Achilles' heel—two of them, in fact. And the Golden Jihad wasn't above exploiting that to its advantage. The woman and the boy were probably still alive, and would remain so only as long as Anderson was of use to the terrorists. It was added incentive for Bolan to find them quickly.

Suddenly an opening appeared in the vegetation, and Bolan slammed on the brakes. It was the turnoff, at last. Narrower than the road, the grass and weeds that had overgrown it had been flattened recently, the growth still green, not brown as it would have been if any length of time had gone by.

Bolan worked the shift and skewed into the opening.

According to the Feds, the cabin once belonged to Anderson's father. It had been bequeathed to him four years earlier after his father suffered a fatal heart attack. The noncom, busy with his military career and family, rarely went there.

Since it was so remote, it seemed an ideal place for the terrorists to hold Anderson's wife and son.

Bolan had been skeptical when Brognola had first mentioned the cabin. He couldn't see the leader of the Golden Jihad being so obvious. Ahmed Tufayli was a ruthless, crafty killer with a knack for never doing as the authorities expected.

As Bolan recalled, the cabin sat in a clearing at the base of a mountain about half a mile from the turnoff. To maintain the element of stealth, he killed the Jeep's headlights and slowed to a crawl. He soon came to an open area where there was enough space to pull over. He did so, flicking the ignition key.

Silence descended. Bolan stayed where he was, tuning his senses to the rhythm of the night.

Grabbing the duffel bag, he slid out of the Jeep. The keys went into his pocket.

Nothing stirred in the woods. The Executioner glided into them, stopping behind a pine to strip off his lightweight jacket and pants and don the blacksuit. A holster holding the Desert Eagle went around his waist. A Ka-bar fighting knife was strapped low down on his right leg. As a last touch, he smeared his cheeks with combat cosmetics. He was ready.

The tangy scent of pine filled his nostrils as he catfooted northward along the edge of the road. His jungle-spawned instincts were primed, alert for trip-wires or electronic surveillance devices.

A minute went by. Bolan heard no sounds foreign to the wilderness, nor did he see any lights. He began to suspect that the Golden Jihad had been there and gone. Then a square of yellow glowed in the distance. The soldier recognized it right away—the light from a lantern spilling through a window.

He advanced until he could make out the silhouette of a low structure. A car sat parked in front of it. Halting, he studied the terrain, deciding on the best approach. It wouldn't do to rush in there, not with the lives of the woman and child at stake.

No sooner did the thought cross Bolan's mind than a shot rang out from inside the cabin.

CHAPTER THREE

The Executioner's first thought was that the terrorists were eliminating Azadeh and Thomas Anderson. Bending low, he moved toward the cabin door, zigzagging as he ran. He was almost to the sedan when a scream erupted. It drew him up short.

The sound wasn't a human one. It rose to a piercing pitch before tapering to a strangled whine.

Gruff laughter served as a split-second warning. Bolan dived flat just as the door opened, framing a lean, bearded figure armed with an Uzi. The man's features matched those of a Turkish mug shot of Hassan Nidal, included in Brognola's file on the Golden Jihad. Nidal was second-in-command, answerable only to Ahmed Tufayli himself.

Nidal said something in Arabic to someone behind him. Chuckling, he emerged and went around the side of the cabin into the woods.

Bolan was tempted to go after the fanatic, but he stayed put. Assessing enemy strength was critical in a firefight. He snaked to the right, toward the opposite side of the cabin. Muted voices told him that at least two more terrorists were still in there.

On the east side was another small window. Dust and grime caked the glass pane. Bolan, his back against the rough log wall, rose high enough to peek in.

There were two of them, all right, seated at a table. One man was cradling a Mossberg Model 590 shotgun. Bolan had fired one on several occasions. It held eight rounds, plus one in the chamber—a virtual cannon at short range.

The other hardman had a Negev on a shoulder sling, the assault version sporting a thirteen-inch barrel instead of the standard eighteen-inch. It was fitted with a 32-round magazine.

As Bolan looked on, the terrorist with the Negev reached under his coat and pulled a 9 mm Walther P-88 pistol from a concealed holster. The man strode to the corner of the single room. Only then did the Executioner see the dog. It lay on its side. Around its neck was a red collar, from which dangled a tag. A leash connected the collar to the frame of a bed. A hole above the dog's ribs oozed a steady stream of blood, which was forming into a puddle on the floor.

The terrorist holding the Walther stood over the dog. Laughing, he kicked it twice, causing the animal to cry out. Then he placed a foot on one of its hind legs and applied all his weight. Yipping, the dog tried to rise, but lacked the strength.

Bolan felt sorry for the animal, but there was nothing he could do at the moment. His top priority was the backpack nukes. Second in importance were the Andersons. Since neither the devices nor the family seemed to be present, he had to find out where they'd been spirited. To that end, it was imperative he take the terrorists alive.

As Bolan started to draw back from the window, the man still at the table idly glanced up, catching sight of him. The soldier threw himself to the right.

The Mossberg boomed four times. Holes the size of melons exploded in the cabin wall, showering pieces of wood on Bolan.

On his elbows and knees, the big man crawled to the far corner. As he reached it, the window was knocked out and a head appeared. It would've been child's play for Bolan to pick off the Jihad hardman, but that would mean one less chance to learn the critical information Brognola needed. He held his fire.

The same couldn't be said for the terrorists. At a shout from the man at the window, they let loose. Shotgun and subgun blasted in thunderous concert, peppering the wall.

Bolan was in motion a split second before they fired. He outraced a hail of lead, reached the northwest corner and sped on into the trees. Crouching behind a pine, he sought some sign of Hassan Nidal. The terrorist had to have heard the shooting, and would no doubt come to aid his comrades.

There was no movement in the trees. The only noise was a commotion in the cabin. Bolan heard glass shatter, and something heavy crashed to the floor.

Suddenly the pair made a break for it. Instead of waiting for Nidal, Bolan saw them hurtle from the doorway and sprint toward the car. Back to back, their weapons leveled, they gained the driver's side. The gunner with the Mossberg slid in first.

Bolan had to stop them. Wary of getting a slug in the back from Nidal, he paralleled the tree line until he was as near to the car as he could get without being seen. Aiming at the rear tire, he flipped the selector lever on the M-16 from full-auto to semiauto, then stroked the trigger three times. The tire ruptured with a loud pop. Swiveling, Bolan gave the front tire the same treatment.

The M-16 was fitted with a flash suppressor, but that didn't stop the terrorists from pinpointing the warrior's position. The man holding the Negev swung toward him and fired on full-auto.

Leaden hornets buzzed overhead as Bolan hit the dirt. More slugs chewed into the ground around him. In another second or two he'd be dead. Bolan had no choice. He fixed a hasty bead on the gunner and sent four 5.56 mm rounds into the guy's chest.

The impact flung the terrorist back against the sedan. He then melted to the ground, before tipping over onto his forehead. The subgun fell from his limp fingers.

Bolan brought up the M-16 to cover the other man, but the terrorist was no longer in the car. He had slipped out the opposite door and was making a beeline for the forest.

The Executioner lingered for half a minute, but when Nidal still hadn't put in an appearance, he took off after him. Speeding around the car, he angled toward the weed-choked turnoff. The terrorist was bound to rely on the quickest route to safety.

Bolan knew how vital it was to come up with a lead. He settled into a smooth, mile-eating run, the rubber soles of his combat boots making little noise.

A hundred yards fell behind him, then two hundred. A form took shape in front of him. It was Shotgun, lumbering along at a plodding trot. Every now and then the man glanced over his shoulder, the upper half of his face a pale contrast to the night.

Bolan wasn't worried about being seen. His blacksuit was perfect camouflage. At that distance, he blended into the background so well that he seemed part of it.

The soldier slowly closed the gap until sixty feet separated them. He veered nearer to the pines in case the man unexpectedly turned. Sooner or later the terrorist would grow winded and stop, and that was when the Executioner would make his move.

Then a metallic growl rent the night. Shotgun halted, his head cocked, trying to make sense of the sound.

Bolan knew what it was. Someone was trying to start his Jeep, and there was only one person it could be.

Hassan Nidal was no fool. At the outbreak of shots back at the cabin, he had to have figured that the police or government forces were closing in. He'd probably circled wide around the cabin and made good his escape, deserting his two companions to save his own skin.

Another growl arose, then the engine sputtered and died. A few more tries and Nidal would have the Jeep hot-wired.

Bolan poured on the speed. Ahead of him, Shotgun was doing the same. Whether the man had deduced the truth or was just eager to get his hands on the vehicle was irrelevant. The soldier couldn't let either of them get away. He sprinted flat out, eating up the distance twice as fast as Shotgun.

The terrorist was so intent on reaching the Jeep that he didn't check behind him. Yard by yard, Bolan gained ground. Soon he was close enough to hear Shotgun wheezing like a bellows.

Bolan firmed his grip on the M-16 in preparation for swinging the stock against the terrorist's head. Shotgun slowed slightly, enabling the soldier to draw within eight feet of him. He hiked the assault rifle for the buttstroke. Just as he did, his right boot crunched onto a twig, which snapped with the crack of a bullwhip.

Shotgun shot a glance over his shoulder. Instantly he halted and spun, bringing the Mossberg to bear.

Bolan reached him in a single long stride. Slashing the M-16 downward, he knocked the shotgun aside just as it went off, the blast tearing a chunk out of a tree beside the road.

Snarling like an enraged beast, Shotgun backpedaled to bring his weapon into play again. Bolan drove the M-16 against the terrorist's wrist.

The hardman cried out, lost his grip and tried to regain it. The Executioner slammed his other wrist.

The terrorist roared in pain as the Mossberg fell to the ground. As the man made to grab something from under his coat, the Executioner speared the butt of his rifle into his gut, causing him to double over. Sweeping his rifle upward, Bolan caught his adversary flush on the forehead. The terrorist crumpled.

The soldier heard the Jeep's engine churn a third time. He started toward the vehicle, when suddenly Shotgun heaved to his knees, holding a slender dagger. Bolan felt a stinging sensation in the back of his leg. The killer had tried to hamstring him but merely nicked his flesh. Whirling, the soldier rammed the M-16 into his adversary's head a second time.

That should have done the trick, but clearly Shotgun had a hard head. He swayed, then lunged, lancing the dagger at his enemy's stomach.

Bolan batted the blade aside. He undercut the rifle stock into the man's shoulder, hitting a nerve point and rendering his knife arm useless.

Shotgun didn't let that stop him. He grabbed Bolan's lower legs with his other arm and heaved. Before the Executioner could set himself, he was upended, his shoulders taking the brunt of his fall. The terrorist clawed at Bolan's chest, his lips drawn back as if he intended to sink his teeth into his adversary's exposed throat.

Bolan had gone easy on the man in order to take him alive with a minimum of bodily damage, but enough was enough. Arcing his left elbow up and around, he smashed it against Shotgun's nose. Cartilage crackled and blood spurted.

Shotgun reared. Bolan spiked a palm-heel thrust into his adversary's lower jaw, snapping his head back. Making both hands rigid, he boxed Shotgun on the ears. Then, as the terrorist attempted to push off him and rise, the soldier swept up both his legs. His ankles forked Shotgun's neck and locked. Exerting all the power in his muscled frame, Bolan slammed the man into the hard ground, headfirst.

At last the hardman went limp, sprawling onto his face when Bolan let go. Standing, the Executioner retrieved the M-16 and took off down the road. He could no longer hear the Jeep.

In the heat of battle, he hadn't noticed if Nidal had turned the engine over and driven off. He approached the grassy area, slowed to a walk and entered the woods on his right. Darting from trunk to trunk, he looped to the southeast to come up on Nidal from a direction the fanatic wouldn't expect. He was almost to the nook where he'd left the Jeep when he saw the vehicle, the hood propped open, the driver's door flung wide.

Nidal had either failed to jump start the vehicle, or he was lying low, waiting for someone to show. Bending, Bolan could see that no one lurked under the vehicle. He scoured the shadows on all sides. Only when he was convinced it was safe did he warily step from concealment. No shots rang out.

Nidal had made good his escape.

Bolan wasted no time on self-recrimination. He'd done the best he could. Closing the hood, he pulled out the keys, fired up the Jeep and headed for Shotgun. Tightly knotted cord and a gag ensured the man would give him no more trouble.

The soldier dumped his catch in the back of the Jeep, then drove on to the cabin. He searched the dead gunner and found a wallet containing some cash plus a phony ID identifying the bearer as Jesse Stuart of Watertown, New York. In his pants pocket he also discovered the keys to the sedan. A check of its trunk turned up a cache of automatic weapons that would satisfy any terrorist.

Before entering the cabin, Bolan swept the area. He wouldn't put it past the Golden Jihad to have rigged a nasty surprise, but his trained gaze located nothing.

The place was a mess. A mountain of dirty dishes were stacked on a wood-burning stove. Crumpled clothes lay piled in two corners, with dirty bedding beside the sole closet. Inside it hung several skirts and blouses and a few outfits for a child.

The signs were clear. The Golden Jihad had been holding the mother and child there, but most of the band had left before Bolan showed up. Nidal and the other two had probably meant to leave soon. It was pure luck that the soldier had caught them before they did.

A pathetic whine reminded Bolan that he wasn't alone. The dog was still alive, but it was so weak that it could barely lift its head to look at Bolan when he squatted. "Easy, fella," he said softly.

He reached out, and the dog whimpered. He stroked its head and neck, then took hold of the tag on its collar. "King," he read aloud. "So that's your name." Flipping over the tag, Bolan noted the name and address of the owners. "Dan and Azadeh Anderson."

It puzzled him. Why had the terrorists bothered to bring the dog along? Just so they could torture it later, or had there been a practical consideration? Odds were, Tufayli had kidnapped the woman and the boy before the nukes were swiped, so he hadn't wanted to risk the animal being found at the Anderson's residence.

There was no hope for the poor animal. The hollowpoint slug had made a mess of its insides and left an exit wound the size of a baseball.

Bolan set down the M-16 and slowly drew his Beretta. The 93-R was fitted with a sound suppressor, which he pressed snugly against the base of the dog's skull.

The Beretta chugged once.

MANY MILES TO THE SOUTH, Sergeant Dan Anderson sat slumped on a concrete floor, his hands bound behind his back and his ankles in shackles.

A blindfold prevented him from taking stock of his surroundings, but based on the dank air and lack of noise, he guessed he was in a basement. Where the building might be located, he had no idea. The Golden Jihad had shuttled him from one hiding place to another after whisking him from the Special Warfare Center at Spartanburg. He didn't even know what state he was in.

Of more importance to the man was the fate of his family. Fear for their lives made the waiting an unbearable hell. If they'd been killed, then his betrayal of his country would have been for nothing. It was a thought that gnawed at his soul.

He heard the rasp of a latch. Footsteps thudded on a flight of stairs, drawing closer, until they sounded on the concrete floor.

"Is that you, Ahmed?" Anderson called. "Are they here yet?"

The most wanted terrorist on the globe straddled a rickety wooden chair and regarded his prisoner with contempt.

Ahmed Tufayli hated Americans. He hated their country, their way of life, every little thing about them. America was the Great Satan, a vile imperialist cesspool that sought to impose its degenerate culture on all others.

Six years earlier Tufayli had launched a one-man crusade to bring America to its knees, to make it pay for its crimes against the Muslim world. So far he had seventy-eight deaths to his credit and nine successful bombings.

Leaning forward, Tufayli undid Anderson's blindfold and tossed it onto a nearby dusty workbench littered with long-neglected tools. "Is that better?" he asked.

Tufayli wasn't foolish enough to let his true feelings show. He had learned that it was often easier to get his enemies to do what he wanted if he treated them as if he actually gave a damn about their miserable lives. The sham revolted him, but it got the job done.

He was good at psychological warfare. Before taking up the Holy War, he'd been a psychology major at a university in Ankara, Turkey. He wasn't Turkish, but he knew the authorities thought he was, so he acted the part in order to conceal his true background. It pleased him to make fools of every Intelligence agency on three continents.

Anderson blinked in the glare of the overhead light. His blindfold had been on so long that it took awhile for his eyes to adjust. As he'd deduced, he was in a basement. Across from him stood a washer and dryer. To his right was a cabinet lined with cans.

"Where is my family?" the noncom asked. "Why didn't you bring them down here with you?"

Tufayli smiled, adopting a kind air. "Nothing would please me more than to see you reunited with your loved ones," he said in perfect English, "but there are a few matters we must get straight first."

Panic welled up in Anderson. "What do you mean? I've done everything you wanted. You have the two backpack nukes, don't you? Our agreement was that you'd let me see Azadeh and Thomas once you did."

"True," Tufayli conceded. A tall, powerfully built man, with broad shoulders, he dwarfed the chair in which he sat. "But now that we are ready to move on to the next phase, we must come to a new agreement."

Anderson didn't hesitate. "Anything you want. Just don't hurt my wife and son."

Tufayli had to look away so his prisoner wouldn't see the disgust on his face. Americans were such weak, spineless creatures. It never ceased to amaze him that their country had held sway in world affairs for so many decades.

Anderson misconstrued the Jihad leader's silence. "What's wrong? Did something happen to them?"

"Calm yourself, Sergeant," Tufayli said. "Your woman and the child are fine." He paused for effect. "But they will stay fine only as long as you continue to do as I ask."

"Just tell me what you need."

Tufayli took a pack of Turkish cigarettes from his shirt pocket and lit one. He was in no rush. Making the American squirm was very satisfying. "You have four days in which to teach us how to operate the backpack nukes. If you fail, your wife and child will die the most horrible deaths you can imagine."

"Four days! Do you have any idea how complicated the procedure is? I had to go through three months of intensive training, not to mention the extra—"

Tufayli cut off his protest. "Four days are all I can spare. For safety's sake, we cannot stay in one place any longer than that. Five days from now the bombs will be detonated in the heart of two major American cities."

Anderson tried telling himself that it would be best if he didn't know which ones, but he couldn't stop himself from asking.

Tufayli saw no reason not to tell him, since the noncom wouldn't live to pass on the information. "Let me put it this way. By next week, the Big Apple and the Beltway, as you Americans call them, will never be the same again."

CHAPTER FOUR

The device sat on the large table in the War Room. As black as night, it was exactly the size Cowboy Kissinger had said it would be. The master detonator rod, the arming initiation clock, the detonation timer clock and the electronic fingerprint-reading pad were all at the top of the gun barrel. The zeroes on the digital displays glowed bright red.

Barbara Price regarded the device thoughtfully. "Do you ever get the idea that there's no end to humankind's capacity for self-destruction?"

"Someone's always trying to build a more lethal weapon," Bolan replied.

"You'd think we would've learned our lesson by now," Price said.

"We will eventually."

"Do you really think so?"

Bolan nodded. "If I didn't, I wouldn't be doing what I do. The day each of us draws a line and refuses to be pushed past it, is the day we start to make our world a better place in which to live."

Cowboy Kissinger bustled into the room. "Sorry to keep you two twiddling your thumbs," he said. "I had to wait for Hal to get off the telephone with General Wilson. The old boy wasn't all that eager to give us the current self-destruct codes."

"He wasn't very happy about loaning us this training mock-up or the op manual, either," Price pointed out.

Kissinger stopped in front of the device and ran a hand over the smooth plastic. "Put yourself in his shoes. Even though he wasn't at Spartanburg when the manure hit the fan, the buck stops at his door. He's the head of the SADM unit, so he has to take all the flak. Even if the two nukes are safely retrieved, Wilson'll be lucky if he's not demoted and given a desk job in a subbasement of the Pentagon."

Bolan was more interested in the outcome of Brognola's telephone call. "Do we have everything we need?"

Kissinger pulled a small notebook from his pocket. "You bet. The initiation sequence, the arming code, the self-destruct code—everything you require to blow up the nukes if you have to." He tapped the master digit locking switch. "The only hitch is the fingerprint verification access pad. If your prints had been fed into the Gun, you could set it to self-destruct in no time. As things stand, you'll have to go through a long code override sequence."

"Let's hope it doesn't come to that," Price said. "We want to get both nukes back intact, if at all possible."

Bolan stood next to the weaponsmith. "Let's get to it."

For the next two hours Kissinger gave Bolan a crash course in the proper operation and demolition of a Gun nuke. The soldier had to learn how to deactivate the device in order to be able to stop a countdown, if he should find that either of the stolen pair had been primed.

As for the self-destruct sequence, it was a drawn out process that involved overriding the detonation timer clocks. There were three of them, arranged in a row on top of the barrel.

Memorizing the code was only half the task. It had to be fed into the Gun in a precise manner. Each action had to be done in a certain sequence. If not performed exactly, a fail-safe mechanism would kick in and override the override, forcing the operator to go through the whole procedure again from the beginning.

At one point Kissinger remarked, "The SF boys who go through this have to drill for days on end, until they can practically do it in their sleep. It's too bad we don't have that luxury."

Bolan's fingers were aching by the time they were done. He sat and sipped black coffee as Kissinger examined the mock-up.

"We're lucky in one respect," he said. "In the old days it took two men to disarm one of these babies."

Bolan had been pondering something. "About the arming procedure for the bomb itself," he said. "If I understood you, it can't be activated without fingerprint verification."

"Correct."

"Then since Sergeant Anderson is the only one whose prints the Guns will accept, the Golden Jihad has to keep him alive so he can activate both nukes."

"Not necessarily," Kissinger said. "Sure, only his fingerprints will trigger the switching sequence. But the terrorists can feed in the arming code once he's done that, and they can set the timer in advance."

"How far in advance?" Price asked.

"Ten days," Kissinger replied. "In technical terms, we call that the window of detonation. They could have Anderson start the sequence, then program the detonator clock for the full ten days, giving them time to skip the country."

"They won't want to wait that long," Bolan said.

Kissinger cocked an eyebrow. "How can you be sure?"

"The longer the window, the more risk they run of us tracking down the nukes before the devices go off."

"I agree," Price said. "I've gone over the HUMINT file on their leader. According to Tufayli's psych profile, he likes to play it safe. He's a meticulous planner, down to the least little detail. You can bet that he'll resort to a short window of detonation to reduce the likelihood of being stopped."

Hal Brognola entered the War Room and headed straight for the coffee. He didn't speak until he'd downed a cup in large gulps. "Where would civilization be without caffeine?" he asked no one in particular.

"Have we learned anything from our guest?" Bolan asked.

"Not enough, I'm sorry to say." Brognola slumped into a chair and ran a hand through his hair. "Tufayli is playing this one close to the vest. Those under him haven't been told much about the overall plan. They don't even know where he intends to detonate the backpack nukes."

Kissinger's brow wrinkled. "Could that telephone call to the Associated Press have been a ruse to throw us off the scent? Maybe Tufayli doesn't intend to use the Guns here in the States. Maybe he's planning to smuggle them overseas, possibly for use against Israel."

Brognola shook his head. "On that score we're positive. The man Striker nabbed, Abdullah Hawatmeh, says that Tufayli swore that the Golden Jihad would go down in the history books as the group who brought the Great Satan America to its knees."

Bolan didn't like the idea of sitting around waiting for something to happen. "There must be something we can do. Didn't your people learn anything from Hawatmeh?"

"As a matter of fact, they did," Brognola said. "I was getting to it next." Rising, he walked around the table to a wall-sized map of the United States. "You've been to New Orleans a few times, as I recall."

"And I'm going again, I take it."

The big Fed used a pointer to tap the city. "Hawatmeh and five other members of the Golden Jihad were smuggled into the country on board a freighter that docked there more than a week ago. For two days after their arrival, they hid out at the home of an exporter by the name of Mehmet Akbar."

"What do we know about him?"

"Akbar is fifty-two years old. He was born in Iraq, but came to the U.S. with his parents when he was ten and has been here ever since. His firm exports building materials. He has no criminal record. We've never even had reason to put him under surveillance." Brognola paused. "We're hoping that the Golden Jihad went back to his place after snatching the nukes. It's a long shot, but it's the only lead we have at this point."

Bolan rose. "I'll be ready to go in ten minutes."

"Good. Grimaldi's preparing for takeoff."

True to his word, Bolan was at the landing strip in under ten minutes, his duffel bag in hand. Jack Grimaldi, Stony Man Farm's ace pilot, gave him the thumbs-up sign as he hurried to the F-111F jet. The whine of the twin Pratt & Whitney TF30-PW-100 turbofans was ear-splitting.

The appearance of the landing strip, like everything else at Stony Man, was deceptive. Located in the northwest sector, it seemed to be a run-of-the-mill dirt strip. But just under an outer cover of dirt and grass lay a solid concrete runway, able to handle everything from Piper Cubs to jet aircraft like the F-111F.

Bolan strapped himself into a seat next to Grimaldi. The duffel bag had gone into a storage compartment behind them.

Grimaldi closed the canopy, flicked a few switches, then glanced at Bolan and grinned. "Ready to ride the range again, Sarge?"

Before Bolan could answer, the pilot punched the throttle and the sleek aircraft hurtled toward the far end of the runway. In seconds the whine of the engines rose to a rumbling roar.

As the powerful jet arced into the azure sky, Grimaldi tossed back his head and let out with a boisterous, "Yahoo! Look out, Crescent City! Here we come!"

AHMED TUFAYLI WASN'T a happy man. Seated across a small kitchen table from him was his second-in-command, the one man he'd thought he could always rely on. "How could you let it happen?" he demanded.

Hassan Nidal scratched his thin beard. His eyes narrowed. "What else was I to do? Let myself be caught, or worse?"

"No," Tufayli agreed sullenly. The loss of two Jihad members was a major setback, but it wouldn't delay him in carrying out his plan. He could make do with two five-man teams, instead of having six on each. "You are certain they are both dead?"

"Yes," Nidal lied. He hadn't actually seen either of his comrades go down, but he wasn't about to admit as much and have to face Tufayli's wrath. As part of the pledge each man took when he joined the Golden Jihad, he vowed never to be taken alive, and to never let any of his fellows be taken, either. Tufayli took that vow seriously. Violators paid with their lives.

"I will miss them," Tufayli said for the benefit of the other men in the room. "They were both devoted to our cause. Now, more than ever, we must see that nothing stands in our way. We must pay the Americans back for what they have done."

Nayif Nasrallah, the youngest of the Jihad, and a hothead, raised his fist. "Down with the imperialist pigs! May they all burn in hell for their evil ways!"

Tufayli got up and walked to the basement door and slowly descended the stairs.

Sergeant Anderson didn't hear the footsteps this time. He was dozing, his back against the concrete wall, his wife's head resting on his shoulder. It was the first time he'd slept since his wife and son had been abducted.

A searing pain racked the noncom's side and he snapped awake to find the terrorist leader looming over him, drawing back his leg to kick him again. "What's the matter?" Anderson blurted. "Why are you kicking me?"

"Because you are American," Tufayli said, sneering. The loss of two of his men had rekindled the flame of hatred that burned in his heart. He was close to flying into one of his periodic rages and losing control.

Azadeh Anderson, a petite, raven-haired woman who couldn't hide her terror, drew to one side, shielding her infant son with her body. "Don't hurt us!" she cried.

"Hurt?" Tufayli said through clenched teeth. "You do not know the meaning of the word, whore!" Seizing her by the hair, he cocked a fist to smash her in the mouth.

"No!" Anderson shouted. Although his wrists were bound and his ankles shackled, he could move a few feet in any given direction. Coiling his knees under him, he propelled himself at the terrorist, lowering his head to ram into Tufayli's abdomen.

The Jihad leader was much too quick. Casting the woman aside, he sidestepped the soldier's lunge, twisted and looped an arm around Anderson's neck. His muscles tightened. A sharp wrench was all it would take to snap the man's neck like a dry twig.

A hand clamped onto Tufayli's shoulder. Hassan Nidal, knowing his leader better than any other member of the Golden Jihad, had followed him. Nidal had seen Tufayli fly into a rage too many times not to recognize the signs. "Do not, brother," he said in Arabic. "We need him, remember? Without this swine, we cannot set off the bombs."

Nidal's soothing tone had the desired effect. Tufayli blinked. The red haze in front of his eyes cleared. He looked at the soldier and abruptly let him go. He realized the awful mistake he'd been about to make and pressed a hand to his perspiring brow. "Thank you, brother. I came close."

Anderson used his shoulder for leverage and pushed to his knees. He was shocked by the unprovoked attack. Until that moment, none of the terrorists had laid a finger on him. Tufayli, in fact, had been the friendliest of them all.

Their humane treatment, more than anything else, had helped Anderson convince himself that maybe the terrorists would do as Tufayli claimed and let his family live when it was all over. But there had always been a tiny voice that had warned Anderson he was deluding himself, that as soon as he had served his purpose, he would be eliminated.

Still, he'd clung to hope. He had his wife and son to think of. As long as he obeyed, they stayed alive. It was that simple.

Now Anderson saw Tufayli in a new, true light. With terrible certainty he knew his days, and those of Azadeh and Thomas, were numbered.

It changed everything. Anderson couldn't let his family die. Somehow, he would find a way for all three of them to escape.

Tufayli saw something in the soldier's eyes that made him realize how grave a mistake he had made. The loss of his two men had fanned his rabid hatred of all things American and provoked him into the blunder. What little trust he'd earned from the noncom had just been lost.

But he wasn't one to linger over a mistake. Immediately he sought to turn it to his advantage. "I apologize, Sergeant," he said as humbly as he could act. "I just learned that two of my men were slain by your countrymen, and I lost my head."

The admission confused Anderson. The last thing he'd expected was for the terrorist to say he was sorry.

"It will not happen again," Tufayli declared, and meant it. He could ill afford another mistake, not when they were so close to striking the greatest blow ever against the Great Satan, even greater than the Oklahoma truck bombing had been.

With Nidal in tow, Tufayli headed upstairs. Near the top he slowed to whisper, "We will let the dog stay with his woman for half an hour more, then you will bring him up and the training sessions will begin."

"He might try to deceive us," Nidal said.

"There is always that chance, but as long as we have the woman and the child, I believe he will cooperate."

"What do you plan to do with them when this is all over?"

"Need you ask?" Tufayli placed a hand on the latch. "I will allow Nayif and whoever else is interested to have their way with the whore. Then we will kill her."

"And the sergeant?"

"I will start by gouging out his eyes, then work my way down from there. He will grovel for mercy before I am done." Tufayli pulled on the door. "Mark my words."

Nidal had one last query. "And what about the infant, my friend?"

Tufayli gazed down at the threesome. "What do you think?" he said. "It is too bad, though. My first thought was to take it back with us."

"Whatever for?"

"My cousin lost her son to an Israeli security patrol a while back, so I toyed with the idea of asking her to raise this one as her own." He grinned. "It would have been poetic justice, would it not, to rear an American brat to hate America? One day he might even have become the leader of the Jihad."

Nidal, a man who rarely found cause to laugh, roared.

MACK BOLAN, DRESSED in casual clothes, his duffel bag draped over a broad shoulder, strolled along Canal Street, New Orleans's main thoroughfare. Off to the right was the French Quarter, to his left the business and financial district.

According to the intel relayed by Brognola, Mehmet Akbar had an office in the business district, a warehouse down by the waterfront and a plush home uptown, in an upscale residential area not far from Audubon Park.

In keeping with the President's wish to maintain a low profile, Bolan was on his own, which was how he preferred it. Brognola had also made it clear that he had a free rein.

Bolan took a left at the next corner. The sidewalk bustled with pedestrians. He came to a side street and had to stop while a funeral procession, led by a jazz quartet, passed.

The soldier went on. Several times he stopped in front of store windows and made a show of studying the merchandise. In reality, he used the windows as mirrors to check for a tail. No one knew he was in New Orleans so he doubted anyone would be shadowing him, but he'd never been one to take anything for granted.

It was early afternoon when he halted before a seven-story office building. Listed on the directory in the lobby were dozens of businesses, everything from attorneys to a floral shop. A name on the top floor caught Bolan's eye: Mehmet Akbar and Sons, Exporters.

The Justice Department had learned that Akbar had four sons, the youngest in his early twenties. Bolan thought it likely that Mehmet Akbar included them in his shady dealings.

Rather than use the elevator, Bolan took the stairs. On the top landing, he cracked the door enough to scan the carpeted corridor. Offices lined both sides. According to a sign jutting out from the wall, the one he wanted was halfway down the hall.

Adopting a casual air, Bolan ambled toward it, pretending to read the office numbers. He didn't look directly inside when he went by Akbar's office, but out the corner of his eye he noted a glass door, a cubicle where a secretary sat typing on a computer keyboard and an inner wood door, closed tight, that bore Akbar's name.

It was enough to tell Bolan that the terrorists weren't hiding there. The offices were just too small.

He was almost past when the inner door abruptly opened. Out came a portly man of Middle Eastern complexion, carrying a file. Curly hair, tinged gray at the temples, crowned an oval face with plump cheeks and a thick mustache.

Mehmet Akbar looked just like he had the day his driver's license photo had been taken. He turned toward the glass door, but by then Bolan was safely by. The Executioner decided to take the elevator rather than go back past the office and risk Akbar's seeing him.

Bolan stabbed the elevator button twice before the car arrived. A woman and two men had joined him by then. As the door slid open, someone called out behind them.

"Hold that for me, would you, please?"

It was Mehmet Akbar. Bolan moved to the back of the car and tucked his chin into his chest. Akbar entered, holding a briefcase. He thanked the man who'd kept the door open, and smiled at each of them. The car started to descend.

Bolan couldn't believe his luck. If Akbar spotted him later hanging around the warehouse or prowling the neighborhood where he lived, the man might recognize him and grow suspicious.

The soldier stayed in the rear of the car when it reached the ground, letting the others get off first. Four people were waiting to get on, or he would've remained in the elevator until Akbar was out of sight. As it was, he remained where he was long enough for the exporter to reach the building's entrance.

Akbar appeared to be in a hurry. Dashing to the curb, he looked both ways, then urgently beckoned a taxi. When it cruised past without stopping, he stepped into the street to flag another.

Bolan's curiosity was piqued. It was possible that Akbar was on his way to see the terrorists. Pushing through the revolving door, he saw the exporter hop into the second cab. As it gained speed, the soldier searched for one he could take. To his annoyance, there was none.

A red light halted Akbar's taxi a block away, buying Bolan a few precious moments. Around a corner squealed an old-model taxi with its overhead light off. Taking a gamble, the Executioner darted in front of it.

The driver slammed on the brakes in the nick of time. Poking his head out of the window, he bellowed, ''What the hell is wrong with you, mister? Do you have a death wish or something?''

Bolan pulled out a wad of bills and peeled off thirty dollars. "This is your tip if you'll follow that cab," he said, pointing at the one that had picked up Akbar.

"What is this, mister, a joke?"

Bolan was about to assure the driver he was serious, when a hard object jammed into the base of his spine. He didn't need to look over his shoulder to know that it was a gun barrel.

CHAPTER FIVE

Usually Hal Brognola liked his job. He liked making a difference, doing work that saved lives and helped safeguard the country he held so dear.

Being director of the Justice Department's Sensitive Operations Group had its good days and its bad days. It also had days straight from hell, and this was one of them.

The big Fed haunted Communications for word from Bolan. The stakes this time were so high that he had to be ready to act at a moment's notice if a break came their way.

For years, experts in terrorism had predicted that radical groups were bound to target the United States. The tendency had been to downplay the predictions until the World Trade Center attack. Even then, most of Brognola's peers had shrugged off the notion that the United States could become another Lebanon or Dublin.

Oklahoma City had been the wake up call. It had shown everyone that American soil was no longer sacred, that Americans were no longer safe from the horrors that had ravaged so much of the world for so many years.

Terrorism was the wave of the future, the experts said. Get used to it, was their advice. The picture they painted was of a country under siege, where no one would be safe from one day to the next.

Even so, Brognola would never give up. As long as there were men like Mack Bolan willing to sacrifice everything for the cause of freedom, America had a prayer. As long as people still cared about their future, and the future they were passing on, there was hope for humanity.

"Mr. Brognola? Sir?"

The big Fed realized that one of the computer techs had been trying to get his attention for some time. "Yes, Josh. What is it?"

"Here's that report you wanted, sir." The young man handed over a slim file. "We did the best we could on such short notice. It's not one hundred percent accurate. The stats are ballpark figures."

"I'm sure you've done a fine job," Brognola said.

"Mr. Kurtzman helped with the projections. He came in while we were working on them, and the next thing we knew, he was pretty much running the show."

Brognola grinned. That sounded just like the Bear, as everyone called Aaron Kurtzman, Stony Man's resident computer wizard. If anyone could come up with reliable projections, he was the one.

Brognola left Communications. He wanted to be alone for a while to examine the report. It contained the answer to a very important question, one that had been bandied about in the War Room, but for which no one had a definite answer: namely, exactly how many lives would be lost and how much damage would result if one of the backpack nukes was to be set off in a heavily populated city?

He took the stairs to the basement level and locked himself in the office he often used when at the Farm. Sitting down, he flipped open the file and scanned the data.

It took a few minutes for the enormity of the stats to sink in. Brognola felt an invisible icy hand constrict his chest. He ran his finger down the page, then turned to the next.

Someone had sketched a diagram of a probable blast radius. Primary damage caused by the thermal effect, collateral damage caused by the shock wave and tertiary damage caused by flying glass and debris were all assessed.

On the third page, the radiation produced was broken down into three phases. First came the initial radiation caused by the explosion. Then came the fallout that would descend over a wide area. Lastly were the radioactive elements such as iodine-131, strontium-90 and barium-140 that would cause long-term problems with bone cancer, anemia and leukemia.

The report was mind-boggling. Brognola leaned back and tried to come to grips with Kurtzman's so-called conservative estimate of a quarter of a million deaths. Depending on the prevailing winds and other factors, the total could climb a lot higher.

Oklahoma City would pale in comparison.

MACK BOLAN FROZE. Too many innocent bystanders were around for him to resist. Someone leaned close to him and a voice whispered in his ear.

"Don't move and don't speak. You will die here and now if you do."

There were two of them. As the gunner spoke, a husky man in a trench coat stepped into view and grinned at the taxi driver, who still had his eyes on the bills Bolan had given him. "Our friend has changed his mind," the husky man said. "He forgot an important appointment. You can go on about your business."

"What about this money?" the driver asked.

The husky man glanced at Bolan and smirked. "Keep it. With his compliments."

The driver looked up. "Thanks, mister," he said. With a wave of the greenbacks, he drove off.

A gleam came into the husky man's dark eyes. "Let's find someplace quiet where we can have a little chat." Gazing both ways, he pointed at an alley to the left of the office building. "Down there, Amal," he directed the gunman.

Prodded by the pistol, Bolan was steered into the alley and forced to walk its entire length to a high wire fence.

Trash cans, boxes and empty crates lined both sides of the alley. Tall buildings hemmed them in, except beyond the fence, which flanked the rear of a two-story brick building. There was no one else around.

Gripping the duffel bag over his shoulder, Bolan slowly turned.

Amal also wore a trench coat. In his right hand was an Astra A-70, a 9-mm import, nickel plated with black synthetic grips. The flap of his coat had hidden it from passersby out on the street, but now he extended it into plain view. He was taller and thinner than the other man, but their features were so alike that Bolan suspected they were related, possibly brothers.

The man didn't draw a weapon. Evidently he had complete confidence in Amal. Placing his hands on his hips, he said, "All right, start talking. Who are you and why are you so interested in our father?"

Bolan adopted a poker face. "I don't have any idea what you're talking about."

The hardman struck with the speed of a cobra. One moment he was standing still, the next his fist had sunk into the Executioner's gut. Bolan doubled over, gasping, then dropped onto his right knee. He hunched over, clutching his stomach as if he were in agony.

"You want to play games?" the man snapped. He grabbed Bolan by the hair and jerked his head up. "Do you have any idea who we are?"

The soldier tried to shake his head, but the hardman had a grip like a vise. "No," he said.

"We're two of Mehmet Akbar's sons. We have the office right across from his—Crescent Security."

Bolan recalled seeing the sign on the door. At the time, he hadn't paid it much attention. According to the registry on the front of the building, two private security firms had their offices there.

"We have surveillance cameras in the fake potted plants at both ends of the hall," the man went on. "The second you came out of the stairwell, we picked you up."

Bolan had to hand it to Mehmet Akbar. No one would be more protective of him than the man's own sons. Setting them up in their own security business right across from the export office was clever. It indicated Akbar's operation was much more sophisticated than Bolan had thought.

The younger Akbar gave him a rough shake. "You acted real suspicious, the way you were eyeing our father's office. So we decided to follow you."

Bolan chided himself. He'd been so intent on not losing Akbar that he'd neglected to watch his own back. It was a rare lapse that he hoped wouldn't prove fatal.

"Now, I'm going to ask you one more time," the man said, gouging a fingernail into Bolan's cheek. "Who are you, and why were you spying on our father?"

All the while the younger Akbar had been talking, Bolan had been girding himself. His legs were coiled to spring, his right arm poised. Just as he was ready to explode into action, a shout rang out from the mouth of the alley.

"This is the police! What's going on back there?"

Both Akbars did what anyone else would have done. They stiffened and swung toward the alley entrance.

Bolan sprang. Whipping the duffel bag like an oversize bat, he slammed it into the man, sending him flying into the left-hand wall. His brother spun, bringing up the Astra. The soldier caught him full on the chest with a reverse swing. The 9-mm pistol cracked, the slug chewing into the asphalt, and Amal crashed down on top of a crate, shattering the wood to splinters.

The pair was momentarily dazed. Up the alley, two of New Orleans's finest drew their weapons and advanced on the run.

Bolan could ill afford to spend hours in police custody. Pivoting, he dashed to the wire fence. He threw his bag over, then, taking a step back, he launched himself at the barrier and began to climb it swiftly.

"Hold it right there!"

Bolan ignored the command. He gained the top. The fence swayed under his weight as he forked a leg over the uppermost wire and heaved. For an instant it felt as if the whole section of fence would buckle and send him toppling, but it held and the next second he dropped lightly beside his bag.

"Freeze, mister!"

The fleet officer was a dozen yards away, his gun trained on Bolan's chest.

The Executioner snagged the duffel bag and angled toward the corner of the brick building. The officer swore vehemently. Looking back, Bolan saw the policeman start to clumsily climb the fence. He wasn't quite halfway up when the second officer got there and said something that convinced the first one to give up the chase. They turned to the Akbars.

Bolan didn't slow down until he came to the next street. Blending into the pedestrian flow, he headed west for two blocks, then turned to the north. For more than fifteen minutes he traveled in a random pattern, never going very far in any one direction.

At length the soldier relaxed. He had given them the slip, but his mission had become a lot more complicated.

No doubt the police would run in Akbar's sons for questioning. But since no crime had been committed, other than the discharge of a firearm within the city limits, a pistol Amal Akbar was probably licensed to carry, they'd be back out on the street in no time.

Now that the Akbars were alerted to his presence, Bolan knew they would take steps to keep him from meddling in their affairs. Security at their warehouse and Mehmet Akbar's home would be tightened. Akbar might even go into hiding. Finding the Golden Jihad, if the terrorists were indeed in the city, would be next to impossible.

Bolan wasn't about to give up, though, not with the stakes being what they were.

He had four hours to kill until nightfall. Making a hard probe of the warehouse or Akbar's residence in broad daylight, with the other side forewarned, would be certain suicide.

He took a leisurely stroll through the French Quarter. The narrow streets and shady passageways made it easy for him to verify no one was shadowing him.

As the sun dipped to the western horizon, he made his way to the waterfront. He stopped at a pay phone to put in a collect call to Stony Man Farm.

Hal Brognola had nothing new to report. Every last resource of the federal government had been brought to bear, yet the Feds might as well have been hunting for the proverbial needle in a haystack, for all the good it was doing them.

So far, no word of the theft of the backpack nukes had been leaked to the media. The President was holding off until there was no other choice, Brognola told Bolan. The Man still feared having a nationwide panic on his hands.

Bolan ended the call, reassuring Brognola that he'd be careful.

The wharves still bustled with activity, the port of New Orleans being one of the busiest in the world.

He discovered that the warehouse belonging to Mehmet Akbar was less than a block from the shore. On one side lay a vacant lot choked with weeds; on the other stood a bigger warehouse that belonged to a different company. He made a wide circuit of both.

According to a sign in the front window, Akbar's place was closed for business. No lights showed inside.

Bolan let the shadows lengthen before he slipped between the two warehouses. A parked forklift offered a convenient place to drop low. He plucked the Desert Eagle from his duffel bag and strapped the big pistol around his waist. He then readied the M-16, reattaching the upper and lower receiver groups and reseating the receiver pivot pin. Next, he slapped in a magazine.

The soldier noticed a side door to Akbar's warehouse. It prompted him to remove another item, a vibrating pick, before he hid the duffel bag under the forklift. Moving stealthily to the door, he tested the knob. Locked.

Squatting, he inserted the thin pick into the keyhole and pressed the black switch on the metal cylinder. Battery powered, the cylinder hummed as the pick shimmied the tumblers into position.

A vibrating pick took a lot longer than C-4 to open a locked door, but it was a lot quieter. Minutes ticked by as the pick throbbed. Now and again Bolan tried the knob. Just when he'd begun to think he'd have to rely on plastic explosive, the door opened.

He flicked off the pick and shoved it into a back pocket. Cracking the door with the barrel of his rifle, he pulled out a pencil flashlight and swiveled the head. The thin, bright beam speared the darkness ahead of him. He confirmed that no tripwires had been set before he eased inside.

Hugging the wall, he hunkered down and strained his ears. He could make out pallets stacked high with building supplies. Tucking the rifle stock to his shoulder, he crept down an aisle in a crouch.

Reaching a junction, Bolan spied a small office near the main entrance. He hastened down the side aisle, passing pallets of lumber and piled bags of cement mix. The office door was open. Bolan went through a desk and a file cabinet, neither containing anything out of the ordinary. He'd turned to the doorway, when a huge corrugated metal door on the other side of the office began to rise.

The soldier was out of the office in a flash. Ducking behind a pallet piled high with plywood, he turned off his flashlight. No sooner had he done so than the door rose high enough for the headlights of a car to pierce the interior.

A black four-door wheeled into the warehouse, followed by a tan sedan. They parked next to each other and hardmen spilled out.

Akbar's sons, Hadji and Amal, stepped from the black vehicle. They barked orders and overhead lights flared to life. The corrugated door was quickly closed, and the six gunners lined up in front of it. Amal stepped to a nearby crate, opened the lid and passed out subguns to the waiting men.

Bolan had to get out of there before he was discovered. He rose into a crouch, but paused when Hadji Akbar spoke.

"You all know what to do. Sooner or later the bastard who got away from my brother and me will show up, either here or at the house. When he does, he'll be in for a very big surprise."

"Do you want us to take him alive?" a gunner asked.

"We want him to look like a sieve when it is over," Amal stated.

Bolan didn't linger to hear any more. Bent low, he scooted between two pallets, then hastened along a narrow aisle toward the side of the building. He was halfway to the door he'd picked open when a gravelly voice bellowed from its vicinity.

"Hadji! Amal! The side door has been opened!"

"What?" Hadji Akbar shouted. "Maybe the man we want is already here! Spread out! Search for him! Remember, five hundred dollars goes to whichever one of you brings him down!"

CHAPTER SIX

The training sessions weren't going well, and Ahmed Tufayli was angry. He glared at the members of the Golden Jihad. "What is the matter with all of you, brothers?" he demanded in Arabic so Anderson wouldn't understand.

Nayif Nasrallah was the only one brave enough to say what all of them were thinking. "It is too complicated, Ahmed."

Tufayli leaned against the picture window in the living room. The curtains were drawn, so he wasn't afraid of being seen from outside. Folding his arms, he said with contempt, "Are you saying that Americans are smarter than we are? Are you telling me that you are too dumb to learn the arming sequence?"

Nasrallah bristled. "I am the equal of any American swine! But I have never been good at memorizing numbers. It gives me a headache!"

Tufayli faced his lieutenant. "And you, Hassan? Does it give you a headache, as well?"

Nidal didn't like being criticized in front of the others. Especially since he'd been doing better than most of them in getting the proper sequence down. "No, Ahmed," he answered. "We are all trying our best. We all want to see the Americans suffer. It is just that we need more time. Four days will not be enough. You said yourself that the soldier trained for months."

Tufayli frowned. Having his own words thrown back at him fueled his anger. "And you know that we should not stay in one place more than three days. To do so increases the odds of the Americans finding us."

"I know," Nidal said wearily. Their leader constantly drummed that fact into them.

"I have made an exception this time," Tufayli went on, "against my better judgment. We will stay here four days, but no longer."

Striding to the middle of the room, Tufayli towered over Sergeant Anderson. "Look at this stupid scum," he said, jabbing a finger at the noncom. "So what if it took him weeks to learn the procedure? We are more intelligent than the average American. We can do it in far less time."

Anderson was trying to figure out what his captors were talking about, but he was at a loss. When their leader pointed at him and a handful of them sneered, he gathered that he was the subject and that he'd just been insulted. But he wasn't about to speak up, not when his wife and son were downstairs and defiance might cost them their lives.

He shifted his attention to the Gun nukes. There were times when he wished that he'd never set eyes on them, when he regretted ever being picked for the SADM program.

His big mistake, Anderson realized, had been in bragging about it to Azadeh. The SADM unit was one of the most closely guarded secrets in the U.S. military. It was classified Top Secret—Eyes Only. Members of the two teams weren't supposed to tell a living soul, not even their families.

Anderson had been with the program for about four months when he'd let it slip. Azadeh and he had gone out on the town, their first evening out since the birth of their son. The sergeant had had quite a bit to drink, and before he'd quite realized what he was doing, he'd told his wife everything. He'd made her promise never to tell a living soul.

But Azadeh was only human. She'd written a letter to her parents in Kuwait, boasting of her husband's new job. They, in turn, had confided in a dozen or so close relatives. A cousin happened to unwittingly mention it to an friend with connections to the terrorist underground. The friend then passed on the information, for a price.

Or so Ahmed Tufayli had claimed when Anderson asked him how the Golden Jihad had found out about him.

A nudge on his shoulder made Anderson look up. "We are ready to go on," Tufayli said. "My men will not complain anymore, but you must do your part, Sergeant. You must not make it any harder on them than it has to be."

"I'm doing my best," Anderson said.

Tufayli's smile was as cold as ice. "I hope so, American. If I suspect that you are trying to trick us, I will go downstairs and personally cut your wife's tongue out. Do I make myself clear?"

Anderson's heart skipped a beat. His mouth went dry, and he had to swallow before he could reply. "Perfectly clear."

"Good. Let us proceed."

THE EXECUTIONER WAS in a tight spot. Eight hardmen were fanning out across the front of the warehouse door. Several more had come in by the side entrance and were doing the same. He was trapped in the middle. It was only a matter of time before a gunner spotted him.

An old adage said that in combat, it was always wise to take to the high ground. As a former sniper, Bolan knew the strategy was sound. Surrounded, he looked for a vantage point that would give him a clear field of fire, but limit the return fire of his enemies.

A small mountain of cinder blocks was stacked on a nearby pallet. Bolan moved around to the far side of it, slung his M-16 and climbed. The holes in the blocks made convenient handholds. In moments he was stretched out flat on top.

Inching to the edge, the soldier checked on the triggermen who had entered through the side. There were four of them, all armed to the tooth. Each advanced slowly up a different aisle.

Hadji and Amal Akbar and the men with them had divided into pairs. They scoured the main aisles, searching behind every pallet.

Bolan noticed that none of them thought to look up. He held his fire, hoping that once they'd covered the warehouse and not found him, they'd give up and he could slip from the building undetected. He should've known it wouldn't be that easy.

The two groups came within sight of each other. Hadji called to a thickset blond shooter. "Anything, Harry?"

"No, sir. Not a sign."

Amal stopped and lowered the Bushmaster he held. "We've looked everywhere."

Harry had a Colt AR-15 carbine with a collapsible stock. He went to cradle it in the crook of his left elbow but stopped when his eyes drifted to the top of a pallet piled high with boxes. "Not quite everywhere, boss," he said, and nodded.

Hadji caught on right away. At a gesture from him, three hardmen moved to the pallets and began to scale them.

Bolan aligned the sights of his M-16 on the fastest climber. The gunner clambered into full view, knelt and swiveled in a three-hundred-and-sixty-degree turn. The instant the man saw Bolan, he opened his mouth to alert the others. At a range of seventy-five feet, the soldier put a round through the hardman's tonsils.

A second gunner was just scrabbling onto the top of a pallet holding bags of cement mix. The next instant the back of his cranium burst outward, showering brains, blood and gore on Amal Akbar.

The third climber was more cautious. He risked a peek over the top of the pallet he was climbing, and lost an eye to the sting of a 5.56 mm hornet.

It all happened so swiftly that the three gunners were down before Hadji Akbar could bellow for the rest of his men to take cover. He dived behind a pallet. "Get the bastard!" he roared, and cut loose with his Uzi.

A thunderous din rocked the building as the remaining nine men unleashed a blistering firestorm of lead on the mountain of cinder blocks. Fanning out as they fired, they encircled the pallet to prevent their quarry from getting away.

Hadji emptied one magazine and slapped in another. Firing a sustained burst, he charged closer. Every gunner was doing likewise. Empty shells rained down, and magazines littered the floor.

The cinder blocks began to disappear in the hail of lead, bits and pieces flying in all directions. The top layers were soon cracked or split clear through.

Hadji was on his third magazine when it dawned on him that there was no return fire from the guy they'd cornered. "Stop shooting!" he yelled. He had to repeat himself before the gunfire tapered and died. He caught his brother's eye. Together, they raced to the pallet, shattered cinder fragments crunching under their feet.

Hadji beckoned Harry over and pointed upward. Without hesitation, the blond shooter set down the Colt AR-15, drew a pistol and climbed. Hadji glued his eyes to the rim, waiting for his enemy to show himself so he could blow the man's brains out. Harry reached the top without a shot being fired.

"He's gone, boss."

"That's impossible!" Amal responded. "Where the hell could he have got to?"

Only Bolan knew the answer, and he was outside the warehouse. A heartbeat after picking off the third climber, he'd slid to the corner farthest from the hardmen, let his legs dangle and dropped. He'd hit the floor just as Hadji gave the order to open fire. Then, ducking behind another pallet, he'd carefully worked his way to the side door. Hadji and Amal were rushing the cinder blocks when he slipped outside.

Pausing long enough to retrieve the duffel bag, Bolan sprinted to the end of the building. He crossed a narrow street to a high wooden fence bordered by overgrown shrubs. Plunging into the heart of the bushes, he crouched with his back to the fence.

There was the sound of heavy footfalls. Harry and four shooters appeared under the sole streetlight between the warehouse and the sidewalk. They scanned both directions, then Harry cursed. The men spread out, two of them making for the shrubbery. They made no attempt to conceal their hardware.

With only the streetlight providing illumination, Bolan doubted they would spot him, but he was ready, just in case.

The two gunners stayed close together, halting when they were a stone's throw from the bushes. One sank into a crouch to peer into the shadows while the other covered him. They were pros. At the slightest sound or hint of movement, they would open fire.

Bolan was no more than thirty feet from them. He didn't have on his blacksuit, but his clothes were dark enough that unless one of the gunners had a flashlight, he was safe.

As if on cue, the triggerman who had crouched produced a small flashlight. He flicked it on and played the beam over the shrubbery.

The light missed Bolan by no more than a few feet. The beam roved to the left, away from him, and then to the right, back toward him. It was so close that his elbow was caught in the glare, but a shout from the warehouse caused the gunner to twist to look behind him. The beam dipped to the ground.

"The boss wants everyone back inside! Now!"

Harry and his companions regrouped and moved off.

Bolan remained where he was. Until he could be sure they hadn't posted a lookout, he was content to bide his time. Soon car engines rumbled within the building. One of the vehicles left, but it was too far off and too dark for the soldier to tell which one.

The rattle of the corrugated door galvanized him into breaking down the M-16 and stowing it in his bag, together with the Desert Eagle and holster.

Keeping close to the wooden fence, he traveled more than a hundred yards before leaving cover. His penetration of the warehouse hadn't been a total waste. He knew the Golden Jihad wasn't hiding there, nor were the terrorists at the downtown office. By process of elimination, that left Mehmet Akbar's house.

Bolan reached the waterfront. Nearby, a freighter was being unloaded. Several men in suits watched from the dock, staring at the Executioner as he went by. He returned their looks, thinking they might be gunners from the warehouse, but none of them seemed familiar.

There was a pay phone at the next corner, and Bolan decided to put in a call to Brognola.

"Striker?" the big Fed said when he came on the line. "Anything new?"

"I was about to ask you the same thing," Bolan said.

Brognola sighed. "It's as if the Golden Jihad has vanished off the face of the earth. Without being specific about the reason we want them brought in, I've had the FBI put out a nationwide alert. So far, there's been no result. I don't mind telling you, I'm getting real worried."

"That makes two of us," Bolan admitted.

"What's the latest at your end?"

He filled Brognola in, ending with, "I'm on my way to Mehmet Akbar's place now. If the terrorists aren't there, we're back at square one."

"In more ways than you know. The forensics team I sent to the Poconos is back. They went over Anderson's cabin with a fine-tooth comb."

"Let me guess. They found nothing."

"Fingerprints, mostly. They were able to confirm that the woman and the child were held there awhile. Several of the prints we lifted belong to known members of the Jihad. A few are new to us. We're running them through Interpol and Scotland Yard."

Four or five vehicles had gone by while Bolan talked. He'd checked each one and seen no cause for alarm. Then he heard the metallic growl of another oncoming car, and he shifted to see it better. It was already quite close. As he turned, the engine revved even higher.

For a few heartbeats, the Executioner was held in the wash of headlights from the black sedan as it leaped the curb and rocketed toward the phone booth. Dropping the receiver, Bolan whipped open the door and dived to the side. He had no time to grab the duffel bag.

The sedan had been doing over seventy miles an hour. It smashed into the booth with the force of a battering ram, causing glass to explode and metal to crumple. The car bounced high as it shot over the tangled wreckage.

Bolan came down on his right shoulder. Rolling into a crouch, he palmed the Beretta and tracked the vehicle as it slewed into a turn to come back at him. His finger stroked the trigger twice, but instead of holes appearing in the windshield, the rounds merely nicked the glass, whining off into the darkness.

The soldier aimed a round at the front passenger door, but the slug splatted uselessly on armor plating.

Bolan hadn't counted on Akbar going to the expense of turning his vehicles into tanks. The more Bolan learned about the man's operation, the clearer it became that the exporter was no run-of-the-mill criminal. It made him wonder if Akbar was more involved in the terrorist network than the Feds had first suspected.

The driver of the black sedan had gotten the vehicle under control. Bolan rose and ran as the car barreled toward him. He reached the parking lot of a convenience store.

Two store customers had heard the crash of the phone booth, and they stood at the plate-glass window, gaping.

Bolan raced flat out. The sedan streaked toward him, tires squealing. He sprinted past a parked van. Ahead was a sidewalk and the storefront. There was nowhere to hide.

Whirling, the Executioner planted both feet and faced the vehicle head-on, holding the pistol straight out in front of him. He aimed at the driver.

The suppressor coughed four times. Bolan knew the 9-mm automatic didn't have the penetrating power of the Desert Eagle. The best he could hope for was to spiderweb the glass, or to cause the driver to duck. Either would do the trick.

It proved to be the latter. The gunner behind the wheel recoiled as the lead smacked close to his face. For a few critical seconds he was distracted, his eyes drawn away.

The Executioner sprang from the hurtling vehicle's path. It missed him by a full yard, bounced up over the sidewalk and struck the front of the convenience store with a tremendous crash.

Plate glass exploded every which way as the car plowed on. The two customers darted to safety, the woman shrieking in terror. The sedan smashed into a display, pulverizing it. Momentum carried the vehicle into a second row of shelves, where it came to rest, its engine still running.

Bolan didn't stay to see more. He sprinted toward what was left of the phone booth. The noise had drawn the attention of the longshoremen, and they were leaving the docks to investigate. It wouldn't be long before the police were summoned. The soldier needed to be long gone when the cops got there.

The duffel bag was buried under debris but seemed to be intact. Bolan kicked a jagged panel of broken glass out of the way and reclaimed his private arsenal.

By now the sedan was backing out of the store. The owner raged at the men inside, throwing broken items at the grille. The gunners ignored him. Burning rubber, the car looped around so that the front end pointed at the Executioner.

Bolan was right back where he'd started, caught flat-footed in the open. Fingers flying, he opened the bag. As the black sedan roared toward him again, he scooped out the Desert Eagle. He adopted a two-handed Weaver stance, but he didn't fire. Not yet.

The car crossed the parking lot in a blur, its engine a metallic banshee, a sadistic grin lighting the driver's face.

Bolan knew that so-called bulletproof glass came in different densities. Some could hold up to an Uzi at point-blank range, while others would only withstand small-caliber firearms.

The windshield on the sedan was impervious to the Beretta, but Bolan was about to test it against a .44 Magnum Desert Eagle, one of the most powerful handguns on the face of the planet.

He squeezed the trigger twice, and the twin blasts were like claps of thunder. Wide pockmarks appeared on the windshield, but the car kept coming. Bolan steadied his arms and fired twice more, aiming for the pockmarks where the stressed glass would be weakest.

The windshield splintered. The driver screamed and threw his hands over his face. The sedan veered out of control, shooting past the Executioner and out into the street.

Bolan glimpsed the gunners in the back seat trying to get their hands on the steering wheel, but the driver had slumped over it. Evidently his foot had tramped on the gas pedal because instead of slowing, the vehicle picked up speed. It careered up and over the far curb, tossing the passengers around as if they were straw dolls. The oil pan bottomed out with a piercing shriek. Sparks flew as metal grated on concrete. The sedan sped across a strip of pier, crashed through a restraining barrier and became airborne.

The soldier didn't linger to see the car pancake. Grabbing his bag, he spun and jogged off down the street. At the next corner he cut to the right, where there were fewer lights and less traffic. He checked behind him, but no one was in pursuit.

Bolan had traveled two blocks when the wail of sirens heralded the approach of the police. Darting into an alley, he clung to the shadows until he came to a nearly deserted side street.

He slowed to a walk. The police would be busy for a while, fishing the sedan out of the river and questioning eyewitnesses. He was safe enough, but he had to get out of that section of the city, and quickly.

A cruising cab offered Bolan the means. He gave the driver directions and leaned back against the seat.

As bloody as the first skirmish with the Akbar clan had been, something told Bolan that the worst was yet to come.

CHAPTER SEVEN

Anderson was going over the arming procedure for what seemed to be the hundredth time.

The terrorists were slow learners. A few, such as Hassan Nidal, had half of the sequence down and could perform it with fair accuracy. But the rest had to struggle to memorize the codes, and they forgot from one hour to the next what they had already learned.

Anderson was patient with them. Every time they bungled it, he thought of his wife and son. It didn't help matters any that the terrorist leader hovered over him like a hawk, monitoring his every move.

They had been at it for ninety minutes when Ahmed Tufayli told them to take a break. Anderson was on the floor between the two Gun nukes. Slumping with exhaustion, he stared at the detonation time clocks on one of the devices. He was thinking of the horrible loss of life that would result once those clocks were set, when suddenly the idea came to him.

Anderson knew very little of Tufayli's master plan, other than where the Golden Jihad was going to set off the backpack nukes. He assumed that both devices would be timed to detonate simultaneously. He also assumed that the terrorists would allow themselves a safety margin of hours or even days between the time the nukes were armed and the actual detonation.

If that was the case, then Anderson saw a way to foil them without giving himself away. The terrorists had no way of knowing that once the nukes were armed and the detonation time clocks set, there was an added step that had to be taken in order for the bombs to go off. It involved setting the detonation time clock lock.

The lock feature was the last in a series of failsafe procedures. A simple press of a button was all it took. If it wasn't pressed, the clock would tick down to the time set for the blast, then automatically reset at zero without the nuke going off.

Anderson started to smile and caught himself. If he could pull this off, it would prevent countless thousands from being killed. And if he played his cards right, it might buy his family time to give the terrorists the slip.

At that moment, Ahmed Tufayli's shadow fell across him. Anderson panicked, fearful he had somehow given his thoughts away by his expression. "What's up?" he asked, his voice cracking.

Tufayli enjoyed seeing the fear in the American's eyes. As long as the soldier was afraid of him, he could bend Anderson to his will.

Taking a seat, Tufayli asked, "Which five of my men are learning the arming procedure the fastest?"

The only one whose name Anderson knew was Hassan Nidal. He mentioned the lieutenant's name, then pointed out four others who were doing almost as well.

Tufayli nodded. "I agree with you. I have been watching them closely, and they are the best." Reaching out, he patted one of the nukes. "I will have them set off the first of these beauties."

Only by sheer force of will was Anderson able to keep his tone even as he asked, "You're not setting them both off at the same time?"

"Of course not," Tufayli said. "The effect on the American people will be twice as devastating if two cities are struck twenty-four hours apart. Wouldn't you agree?"

Anderson nodded. His scheme to turn the tables was unraveling before he could even put it into effect.

"Besides," Tufayli added, "I wouldn't put it past you to try and dupe us. This way, if the first nuke doesn't go off when it should, I can take steps to persuade you to correct your mistake with the second one." His smile was as smug as only a madman's could be.

"You don't miss a trick," Anderson said, despairing of ever getting himself and his family out of this mess. No matter what he did, he stood to lose his life and those who meant more to him than anything.

Tufayli stood. "All right, brothers," he declared in Arabic, "back to work. Remember, learn your jobs well so that soon you will have the distinction of going down in history as the noble warriors who brought America to its knees."

AUDUBON PARK WAS much bigger than Bolan had thought it would be—three hundred and fifteen lush acres that stretched between the Mississippi River and St. Charles Avenue. It was so big that it included a zoo and a golf course.

Bolan was let off on St. Charles. He headed for the man-made hill put in by the city fathers to show the people of flat New Orleans what a hill looked like. From its summit he enjoyed a sweeping vista of the city.

Of special interest was the quiet residential area east of the park. Bolan didn't like the notion of engaging in a firefight in a city. Too many innocent bystanders were at risk. But it seemed he couldn't avoid it in this instance.

He reminded himself of what was at stake. Unless the backpack nukes were recovered, the cost in human lives would be atrocious. He had to weigh them in the balance with the few that might be lost if he made a hard penetration of Mehmet Akbar's estate.

Suddenly he saw a city beat cop strolling toward him. He shifted, gazing to the north. Spying on the officer out of the corner of his eye, he hoped there wasn't an APB out for someone answering to his description.

Other people were on the hill, and Bolan blended in among them, trying to be inconspicuous. Slouching to disguise his six-foot-three-inch height, he ambled to the east.

The patrolman reached the crest and looked around. Showing no interest in Bolan, he grinned when a small boy bounced up to him to admire his uniform.

The soldier was soon out of sight in the trees. He avoided walkways and congested areas, going on until he left the park. Akbar's house number was etched in his memory. When he judged that he was about two blocks away, he circled to the south. A reconnaissance was in order.

The neighborhood resembled any other. Most of the homes were well lit and it all seemed perfectly normal. There were no cars crammed with hardmen parked on the street corners, waiting for Bolan to show, and no gunners were making the rounds of the neighborhood. Mehmet Akbar was keeping a low profile.

Turning onto Akbar's street, he slowly walked toward the residence. It was the biggest one on the block, an older Spanish-style house with a large, neatly kept lawn flanked by four high stone walls.

There was no sign of security cameras, but that didn't mean there was none. A closed wrought-iron gate appeared to be the only way in. Bolan noticed an intercom speaker and a buzzer mounted on the wall beside it. No guards had been posted.

A circle drive looped in front of the house, empty of cars. The house itself was dark, giving the impression no one was home.

Bolan passed the gate, came to the street corner and scanned the block to make sure no one was watching him. Ducking around the wall, he moved into deep shadow and squatted.

Something wasn't quite right. Back at the warehouse, Hadji Akbar had mentioned that welcome committees had been set up at both places. Yet no one was at the residence. Bolan saw two explanations. Either Akbar had fled, or the house wasn't really deserted.

There was only one way to find out.

In short order Bolan once again had the Desert Eagle holstered on his hip and the M-16 locked and loaded. A few extra items went into his pockets. Stowing the duffel bag in a patch of high grass, he stalked toward the rear of the property.

The stone wall was eight feet high, and no trees grew close to it. Bolan slung the rifle, paced off ten steps and faced the corner. Breaking into a dead run, he flew toward the wall. At just the right moment, he leaped, his arms outstretched. His grasping fingers caught hold of the rough lip, and he quickly hoisted himself onto his elbows. From there it was an easy matter to swing both legs onto the top.

The soldier paused. A small stand of trees grew farther in. Between them and the house was an idle white fountain ringed by marble benches, a gazebo to its right. Nothing moved, and all the windows were as dark as those out front.

He went over the side, landing lightly on the balls of his feet. Unslinging the M-16, he hugged the left wall as he glided forward.

Once more, no security devices were obvious, yet Bolan couldn't shake a nagging feeling that he was being observed. Coming abreast of the trees, he darted into them, went prone and slithered to a spot where he could see the whole house.

Bolan let some time go by. Barging into a trap wasn't to his liking. When he saw no activity inside and no lights appeared, he set the M-16 on semiautomatic and crept to the back door.

Made of thick oak, it could probably withstand a portable police battering ram. Bolan stepped to a window, which was barred. So was the next. He checked each one as far as the corner. Peering around it, he froze.

A pair of Dobermans was lying near the front of the house. One of them suddenly raised its head and sniffed the air. Both dogs turned toward him.

Bolan didn't wait to see if they had caught his scent. Wheeling, he sprinted to the opposite end of the house. He was barely out of sight, his eye pressed to the corner of the house wall, when the Dobermans trotted into view. They stopped and sniffed at where he'd stood. One growled softly and they came on at a brisk trot, their noses low to the ground.

The grounds offered nowhere to hide, nor could he reach the front gate before the dogs overtook him. Then Bolan saw that ivy covered much of that side of the house. It rose as high as the second-story windows, and none of the windows on that level was barred.

Slinging the M-16 over his right shoulder, Bolan coiled, then jumped as high as he could. He didn't know if the ivy would bear his weight. If not, he'd have to kill the dogs before they got close enough to kill him. And he was reluctant to kill animals that were doing what they'd been trained for.

The big man's fingers wrapped around the clinging vines, and he held on for all he was worth. The ivy sagged. He thought it would rip right off the wall, but then it steadied. Hand over hand, he went higher, the leaves rustling under him. He was careful not to put too much strain on any one strand. Halfway up, a low snarl made him look down.

The Dobermans sat on their haunches at the base of the wall, their thin lips drawn back to reveal their gleaming teeth.

Bolan hoped they wouldn't bark. They began to pace, growling low in their throats, but they didn't make enough noise to rouse any of the neighbors.

The Executioner had to lean out from the wall to snag the windowsill, which was broad and dusty. He held on tight with one hand, then let go of the vines to lift his other arm. His hand on the sill slipped, and he started to fall. Thrusting both arms into the vines, he brought himself to a lurching stop, but in so doing, some of the vines broke. His body canted backward. The Dobermans were on their feet, growling in anticipation.

Bolan threw himself against the wall, gouging purchase for his feet. This time the vines held firm.

Exhaling in relief, he climbed back up to the sill. This time he was more careful, first brushing off any dust, then wiping his hand on his shirt. Getting as good a hold as he could, he slowly pulled himself high enough to prop both arms on top of the sill.

The room within lay dark and still. Bolan pushed up on the bottom of the window and was surprised when it rose easily and silently. It seemed strange that Akbar had put bars on the windows on the first floor, but hadn't bothered to secure those on the second. Then again, with the dogs roving the grounds, perhaps it hadn't seemed necessary.

With a deft flip, Bolan was inside, crouched and alert, the Beretta snug in his right hand. A night-vision device would have come in handy. The room was pitch black except for near the window. Vaguely he made out the outline of a bed and a vanity. The fragrance of a musky perfume hung in the air.

Bolan was in a woman's bedroom. He listened but heard nothing. Apparently the house really was vacant. In that case, he figured he'd make a sweep of all three floors and see what he turned up. If the Golden Jihad had been there, he should find a clue.

Moving to the door, Bolan tested the knob. It turned, and he carefully stepped out. A corridor ran the length of the house, and thick pile carpet made moving stealthily a breeze.

Soon Bolan came to a mahogany table bearing a large Middle Eastern vase. Beside the table was a bannister. Below, a spacious living area unfolded. He moved to the top of a spiral staircase, took three steps down and stopped as bright light bathed the picture window.

Tires crunched on the drive, then car doors slammed.

The soldier ducked behind the table as the front door opened. A switch was flicked and the living room lit up. Someone was talking, a voice Bolan recognized even though he'd only heard the man ever say a few words.

"—damned lucky they were able to fish you out of the river," Mehmet Akbar was grumbling. "It would've served both of you right if you'd gone down with the car and drowned."

The Executioner ventured a look. Behind Akbar came Hadji and Amal, their damp clothes clinging to them. Three gunners dogged their footsteps. Three more men entered seconds later, and one closed the door.

"We were only following your orders," Hadji said.

Mehmet Akbar was a full head shorter than both his sons, as well as thirty pounds lighter. Yet he turned on them, poking each of them in the chest. "*My* orders? I don't recall telling you to turn the streets into a war zone! And I sure as hell didn't tell you to destroy a convenience store!"

Amal cringed. "But—" he began, but got no further.

"But nothing! My instructions were crystal clear! You were to set a trap for the meddler at the warehouse. The idea was to eliminate him with no one being the wiser." He balled a fist as if to strike Amal. "What do you use for brains? Now you'll be in the papers and on the newscasts! If I didn't have one of the best lawyers in New Orleans, you'd both still be sitting in jail."

Hadji shifted from one foot to the other. "We apologize."

Akbar dismissed the apology with a gesture. "A fat lot of good that does us. Our entire operation ran smoothly for so many years because I was smart enough to keep a low profile. Now, in a moment of supreme stupidity, two of my sons have ruined everything.'' He paused. ''Wait until your brothers out at the farm hear the news!''

Bolan's interest rose. The Feds had never mentioned a farm. He wondered if that could be where the Golden Jihad terrorists were lying low. Placing a hand on the floor for balance, he leaned forward to hear better. As he did so, a distinct click came from behind him and something touched his nape.

''I wouldn't move if I were you big man.''

Bolan's first instinct was to hurl himself to one side and blaze away, but the knowledge that he would be dead before he completed the roll rooted him to where he was. Frowning, he let the M-16, the Desert Eagle and the Beretta be taken by a second hardman.

''All right, mister. Stand and move out onto the landing, arms up.''

Bolan did as the gunner said. All eyes lifted toward him. Hadji and Amal glared their hatred, but their father merely smiled.

''Well, Edwards, what do we have here?''

The man behind Bolan, a skinny triggerman partial to a Glock pistol, said, ''We've been monitoring him from the control room ever since he scaled the back wall. He never saw the camera in the fountain.''

Mehmet Akbar strutted up the stairs. "How did he elude Samson and Hercules?"

Edwards snickered. "He came up the vines on the east side. The dogs couldn't reach him." The gunner shook his head in amazement. "You should've seen him, boss. He's a regular Tarzan."

The senior Akbar halted and studied Bolan. His sons climbed the stairs and made to move past him to get at the Executioner. With a resounding slap to Amal's jaw, Akbar brought them to a stop. "What do the two of you think you're doing?"

"He's ours!" Hadji declared. "We owe him! Let us pay him back here and now!"

Amal nodded.

Their father gave both of them a push that nearly tumbled them down the staircase. "What is the matter with you? Did everything I said a minute ago go in one ear and out the other?" He jabbed a finger at the floor. "You would kill him here? In my home?"

Under different circumstances, Bolan might have found the stupefied expressions of the two sons comical.

Akbar sighed. "You boys can learn from Edwards, here. Explain to them, Edwards, why you let our visitor into the house instead of killing him out on the lawn."

"We can't have any of the neighbors notice," the gunner said, showing his teeth. So did several of the others. Hadji and Amal were clearly not held in much esteem by the shooters who worked for the family.

"Did you hear?" Akbar baited his sons.

"We would have done the same," Hadji said sullenly.

"I think not. I think you would have gunned him down out in the open, and my house would now be surrounded by police."

Akbar turned to Bolan. His face hardened. "Enough of them. I want to know who you are, who sent you and why you invaded my house."

Bolan didn't respond. Giving one's name, rank and serial number didn't apply in the war on terrorism.

Amal's temper flared. "All I need is ten minutes with him, Father, and you will have the information you want."

Akbar was nearing the end of his patience. "How would you persuade him? Break his legs? His arms?" He waved a finger in Bolan's face. "Look at him, Amal. This one is not weak. You could beat on him all day with a baseball bat and he still wouldn't tell you anything."

"Then how will we get the truth out of him?"

Akbar chuckled. "There are ways. There are always ways."

To Edwards, he said, "We will take our visitor to the farm. There, we will have all the privacy we need to do this the right way."

A pair of gunners seized Bolan and roughly ushered him to the first floor. Ringed by a half-dozen others, he was pushed toward the front door.

The Akbars were in the lead. Mehmet Akbar paused at the door and looked back at Bolan. "I hope you will make this easy on both of us and change your mind on the ride out. If not . . ." He shrugged, then smiled, "I hope that you are fond of snakes."

CHAPTER EIGHT

Any hope Mack Bolan had of being able to slip free of his captors on the ride to the Akbar farm was dashed the moment they shoved him into the back seat of a beige car and two gunners slid in on either side. Wedged between them, their pistols gouging his ribs, there was nothing the soldier could do.

Mehmet Akbar sat in the front, while Hadji drove. The other son, Amal, rode in a second car with four hardmen.

They took Interstate 10 to Highway 39, and from there followed secondary roads to the southeast. For a while, low ridges paralleled the roadways. In due course the frontlands gave way to marsh. They were entering bayou country.

Taking Bolan prisoner had put Akbar in good spirits. He hummed and whistled the whole trip. When the marshlands appeared, he turned and said, "Take a good look at your final resting place."

Bolan made no comment.

"The bayou never gives up its secrets," Akbar went on. "That is a saying among the Cajuns down here. When I was younger, I never understood what they meant."

Seeking to learn about Akbar's operation, Bolan remarked, "That was obviously before you turned to aiding and abetting mass murderers."

The senior Akbar's fine humor evaporated. "I do not like your tone."

Edwards, who sat on the Executioner's right, dug his pistol into Bolan's ribs. "Be careful what you say. All the boss has to do is nod and this will go off."

A minute went by, then Akbar spoke again. "There is much more to my operation than you know. It is huge. The righteous warriors who fight our Holy War rely heavily on me."

Bolan pondered his statement. Since he doubted Akbar would answer direct questions, he tried an oblique approach. "Was your father involved in the terrorist network too?"

"No. My father loved America. I tried to get him to see the truth, but he died still believing that this is the land of golden opportunity."

"He was right," Bolan said.

Akbar whipped around. "He was a fool! Whenever we went back to Iraq, he refused to admit that Western influences were destroying the old way of life. He was blind to American imperialism, to American deceit.''

''But you weren't,'' Bolan said dryly.

''Damn right I wasn't!'' Akbar grew more excited. ''My grandfather and my cousins opened my eyes. They showed me how evil this country is, how it is trying to mold the world in its own wicked capitalistic image.''

Bolan had heard that lame rationale many times. ''Americans have no desire to conquer the world.''

''Perhaps not with armies. Your leaders rely on political pressure and economic sanctions to force their will on others.'' He snorted. ''It won't work, though. In the end, freedom and truth will win. Those who try to oppress mankind will be punished for their sins.''

Nothing Bolan could say would set such warped logic straight, so he didn't even try. Besides, he'd met fanatics like Akbar before, men who believed only what they wanted to, even when those beliefs flew in the face of reality.

He glanced at Edwards. Most of the gunners were local, which made Bolan wonder how devoted they were to Akbar's cause. ''What about you?'' he asked. ''Are you fighting the Holy War, too?''

The gunner snickered. "I'm in this for the money. Mr. Akbar pays real well."

"So you don't mind being a traitor to your own country?"

Edwards pursed his lips. "I don't think of it that way. To me it's just a job. I do my work, collect my check and that's all." He wagged the Glock. "Offing a few stiffs now and then is no big deal."

"So the deaths of thousands of innocents won't bother you?"

Edwards was clearly puzzled. "What do you mean?"

Akbar turned to stab a finger at Bolan. "Shut up. Another word and I will have you gagged for the remainder of the ride."

Bolan said no more. He had learned what he wanted to. The shooters working for Akbar had no idea their boss was involved in the most diabolical terrorist plot ever hatched. It was food for thought.

Eventually they turned onto a gravel road that became a dirt ribbon winding deep into the bayou. Murky channels of sluggish water laced the lowland, broken here and there by islands of ground, some of them many acres wide.

Twenty minutes after leaving the road, an island rose up out of the marsh in front of them. Buildings became visible, nestled among the trees.

Hadji had to stop to open a closed gate. There were no guards, but a video camera was mounted on a stump nearby.

Close up, Bolan could see the buildings were in poor condition: the paint was blistered and peeling; cracks marred the walls; several windows were broken; a door hung by one hinge. The ancient homestead gave every appearance of being abandoned.

"It looks like a dump, doesn't it?" Akbar said as he climbed out. "Anyone who saw this place from the air would never suspect what goes on inside."

Hadji drove straight for the side of a dilapidated barn. As they neared the wall, it suddenly swiveled out and up, rising on recessed rollers as would an automatic garage door.

Bolan was impressed. Hidden behind the facade of decay and neglect was a building of corrugated metal. A concrete floor was piled high with crates and boxes, just as the warehouse on the waterfront had been. But where those crates had contained building materials, this one was crammed with ordnance of every shape and size. Stenciled labels identified machine guns, rocket launchers, grenades, mortars and more. It was an arms cache worth millions on the black market.

Bolan put two and two together. "You weren't just bragging earlier," he said to Akbar as the gunners hustled him from the vehicle. "You run an arms pipeline to the Middle East."

The man beamed. "It's more than that. I've been selling arms to terrorists all over the world for many years now, without once arousing the suspicions of the federal government. Clever, don't you think? Here I am, one of the largest suppliers of illegal weapons anywhere, operating right under their noses."

Bolan scanned the containers. "Stingers, M-29s, M-60s," he read aloud. "The only way you could get your hands on these is if you have a supplier in the military."

"Whether I have or not is irrelevant to you," Akbar said, "since you will not live long enough to make use of the information."

A half-dozen men had been working at various tasks when the cars pulled in. Now two of them came over. Both were spitting images of Akbar, only twenty to thirty years younger.

Bolan guessed they were the other two sons, a hunch confirmed when Akbar embraced them.

"Subhi. Musa. I have brought a guest. Would you be so kind as to take him into the back. Give him the same treatment you gave that street cop who was sniffing around our operation a while back.''

Subhi was the oldest, a square chunk of a brute who looked as unstoppable as a tank. Musa's dark eyes sparkled at the thought of doing Bolan harm. At a nod from him, Edwards and another gunner seized the Executioner and hauled him toward the rear.

The temptation was strong, but Bolan dared not resist. If he broke free, he'd be gunned down before he went five yards.

A metal door opened into a small, bare room. The only thing in it was a long chain and a meat hook suspended from a high metal girder.

At a word from Musa, Bolan was bound. Edwards looped the rope that bound his wrists over the hook, and he was hoisted up. He dangled a good foot off the floor, the rope biting into his skin.

Subhi Akbar stripped off his shirt, his powerhouse frame rippling with muscle. Flexing his arms, he stepped up to Bolan. "Scream all you want to, mister," he said with a sneer. "The only ones who'll hear don't give a damn whether you live or die.''

Bolan watched the man fold his ham-sized hands into fists, and he tensed for the first blow.

Being mentally prepared in no way lessened the agony that lanced his ribs a moment later.

The brute grinned and rubbed his knuckles. ''That felt good. I haven't had a decent workout in a long time.'' Setting himself into a boxing stance, Subhi began to pound on the Executioner in earnest.

WHERE WAS STRIKER? Brognola checked his watch for the tenth time in as many minutes.

Bolan was supposed to call in at least once every five hours. Forty-five minutes had gone by since the last call was due, and the big Fed couldn't help worrying.

Since their previous contact, Brognola had put the resources of the federal government, as well as those of a number of international agencies, to work on uncovering all they could about Mehmet Akbar. Few concrete leads had been gleaned, but there were enough interesting tidbits for Brognola to piece together part of the picture.

Paper trails revealed that two of Akbar's best customers were in Iraq and Iran. Others were in Syria, Libya, Pakistan and Colombia. Wherever terrorist or anarchist elements flourished, Mehmet Akbar did business.

Exactly what kind of business was unknown, but if Brognola had to hazard a guess, he'd say that Akbar was in the illicit arms trade, and had been for quite some time. It astounded him that the man had gotten away with it for so long.

Brognola had to remember that for all its superior intel-gathering ability, the government didn't, and couldn't, know everything. Some intel was bound to fall through the cracks. Federal agents were only human, and they made mistakes, like everyone else.

Rising from his desk, Brognola left the office. He needed to keep busy, to channel his restless energy until he heard from his friend.

Venturing to the first-floor dining area, Brognola helped himself to a sandwich and coffee. A handful of blacksuits and other Farm employees were scattered at the tables. In a corner, his bulk out of all proportion to his wheelchair, was Aaron Kurtzman.

Brognola went over. "Mind if I join you, Bear?"

The computer expert looked up from the newspaper he'd been reading. "Not at all," he said, scrutinizing the big Fed closely as Brognola eased into a chair. "How goes the war?"

"It's gone better. Striker's late reporting in. I'm giving him another half hour, then I'm sending in a backup squad."

Kurtzman set down his paper. "It seems this one's really getting to you."

"You know the details. So can you blame me?" Brognola took a bite of his sandwich, then dropped it. Suddenly he wasn't so hungry. Being reminded of the potential catastrophe they faced was enough to spoil anyone's appetite.

Kurtzman offered a kindly smile. "Don't be so hard on yourself. You're doing the best you can."

"What if it's not good enough this time?" Brognola said. "You helped the computer crew project casualty losses, so you know what's at stake."

"It's no more than what's at stake any other time."

"How can you say that? It's not as if we're up against a drug lord or a Mafia-type. We're talking nuclear weapons here. There's a hell of a lot more at stake than usual."

Kurtzman spread out the newspaper and began reading the headlines of some of the columns. "'State Department Believes North Korea Has Developed A-Bomb.' 'Thousands Die In Nerve Gas Attack In Japan.' 'Iraq Used Biological Weapons In War.'" He shook his head. "I'm sorry, my friend, but the stakes are always the same. All that changes are the players and the playing field."

"Maybe so, but each year it gets worse out there. The threats grow bigger, the consequences more terrible." He sighed in frustration. "When the cold war ended, I had such high hopes that the worst was behind us. That's not the case. The worst is yet to come."

"It'll be that way until humanity learns to live together in peace."

"I'll doubt whether either of us will live long enough to see that happen."

Kurtzman nodded. "Even so, that's our goal, isn't it? To make this world a better, safer place? Maybe it won't be for us, or even for the next generation. But sooner or later, peace will prevail. We have to believe that, or we might as well give up now."

In his heart, Brognola knew Kurtzman was right, but all that went through his head was the same question he'd been asking for the better part of an hour: Where the hell was Mack Bolan?

SUBHI AKBAR HAD DONE a thorough job. From shoulders to hips, from front to back, he had rained punch after punch on Bolan's body. They were never hard enough to break any bones, but always with enough force to cause excruciating pain.

Initially Bolan had gritted his teeth to keep from crying out, but after Subhi had been at it a while, there'd been no need. Bolan had crossed a threshold that numbed him to the sustained blows. It was as if he had reached a plateau of agony.

Subsequent punches didn't make the pain any worse, but they did cause it to last longer. An hour after the beating, hanging alone in the darkened room, Bolan felt as if Subhi were still right there, pounding on him.

The door opened, letting in light. Bolan shut his eyes against the glare.

"How are you holding up?"

It was Edwards, the skinny gunner. Bolan wasn't about to admit how he really felt, so he kept his mouth shut.

"You are one tough bastard," Edwards said. "I don't know how you kept from screaming your guts out."

Bolan licked his dry lips but still didn't speak.

"The big boss wants to see you," Edwards said. He glanced at the doorway. "Before Bullock gets here to help me, I've got a question." His voice dropped to a whisper. "What was that stuff you were saying about thousands of people dying? Was that some kind of scam?"

"No," Bolan replied.

"Americans?"

"Yes."

Edwards checked the doorway again. "You're sure Akbar is involved? I know he's hooked up with some spooky flakes from overseas, but I never figured he'd import them. How are they planning to do it? Poison gas or something like that?"

The theft of the backpack nukes was supposed to be a closely guarded secret, but Bolan had to come clean. "Nuclear weapons," he said. "Terrorists your boss helped sneak into the country plan to set them off in a major city."

The skinny triggerman swore. "You're not jiving me?"

Bolan looked down at him.

Edwards swallowed hard. "No, I guess you're not. I'll off anyone for the right price, but nuking an American city! Jesus!"

At that instant a shadow filled the doorway. In strolled one of the other shooters, a brawny specimen almost as big as Subhi.

"Give me a hand, Bullock," Edwards directed.

The two men soon had Bolan off the hook. He swayed when his feet made contact with the floor. For a moment he expected to keel over, but Edwards grabbed him by the shoulders and held him until his strength returned.

"Can you walk?"

Bolan nodded. Bullock pushed him toward the door, and the soldier nearly proved himself a liar by stumbling. Righting himself, he walked slowly into the main bay.

Mehmet Akbar and his four sons were waiting.

"I trust you are up to a little walk," the patriarch of the criminal network said. "We have something to show you. Something that will help loosen your tongue, now that Subhi has softened you up."

The Akbars moved toward a door on the north side of the building. Edwards and Bullock accompanied Bolan, their pistols out and cocked.

The big man gained strength with every step. It surprised him to see the sun had risen.

Akbar gestured grandly. "It's hard for me to believe that once I hated the bayou country." He inhaled deeply. "Now I see it as my ally. It cloaks my operations, and helps dispose of my enemies."

Bolan was guided past a dilapidated house and into a grove of cypress trees. They stuck to an old footpath fringed by marsh.

"I can understand now why the Cajuns love this swamp as much as they do," Mehmet Akbar continued. "It is a separate world from the one we know, a world of savage beauty that few outsiders dare to penetrate. It took a man of my genius to see the possibilities here.''

Bolan glanced from the Akbars to the gunners, poised to explode into action the moment his chance came. But Bullock kept him covered the whole time, while Hadji and Subhi watched him like twin birds of prey.

Akbar waved a hand at the marsh. "It looks so peaceful, but it is crawling with all sorts of dangerous creatures, with bogs, quicksand and sinkholes. Most men wouldn't last two minutes out there. How about you?''

Bolan had extensive skill in jungle and swamp survival, a secret best kept to himself. "How many people have you disposed of out here?" he asked for future reference.

Akbar reflected a bit. "Somewhere between twenty and thirty. I've lost count over the years.''

Musa Akbar cleared his throat. "Is it wise, Father, to reveal so much?''

"If it wasn't, I wouldn't do so. Don't worry, our guest won't live long enough to pass on the information." He nodded at the marsh. "Even if he did, the bodies are long gone. In the bayou, even human flesh and bone is biodegradable." He laughed.

Bolan slowed, intending for the Akbars to pull ahead so he'd be alone with Bullock and Edwards, but the muzzle of a Ruger prodded his spine.

"Pick up the pace, Slick," Bullock warned, "or you die that much sooner."

There was a wide clearing around the next bend. Across it, covered by vines and moss, stood an old stone wall that had to have once been part of a dwelling. At its base lay a sinkhole.

Akbar stepped to the edge, then beckoned. "Come take a look, tough guy."

Bolan moved to the brink. The sides were covered with short grass, and a writhing mass of hissing shapes filled the bottom half of the pit—copperheads, scores of them, their forked tongues darting in and out, the hourglass patterns on their skin identifying them clearly.

CHAPTER NINE

Mack Bolan was no coward. Time and again he'd proved his courage in combat. He'd gone up against overwhelming odds and never so much as flinched, even in the face of death.

But the thought of being thrown into that pit, with its slithering mass of venomous reptiles, wasn't appealing. Involuntarily he started to back up. He'd taken only a single step when Bullock's pistol, poking into his shoulder blade, reminded him of the equally lethal two-legged serpents who surrounded him.

"I don't know much about snakes," Akbar said. "I can't say if this hole is a breeding spot. I only know that we almost always find a lot here, and they can be quite entertaining."

The four younger Akbars wore grins of bloodthirsty anticipation.

"I do know a little about copperheads, though," Akbar continued. "The bite of just one is rarely fatal. It'll make a person as sick as a dog, but that's about all." He motioned at the roiling mass. "Being bitten by dozens at the same time, however, is another story. It must be as painful as hell, because everyone we've thrown in there begins screaming bloody murder in no time." He smirked at Bolan. "A tough guy like you might go two minutes, tops."

Hadji rubbed his hands together. "It takes a long while to die, mister. Hours, in fact. First your legs will go numb, and you won't be able to stand. Once you fall, more of them will bite you, in the face, in the neck, everywhere. You'll try to get up, but you won't be able to. Then comes the fun part." He chortled. "You swell up like a balloon, and your face turns black and blue. If you're like most people, you'll beg us to put you out of your misery. But you know what?"

"We won't," Amal finished.

Suddenly Subhi, on Bolan's left, seized him by the wrist, pivoted and heaved.

Bolan tried to jerk loose. He tried to dig in his heels for traction, but his soles found none on the slick grass. Before he knew it, he was flung over the rim and sliding down the short slope toward the squirming, scaly throng.

Harsh laughter erupted above.

The soldier twisted, digging a furrow with his shoes. He lurched to a stop less than a foot from the reptiles. Immediately he froze. There was no reaction from the copperheads. They went on writhing over one another. Then a small one, the yellow tip of its tail quivering, slid toward his right foot.

Bolan did nothing. Stomping the snake might make matters worse. It was bound to thrash about, inciting the others, and he'd be up to his waist in copperheads in no time.

He let the snake reach his shoe. As rigid as steel, he watched it crawl onto the top of his shoe, stop and dart its forked tongue at his leg. Another larger snake poked its head from the mass and regarded him with unblinking eyes.

Up on the rim, Hadji cursed. "This isn't getting us anywhere. Let's push him all the way in."

"Patience, son," Akbar said. "Give our reptile friends a little more time. You know how much they dislike intruders."

As if to emphasize the point, the small copperhead reared up and hissed at Bolan. He was tempted to flick it off, but the bigger specimen had crawled closer, within striking range.

"Come on, you stupid snakes!" Hadji said. "Do something!"

The small copperhead obliged. With lightning speed it struck at Bolan's leg. Its fangs pierced a fold of his pants, but not his flesh. The snake snapped its length from side to side, as if in a fury, then drew back to strike again. For a few seconds it swayed, its tongue testing the air. When its assault went unchallenged, it looped about and slithered back into the roiling mass.

Bolan's mouth had gone as dry as the Sahara. He focused on the larger copperhead. It inched near to his foot. Its tongue brushed his shoe. Hissing, it rose up as if to sink its fangs into him. Bolan braced to fling himself out of the way, knowing that even as fast as he was, his reflexes were no match for the speed of the snake.

Tense moments passed. Inexplicably the copperhead lowered its head to the ground, curled in on itself and rejoined its fellows.

"Hell!" Amal snapped. "This is getting us nowhere."

"I agree," Musa chimed in. "Let's give the stupid snakes a helping hand."

Their father sighed. "Very well. You know what to do."

The Executioner, keeping one eye on the copperheads, ever so slowly pivoted on a heel, turning so he faced the arms dealer and the gunners. They wouldn't take him down without a fight.

Hadji, Amal and Musa had disappeared. Mehmet and Subhi stood with their arms folded, staring at Bolan with contempt. Edwards had lowered the Glock and stood to one side.

Bullock, the other triggerman, aimed his pistol at the Executioner's chest. "One squeeze is all it'll take, boss, and this joker'll be out of your hair for good."

"No," Akbar said. "It would deprive me of the pleasure of seeing him suffer. You aren't to shoot unless I specifically say so."

Disappointed, Bullock dropped his arm to his side.

Bolan saw Hadji returning. The man carried a long tree limb he was stripping of twigs. Amal appeared behind him, doing the same. It didn't take a genius to figure out what they were going to do. Bolan crouched.

Subhi bent, his ham-sized hands on his knees. "Try to make this interesting, pig," he mocked. "I'd like to see you blubber like a baby before the copperheads are done with you."

Hadji and Amal took up positions next to each other. Amal finished trimming the branch. Winking at his brother, he leaned down and jabbed the jagged tip at the Executioner.

Bolan dodged it easily. The youngest Akbar hadn't put much effort into his strike. Amal was toying with him.

Laughing, Hadji bent and speared his limb downward. Like his brother, he didn't try too hard.

Akbar chuckled. Bullock smiled and said, "One push is all it'll take."

Bolan realized that, too. He batted Amal's limb aside, then Hadji's. As long as they were only toying with him, he was safe, but he had to do something before they turned serious.

Hadji took another step, which brought his leg over the brink. Giggling childishly, he drove the branch high, then low.

With a swing of his arm Bolan deflected the first thrust. But instead of repeating the tactic with Hadji's second thrust, Bolan suddenly stooped, gripped the end of the limb in both hands and tugged with all his strength.

The cackle Hadji was voicing died in his throat. His gleeful expression changed to one of pure terror as he lost his footing and was propelled into the pit. He tried to clutch at Bolan, but the soldier neatly sidestepped.

The man screeched as he flew headfirst into the nest of copperheads. His arms flailing wildly, he rose to his knees. Snakes covered his head, shoulders and back. Their fangs seared into him again and again. He babbled insanely, swatting at them in a frenzy.

Bolan was in motion the instant Hadji went flying past him. At that same moment, his younger brother, Amal, had lunged, driving his limb at the Executioner's face. The sight of Hadji plowing into the nest shocked Amal so badly that he stood transfixed, gaping at his brother. It enabled Bolan to grab the limb. But instead of pulling Amal into the pit as he'd done with Hadji, he used the limb for leverage to surge up the slope. He was out of the pit before any of the them could collect their wits.

Then Subhi swung toward him, as Bullock whipped up his pistol.

The soldier grasped Amal by the arm, twisted and hurled him into Subhi, as he lashed out with his left leg, delivering a snap kick to Bullock's kneecap. There was a loud snap and the shooter lost his balance, bellowing in rage and pain. Bolan nailed him with a solid right before running for his life toward the far side of the clearing.

Only Edwards had any hope of stopping Bolan, and he made no move to do so, not even raising the Glock.

Bolan was almost to the footpath when the first shot rang out. His glance showed Bullock on his knees, steadying the pistol to shoot again. Subhi and Musa had begun to pursue him, but a bellow from their father brought them to a halt.

"Where are you going? Your brother is more important! We have to get him out of there!"

A round clipped a cypress next to the trail as Bolan sprinted past the moss-covered bole. Momentarily in the clear, he poured on the speed.

"Bullock! Edwards! I want that son of a bitch!" Akbar thundered. "Get after him while we help Hadji!"

A bend in the path added a slim safety margin. Bolan slowed, stopping beside a cluster of tall reeds. Slipping into them, he crouched. The water rose above his ankles.

The sound of heavy breathing drew Bolan's attention to the footpath. Bullock came around the bend, favoring his hurt knee. His face was beet red.

Bolan hoped the reeds were sufficient cover. He dropped lower, his chin brushing the water.

Bullock barreled closer, near enough for the soldier to see the drops of sweat on his brow. At the same time, the gunner glanced down and spotted him.

Like a missile hurtling from its silo, Bolan shot up out of the reeds. His left hand, formed into a wedge, caught Bullock on the right wrist. The triggerman's gun went cartwheeling into the marsh.

Bullock swung a powerful uppercut. Bolan blocked it with his forearm, then smashed a palm-heel thrust to the gunner's jaw, rocking his head backward. As a follow-up, Bolan threw his entire weight into a knife-hand strike to his adversary's throat.

The shooter staggered, then sank onto his good knee.

Bolan boxed the hardman's ears, a twin palm smash that brought blood pouring from his eardrums. The soldier then darted behind the man, wrapped his arm around Bullock's head, hooking his elbow onto his enemy's jaw. He pressed his other hand against the back of the shooter's skull and wrenched sharply to the left and then the right.

The snap this time was much louder than the one produced by Bullock's kneecap, and his whole body went limp. Bolan let go and the man keeled over, lifeless, his head flopping at an impossible angle.

The Executioner turned, then stopped.

Edwards stood ten feet away, the Glock trained squarely on Bolan. "Those were some real fancy moves you used there, Chief."

The distance was too great for Bolan to reach the skinny gunner before he fired.

"Back up into the marsh and you get to live," Edwards said. "Just be quick about it or I might change my mind."

Bolan did as the man ordered. Water sloshed into his already soaked shoes. He looked around for Bullock's pistol, but it had been swallowed by the thick mud.

Warily Edwards sidled by. When he was in the clear, he paused. "I should have my head examined for doing this, but I'm getting the hell out of here. What you do to Akbar and his boys is up to you."

Bolan studied the gunner. "Why are you doing this?" he asked.

Edwards frowned. "I've offed a lot of dudes in my time, but I don't hire out to waste innocents, including women and kids. Only sickos do that."

A killer with scruples, Bolan mused.

"I never much liked the fact that Akbar was so heavy into the terrorist scene," Edwards went on, "but I was willing to overlook it for the money. Well, not anymore. You'll think I'm crazy, but I won't stand for any of those foreigners nuking our cities. Sure, I work on the wrong side of the law, but I'm still an American."

With a warning to Bolan not to move until he was out of sight, Edwards backed up to another bend, then whirled and sped off.

Bolan climbed onto the footpath. Quickly he frisked Bullock. Experience had taught him that most gunners packed more than one piece of hardware. This one turned out to be no different. In a holster strapped to the small of Bullock's back, Bolan found a backup gun, a 9 mm Intratec Cat with a black matte finish. Eight rounds were in the clip, plus one in the chamber. Hefting it, he raced back up the footpath toward the clearing and his showdown with the Akbar clan.

SERGEANT DAN ANDERSON was exhausted.

The leader of the Golden Jihad had kept him up almost all night training the terrorists, and then had let him sleep for only a little more than four hours.

Fighting a haze of fatigue and anxiety, Anderson hugged his wife and gently caressed his sleeping son. Little Thomas hadn't cried once during their whole ordeal. It was proof positive that if Thomas lived, he would grow up to be quite a man.

Unfortunately the odds of his son reaching maturity were next to nil unless Anderson came up with a plan, and soon. "I love you both so much," he said softly.

Azadeh stroked his arm. "We love you, too." Tears welled in her eyes. "I can't bear to think that we won't grow old together."

"Don't talk like that. Where there's life, there's hope." Anderson mouthed the cliché without much conviction. The longer their captivity lasted, the less optimistic he became.

"Do you think the authorities will find us?" Azadeh asked.

"You want my honest answer?" Anderson said. She nodded, and he shook his head. "If they had any clues at all, they would've busted in the front door by now and given the Jihad a taste of their own medicine."

"What do we do, Danny?"

Danny. That was her pet name for him. She used it only when in the throes of passion, or despair. Anderson looked into the lovely eyes of his wife and admitted, "I honestly don't know. If worse comes to worst, I'll try to hold them off long enough for you and Thomas to escape."

"You are just one man. What chance would you have against so many?"

From the stairs came a grating voice. "I'll answer that for you, Kuwaiti."

Husband and wife spun.

Ahmed Tufayli glowered. He'd overheard enough to know that he didn't have the American cowed to his will yet. Sterner measures were in order. "Your man is a fool. We will crush him like an insect the moment he lifts a finger against us." Reaching the bottom of the stairs, he said, "I believed he was smart enough to realize resistance is futile. I can see I made a mistake. Some discipline is in order."

Anderson pushed to his feet. "What do you mean?"

The Jihad leader called out the names of Hassan Nidal, Nayif Nasrallah and three others. Without delay the men descended.

"What is it, brother?" Nidal asked in Arabic.

Tufayli barked orders in the same language.

"No!" Azadeh Anderson cried, also in Arabic. Springing erect, she said, "I won't let you lay a hand on me!"

Anderson didn't know what was going on. He understood some Arabic, but not enough to catch the rapid-fire exchange between Tufayli and the other terrorists.

The five men who'd come downstairs stepped forward. Anderson moved to intercept them. A brown belt in karate, he assumed a back stance, but having had little food and even less sleep in the past twenty-four hours, he was in no shape to take them on. However, it was obvious they meant to harm his wife, and there was no way he could stand there and do nothing.

Nidal, the second-in-command, grinned and nudged Nasrallah. "Look at this idiot," he said. "What does he think he is doing?"

"He has obviously seen too many Japanese martial-arts movies," Nasrallah said, and leaped to the attack.

Anderson met him halfway. In a blur, he performed a spin kick that sent the young fanatic flying, but before he could set himself, the rest were upon him, their fists raining blows. The sergeant managed to land a solid forearm smash on one of his foes, but that was all. The sheer weight of numbers swept him off his feet and brought him crashing down onto the concrete floor. A fist buried itself in his stomach. Another felt as if it cracked a rib. Two terrorists grabbed his arms, pinning him down.

The others moved toward Azadeh.

"No!" Anderson shouted, struggling furiously. "Don't touch her!"

Tufayli laughed. At a curt nod from him, Nidal pounced. The woman fought like a tigress. For a moment she held the lieutenant at bay, then the rest of the men were on her and she was borne down, kicking and screaming.

Anderson went berserk. With a roar, he hurled one of the terrorists from him and punched the other man in the face. Then free to move, he jumped up and dived at the men holding his wife.

Nasrallah, sporting a bruise from Anderson's spin kick, was eager to repay the American. He released the woman and whirled, bringing up his fists.

The noncom's Special Forces training kicked in. He fought mechanically, striking and defending without conscious thought. He caused the young fanatic to double over with a foot to his inner thigh, while a slashing sword hand to the side of his neck sent him tottering.

A second terrorist rose. Anderson waded into him with the force of a human hurricane. He was acting on pure adrenaline, his movements as automatic as those of a precision clock. A block, a two-finger spear-hand strike, a parry and a bear-hand blow were all it took to dispose of the new opponent.

Tufayli couldn't believe what he was seeing. Four of his men had been taken out of action. He'd never have suspected the American to be capable of such ferocity. Drawing a Bernadelli pistol from under a shoulder holster, he moved in.

Anderson didn't notice the terrorist leader. He had his hands full with the last of the five men, who was proving to be a skilful boxer. He absorbed a right to the jaw that momentarily dazed him. Recovering, he retaliated with a horizontal spear-hand thrust to the man's kidneys. A bottom fist strike to his temple collapsed the boxer like a crumpled piece of cardboard.

He'd done it! His wife was free of their grasp. He extended an arm to help her stand, then saw her eyes go wide. Sensing someone behind him, he spun.

Tufayli brought the barrel of the pistol sweeping down in a vicious arc. It connected above the noncom's ear.

Fireworks went off in Anderson's head. His legs buckled. He heard his wife scream and tried to rise to protect her, reaching out for support that wasn't there. Suddenly three terrorists were upon him, punching and kicking in outrage. Feebly he tried to raise his arms to ward them off, but he had no strength. He lay on the cold concrete floor, gasping for air, pain racking his body.

Nasrallah raised his foot to stomp the American in the throat, but a restraining hand fell on his shoulder.

"No more," Tufayli said. "We need to keep him alive. If you must vent your anger, do it on the woman."

Two terrorists clamped onto Anderson's arms. Horror-stricken, he saw his wife being seized and her dress torn from her body. He shut his eyes, unable to watch, but Tufayli knelt at his side and pried them open.

"You will watch, American! You will learn what it means to defy the Golden Jihad!"

Gradually, Azadeh's screams lessened, to end in choking sobs.

CHAPTER TEN

When the Executioner was almost within sight of the clearing, he left the footpath. Veering once again into the marsh, he circled to the east to come up on the Akbars unseen. Wading from tree to tree, he was careful to stay hidden. Soon the clearing opened up before him, and he saw that he needn't have been so cautious.

The Akbars were otherwise occupied, frantically attempting to get Hadji out of the pit. So far, they hadn't met with success.

Mehmet Akbar stood on the rim. His sons, Amal and Musa, were on either side of him, crouched low, Musa holding a stout tree limb. The three of them were all talking at once, giving advice to Subhi, who had climbed down into the hole, leaving only his head and shoulders visible. All four had their backs to the clearing.

Bolan stalked up out of the marsh, holding the Intratec Cat pistol level.

"Be careful!" Mehmet Akbar was saying to Subhi. "Don't get bitten!"

"Look at them!" Amal declared. "The snakes are so agitated, they are attacking one another!"

Musa wagged the branch. "Grab on to this when you get hold of him, Subhi! We'll pull you out of there before any of the reptiles can strike!"

Subhi bent, then jerked back again. "Damn! That one nearly got me!"

Bolan was halfway across. He was about to call out when a better idea occurred to him. Breaking into a run, he sprinted toward them. From fifteen feet away, he shouted and lowered his right shoulder like a pro linebacker charging an opposing line.

His yell drew the Akbars' attention, and they began to turn in his direction.

Springing, Bolan twisted so that his body was horizontal to the ground, and he slammed into them like a human battering ram. They had no time to react, to dodge aside or to seize hold of him. Father and sons went sailing over the brink.

Amal screamed as he and Musa plowed into the nest of copperheads, landing on top of Hadji. Akbar slammed into Subhi. The powerhouse jackknifed into the snakes as if diving into a pool. The collision arrested Akbar's fall. He landed well shy of the nest and scrambled to his hands and knees.

In an instant, the four sons were covered with copperheads. Writhing and hissing, the enraged reptiles sank their fangs into every square inch of Akbar skin. Hadji was already motionless, his eyes glazed. Amal lay on his side, crying hysterically, too petrified to try to fight off the snakes.

Subhi raged like a grizzly bear. He ripped snakes off him and crushed them with his bare hands. Others he crunched underfoot while plowing toward the edge of the nest. The serpents were so thick that he made slow headway. For every one he killed, he was bitten half a dozen times.

Only Musa made it out of the roiling mass. Still holding the branch, he burst into the clear. Raising it like a spear, he rushed Bolan. "Die, you bastard!" he screamed.

Bolan fired the pistol, and a neat hole materialized between Musa's crazed eyes. He jerked, did a pirouette and toppled back into the pit. The reptiles closed over him, burying him in their slithering coils.

Mehmet Akbar stabbed a hand under his jacket but stopped when Bolan swung the Intratec to cover him.

"Take it out slowly and lose it," the soldier commanded.

Fuming, Akbar unlimbered a Smith & Wesson from a shoulder holster, then threw it out of reach. "Curse you to hell!" he growled.

A strangled cry from Subhi cut short whatever else Akbar was going to say. The powerhouse was on his knees. Copperheads coated his torso, his neck, even his face. He swatted at them wildly, his movements growing weaker by the moment.

"No!" Akbar wailed, and made a move as if to help his son. A snake lunged at him. Flinging himself out of danger, he stared aghast as his four sons were repeatedly bitten. "This can't be happening!"

Bolan made no move to intervene. There was nothing he could do even if he'd wanted to. The Akbars were directly and indirectly responsible for untold deaths over the years—countless innocents who had been sacrificed on the altar of their fanaticism. They were getting their just deserts, and it was long overdue.

It seemed to take forever for Subhi to go down. By then the other three sons were lying still, only partially visible under the tangle of hissing reptiles.

"My poor sons!" Akbar said, slowly standing. Dazed, he shook his head, then turned to Bolan. "And what of me, you son of a bitch? Why have you spared my life but not theirs?"

"Tell me where to find the Golden Jihad."

Akbar blinked. A crafty look came into his eyes. "So that's it." He smiled and stated, "My lips are sealed! Do with me what you will, but you'll never get the information you need."

"We'll find them in time anyway," Bolan said.

"By then it will be too late," Akbar crowed. "The backpack nukes will have been set off. Think of all those who will die, of the widespread destruction! Two cities will experience the ultimate nightmare, and you are helpless to prevent it."

"The Feds might go easier on you if you cooperate."

The man laughed bitterly. "And do what? Sentence me to life in prison instead of sending me to the electric chair? No, thank you, American. I would rather join my sons in Paradise."

Before Bolan could divine the man's intent, Akbar turned and jumped feetfirst into the nest of copperheads. The Executioner started down, then stopped, helpless to prevent the tableau from unfolding.

Snakes were biting Akbar's legs, but he acted as if he didn't notice. Bending, he gripped a thick serpent and raised it level with his eyes. The struggling reptile bit his arms. Again Akbar ignored the pain. A smile curled his lips, and he brought the copperhead close to his face. The snake promptly buried its fangs in his neck. Akbar flinched, then he looked at Bolan and said, "Remember this, American. I am going to show you why we will prevail in the end, why your country is doomed to lose in the great struggle to come."

"Tell me, Akbar," Bolan said. "Which two cities is the Golden Jihad going to hit?"

Akbar didn't reply. Shifting his grip on the copperhead, he abruptly opened his mouth wide and shoved in the snake's head. He gagged, then he coughed, but he kept feeding the reptile into his mouth. His throat bulged. His whole body shook. Suddenly he let the snake go and staggered.

Bolan thought the serpent would slide back out, but it did the opposite. In thunderstruck fascination he watched its rippling form crawl deeper into Akbar's mouth. Half of its body disappeared inside the man, then just its tail was left. With a deft flick, it, too, vanished.

Akbar went into violent convulsions. In the throes of one, he toppled into the pit, where he continued thrashing and kicking as copperheads blanketed him. In under a minute the convulsions ceased. Akbar's mouth fell open, and from it crawled the snake he'd swallowed. Covered with blood and whatever else had been in Akbar's stomach, it entwined with the rest of the reptiles and was soon lost to view.

Bolan lowered the pistol. He'd seen many deaths in his time, but few so sickening. Skirting the edge of the pit, he picked up the Smith & Wesson, a .45-caliber pistol with an 8-round capacity, counting the one in the chamber. It wasn't the Desert Eagle, but it would suffice.

He ran to the footpath. No cries came from the direction of the farm. Maybe the gunners were all indoors and hadn't heard the shot or the screams. Or if they had, they'd assumed he was the one who'd been shot and was doing the screaming.

The temperature had climbed to well above ninety. Combined with the high humidity, Bolan was soaked before he'd covered two hundred yards. When he spotted the tops of the buildings through the trees, he moved more cautiously.

There was no sign of activity from the house. Music wafted from the converted barn. Someone had a radio tuned into a New Orleans jazz station.

As Bolan crept from the bayou, he noticed a car and a pickup truck parked under an enormous willow near the house, the tree's spreading limbs screening them from aerial observation.

He moved to the pickup and checked inside. The keys weren't in the ignition, but someone had left a Mossburg pistol-grip shotgun lying on the floor next to a half-empty box of shells. He inserted four into the weapon and worked the slide to pump a round into the chamber. Cramming the extras into his pockets, he wedged the pistol and the revolver under his belt.

Bolan calculated there were eight hardmen to deal with, unless there were others he didn't know about. He figured they were all in the barn, but he opted to probe the house anyway, to be safe.

The porch floor creaked underfoot even though he stepped lightly. He quietly pulled on a rickety screen door. The inner door hung wide open. With his finger on the trigger of the Mossburg, he slid into the cool interior. It smelled musty. Dust caked the floor, showing a few footprints.

The first room was empty, except for a few broken articles of furniture and a tattered throw rug. The next room was the same. In the kitchen sat a cast-iron stove that hadn't been used in years.

A narrow flight of stairs led to the second floor, but Bolan didn't go up. Only one set of footprints was faintly outlined in the dust, and he guessed they'd been made long ago.

He went out the back, crossed an overgrown garden and scouted the best approach to the barn. Radio music was now being drowned out by the rumble of a forklift.

He was on the point of sprinting to the side door when it suddenly swung outward. A pair of gunners emerged. One held a paper sack, the other a metal lunch box and a Thermos bottle.

Neither saw Bolan go prone. They moved off to a tree and sat with their backs to the trunk. The taller man removed his jacket, revealing a Colt Python in a speed rig under his left arm.

Bolan knew he couldn't take them out without alerting the others. He curbed his impatience and waited for them to finish eating.

They were in no rush. He was contemplating sneaking around behind them, when the door opened again. Out came Harry, the thickset blond shooter from the warehouse who'd shown up at the Akbar residence. He stared off across the bayou, toward the clearing. "Have you guys seen any sign of the boss yet?"

"Nope," the tall man answered.

"He should've been back by now," Harry said.

"Maybe the snakes weren't there. Maybe they tossed that guy into quicksand, like they did Lenny a while back."

Harry wasn't satisfied. "It still shouldn't be taking this long. I want you guys to go look for them."

"Why?" the man with the paper sack asked. "We're on our lunch hour. Can't you send somebody else?"

Harry snorted. "Do you belong to a union I don't know about? Get the hell off your butt, Griggs, and move it. Let the boss know he had a call from overseas. That bigwig in Iran needs to talk to him right away."

"Great," Griggs grumbled, "now I'm a damned errand boy!"

Griggs and the tall gunner took off. Harry watched them until they were out of sight, then went back inside, muttering to himself.

The moment the door closed, Bolan was on his feet. Zigzagging, he ran to the nearest corner of the building. From there he hurried to the door and was just in time to see the blond shooter go past a neatly stacked mountain of grenade cases. Another man was piling crates of ammo. Over by the main bay a pudgy underling operated the forklift. There was no sign of the remaining three hardmen.

Bolan went in fast and low. He squatted in the shelter of a pallet piled high with missile launchers and planned his next move.

The presence of so many explosives made a firefight that much more dangerous. If a round penetrated the wrong crate, the explosion that would result could set off a chain reaction of even bigger blasts that would leave a smoking crater where the corrugated building now stood.

The soldier decided to dispose of the hardmen one at a time, without alerting the rest. It would take much more time and be ten times the challenge, but well worth the effort if the Feds got their hands on the arms cache. Gliding around the missile launchers, he zeroed in on the man stacking the ammo.

Fortunately the forklift and the radio were making enough racket to cover any noise Bolan made. To help matters, the man doing the stacking whistled while he worked. The soldier crept up behind him, looked around to ensure no one had spotted him and brought the shotgun crashing down on the whistler's cranium.

The guy hit the floor without so much as a groan. Bolan dragged him behind the crates and patted him down. The fellow was unarmed.

One down, seven to go, Bolan reflected. He moved off in search of another gunner. The forklift driver he'd save for last since the noise of the machine worked in his favor.

A stack of Stingers offered handy cover. Bolan ducked behind them and peered out. Over by the main door, Harry and a soundman appeared to be checking off items on an inventory sheet, while another hardman was cleaning the windshield of Mehmet Akbar's car. Griggs and the tall gunner had gone in search of their employer, and Bolan didn't expect them back for at least ten minutes.

None of them was close enough for Bolan to reach without being seen, so he stayed where he was, watching like a hawk. After a while the man cleaning the windshield finished and walked away in the general direction of the small room in which Bolan had been beaten.

The Executioner shadowed him. When the man turned to the right and walked through a doorway Bolan hadn't noticed before, he hid until he heard the flush of water. Then he rushed down a narrow aisle, pressing himself against a row of oversized crates the man had to pass on his way back.

The triggerman emerged, adjusting his denim jacket, which concealed a pistol. The man patted the butt and smiled.

Bolan brought the shotgun down on the bridge of the gunner's nose. His second swing caught the shooter in the shoulder, smashing him against one of the crates, causing it to wobble. The hardman was tougher than he looked. Clawing at his pistol, the man was on the verge of yelling for help when Bolan's third and final blow slammed him into the crate again.

The soldier was helpless to prevent gravity from taking over. This time, the heavy crate toppled like a felled redwood. A resounding boom echoed off the metal walls.

"What the hell was that?" someone bellowed.

Bolan didn't waste a second. Stooping, he snagged the unconscious gunner by his jacket and started to drag him. More yells erupted and feet drummed on the concrete floor. The Executioner reached a mound of unmarked metal drums behind which he concealed the hardman.

Harry and two triggermen were converging at a rapid pace, all three with their pistols up and ready. They passed within a dozen yards of Bolan without seeing him.

The soldier's plan to take them out one by one was fast unraveling. He had at most a minute and a half to dispose of the forklift operator.

Evidently a shipment of armament had recently arrived. The man was busy transferring crates from near the main door onto a pallet farther in. He handled the forklift with skill, zipping in tight loops and threading between the aisles at high speed, barely taking five seconds between maneuvers.

Somehow Bolan had to get close enough to strike. Keeping low, he moved to a row of boxes near to where the operator was storing the new ordnance. The man whizzed over to the door, hooked the steel arms of the forklift under a crate, then wheeled the machine around.

Bolan saw his chance. As the machine rolled past him, he leaped out and lifted the shotgun, ready to bash the driver in the back of the head. He made no noise, but something caused the operator to glance over his shoulder.

Jerking a lever, the man braked and swung the forklift completely around so that its large cargo shielded him from the Executioner. He revved the motor, and the machine shot forward.

Bolan was taken off guard, caught in the path of a hurtling metallic juggernaut. He snapped a hasty blast at the top of the crate, hoping it would cause the operator to swerve, but man and machine continued to bear down on him.

"What was that shot?" Bolan heard Harry holler. "Finley, what's going on over there?"

Finley answered, but Bolan didn't hear the man's reply because he was diving to the left and rolling up off the floor. The forklift missed him by a hand's width.

Finley misjudged his speed and smashed into a pile of empty boxes.

Bolan had a clear shot. Taking a bead, he saw the operator twist in his seat, pointing a pistol at him. With a stroke of the trigger, buckshot ripped into Finley's chest, half lifting him out of the forklift and dumping him over the side.

Confirming the kill was unnecessary. At that range, buckshot would blow a hole the size of a melon in a man. Bolan sped into the maze of armament.

Harry and the others were shouting back and forth, but then their words were lost in the sound of a tremendous crash.

Bolan swiftly scaled some crates and discovered that the forklift had kept going, ramming into a row of metal drums. Several had split open, but he was unable to tell what they contained.

Tendrils of black smoke began to curl from the forklift.

The soldier didn't like to think of the result should fire spread through the building. There wouldn't be enough left of it—or anyone inside— to fill a dustpan.

There were still three hardmen to take care of, but Bolan wasn't going to stick around and lose his life in the attempt. Any combat vet worthy of the name knew when to attack and when to beat a strategic retreat.

He turned toward the side door. Twenty feet from him stood a swarthy shooter armed with a Heckler & Koch Model HK-94. Bolan hit the floor. A leaden hailstorm blistered the air above him, pockmarking the crates with holes.

From his prone position, Bolan pumped the shotgun twice. His aim was dead-on, and he was on his feet and racing for the door before the shooter stopped jerking.

A voice yelled at him to halt.

The big man turned into the aisle that led to the exit. A bolt rasped behind him. Again he hit the floor just as a cannon seemed to go off in his ears. The shotgun skidded from his grip. Swiveling, he drew the Intratec in a blur of motion. By the time he'd turned, the Cat was up and out. All he had to do was snap off four rapid rounds that drilled a gunner with an Ithaca Model 37 12-gauge. The man deflated like a punctured tire and Bolan was up and running again.

A thick cloud of smoke wreathed the rafters. Flames had begun to rise from the forklift.

Bolan nailed the door on the fly with his shoulder, his momentum spilling him onto the grass. His fall saved his life. Charging toward him were Griggs and the tall shooter who'd been sent after Akbar. They opened fire too soon. Slugs gouged the turf around the Executioner as he palmed the Smith & Wesson and cut loose with both handguns, blazing away with ambidextrous precision. The men dropped.

Pushing upright, Bolan took off at a run. He covered twenty yards, then thirty. Something told him he needed to put the house between him and the building holding the arms cache. As he reached the corner, he looked back.

Framed in the side door was Harry, the blond gunner. He was sighting down a rifle, but he never got to shoot. At that precise instant, the corrugated building erupted in a fireball, the explosion blowing the structure into a billion bits.

Bolan wasn't quite past the house when the shock wave caught up with him. It was as if he'd been sucked into a tornado. His feet were swept out from under him, his ears deafened by a roar to end all roars. He was thrown head over heels like a matchstick in a maelstrom.

A tree reared in front of him.

CHAPTER ELEVEN

"How are you feeling, Mack?"

It was rare for Hal Brognola to call Bolan by his first name. Bolan knew the big Fed only did so when he was worried about him. "My body feels as if a buffalo used it for a doormat," he admitted, "but otherwise I'm fine. I'm ready to go out again the minute you learn anything."

They were in the first-floor dining room at Stony Man Farm. Bolan had a half empty cup of black coffee in front of him.

Brognola eased his bulk into a chair and set down a brimming cup of coffee. "How about your head? The doc told me you came awful close to suffering a concussion."

"All I hit was a tree," Bolan replied, making light of his mishap. If he let on that he was hurting in any way, Brognola would fuss over him like a mother hen. "There are some people around here who claim that my head is harder than marble, so you have nothing to worry about."

He decided to change the subject. "Have your people come up with any new leads yet?"

"Not yet." Brognola sighed. "Certainly not at the farm in the bayou. The agents on the scene tell me there's a crater there the size of the Grand Canyon. You were lucky to make it out alive, especially after that beating you took."

"How about the other sites? Akbar's house and the warehouse?"

"We're still going over them from top to bottom. It'll take a while."

"It's already been over twenty-four hours."

"I know that," Brognola responded. "I'm also counting every damn minute. But it can't be helped. You saw how large the warehouse is. As for the estate, we've already found two hidden safes and suspect there are probably more, maybe even a hidden room. It could take us a week to go over every square inch."

Bolan said nothing. He didn't need to. They both were well aware that the clock was ticking down and soon they'd be out of time. The Golden Jihad wouldn't wait forever to set off the backpack nukes.

"At least you put Akbar out of business," Brognola said. "From what we can tell, he was one of the biggest arms dealers we've ever stumbled across. You've put a major dent in the whole operation."

"Only until someone else steps in to fill the vacuum," Bolan said.

That was the thing about vermin. Kill one, and there was always another ready to take over where the dead one had left off. It troubled Bolan. He'd eliminate a drug lord one day, and the next a rival would begin supplying the dead man's customers. Or he'd take down an arms dealer like Akbar, and within a week another arms dealer was funneling ordnance through the same pipeline.

There were times when it seemed as if a bottomless cesspool of human scum bubbled just beneath the surface, waiting for the chance to burst out and spread its cancer.

Bolan knew he couldn't give up, though. In his book, quitters might as well dig their own graves and lie down in them, because what they were, in effect, saying to the vermin was "Here I am. Do with me what you will."

He knew, too, that some people believed the only way to win was to compromise with evil, to give an inch in the hope that evil would not gobble up a yard. Bolan saw through that fallacy. The only way to meet evil was head-on. To win the good fight, you had to take the battle to the bad guys, had to hit them on their own turf, where it hurt the most. As every exterminator knew, picking vermin off one by one never had a lasting effect. The best way was to strike at them where they bred, where the evil festered.

"We've had one lucky break," Brognola said, cutting into Bolan's thoughts. "Akbar was big on technology, so he computerized his files. My people have uncovered a few of his account disks at the house. He was smart enough to use a code, but we're confident we can break it. Then, we'll know who his clients were."

"And by then most of them will have learned Akbar is dead, closed up shop and moved elsewhere," Bolan said.

"True, but we're bound to snare a few."

Just then a woman with a no-nonsense air about her joined them. "For you, sir," she said to Brognola, handing over an envelope.

Brognola opened it, read the contents and scowled. "There's no reply. Thank you, Susan."

The woman pivoted on her heel and was gone.

"What is it?" Bolan asked.

"It's from the President," he disclosed. "He's changed his mind about keeping a tight lid on this one. We have forty-eight hours to recover the nukes. If not, he'll go public with the whole deal."

"Why the change of heart?"

Brognola thoughtfully tapped the envelope on the tabletop. "I imagine his inner circle of advisors have been stressing the political liability he faces if one of the nukes goes off. The press will have a field day. They'll crucify him for not alerting the public. They'll claim that less lives would have been lost if word had gotten out in advance. By the time they're done, he'll come across as the political equivalent of Jack the Ripper.''

"Second-guessers always know better than everyone else," Bolan said.

Brognola crumpled the message. "What gets me is that half the time the second-guessers don't have the slightest idea what they're talking about."

At that moment another interruption presented itself in the form of a blacksuit from Security. "My apologies, sir," he addressed Brognola. "Your presence is requested in Security HQ."

"What's up?" Brognola asked, standing.

"We have a perimeter breach."

AHMED TUFAYLI WAS restless. He paced the lower floor of the Golden Jihad's safehouse like a caged cougar, peering out of the covered windows from time to time. He saw no sign of suspicious activity, but that didn't lessen his feeling of unease.

Tufayli couldn't say why he felt as he did. He knew only that there were occasions when his intuition warned him of imminent danger. This was one such occasion.

The Jihad leader was at a window in a side bedroom, staring down the driveway, when his lieutenant joined him. "I do not like it, my friend," he said. "Something is wrong."

Hassan Nidal had known Tufayli long enough to read him like a book. He'd observed his constant pacing with growing concern, and now commented, "Your instincts are rarely wrong. Do you think the Americans know where we are? They could be closing in even as we speak."

"I doubt it, but there's only one way to find out." Tufayli turned away from the window. "Send out two of our men who know some English to check. Have them walk around the entire block. Tell them that if anyone smiles at them or greets them, they are to smile back. I want them to keep a low profile."

"Understood." Nidal left immediately.

Tufayli went down into the basement. His men would assume he was going down for another talk with the soldier. In reality, he wanted to be close to the prisoners in case the house was raided. They would make excellent shields, and even better bargaining tools.

Sergeant Anderson sat huddled in a corner with his wife and son. Azadeh's head rested on his shoulder. Her once lively eyes were fixed on the concrete wall. They were as blank as the wall itself.

Azadeh had been that way since the rape. Try as he might, Anderson could barely get her to respond. He had to virtually force her to eat or drink. Thankfully, after a little prodding, she would mechanically nurse Thomas.

Anderson blamed himself for her condition. It had been the terrorists who'd abused her, but they'd done it to teach *him* a lesson. She'd suffered because he'd plotted to resist their captors instead of keeping his mouth shut.

The noncom's worst fear was that his wife would never recover. She was so lifeless that he feared she would withdraw even deeper inside herself unless she got prompt attention.

Anderson looked up at the sound of footsteps. "Is it time to get back to work already?" he asked Tufayli, who'd been pushing him to get the job done ahead of schedule. The four-day timetable had been cut to three days, and two and a half of them were already gone.

Tufayli shook his head. Inwardly he gloated over the pathetic state of the Kuwaiti woman. In his opinion, any Muslim woman who married an American deserved what she got. "You have a few more minutes," he said. Until he heard that the coast was clear, he would delay the lessons.

Anderson gently stroked his wife's hair. "She needs medical attention."

"There is nothing I can do."

"If we don't get her to a hospital, she'll die."

Tufayli felt no sympathy at all for the American or his woman. "You should've thought of that before you plotted to escape. I warned you what would happen if you didn't cooperate. From the very beginning, I told you that your wife and son would suffer for your mistakes."

Special Forces didn't breed wimps. Anderson had never begged for anything in his life, but he did so now. "Please! Just help her this once, and I'll do everything you want from here on out."

"Save your sniveling. You will do what we want regardless. Remember, she is still alive."

Anderson's face flushed. He told himself that he should've known better. The Jihad leader had made it abundantly clear none of the terrorists gave a damn about his wife. He wanted to leap up and attack Tufayli. He would have, too, had Thomas not begun to squirm. Simmering, he devoted his attention to his son.

The tender scene revolted Tufayli. "By tomorrow morning we will be ready to leave," he stated.

An electric jolt shot through Anderson. Snapping around, he said, "My wife is in no shape to go anywhere! Moving her around could send her over the brink!"

"You should have thought of that."

Tufayli's callousness brought Anderson to his feet. Fists clenched, he took a step forward. "I'll be damned if I'll let you kill her! I'd rather die myself than see any more harm come to her!"

Tufayli saw that he'd pushed the soldier too far. One more wrong word, and the American would wade into him without any regard for the consequences. He also realized that even though he was armed, he was alone. Anderson might reach him before he could get off a fatal shot. He'd seen with his own eyes how fiercely the soldier could fight when pushed to the edge.

Tufayli thought fast. Rather than provoke the American even more, he said, "Calm down, my friend. It is in both our best interests to keep your woman alive. Without her, you would not do as I want."

"She can't be moved!" Anderson insisted.

The Jihad leader regarded the woman for a moment. "All right, let's say I go along with your wishes. Let's say I arrange to keep her here until you have fulfilled your end of the bargain. What do I get in return?"

Anderson had learned his lesson. "How would you arrange to keep her here?" he asked suspiciously.

"Quite easily. Instead of sending five men apiece to New York and Washington, only four men will go to Washington. I will leave one of my trusted helpers, Nayif Nasrallah, here to look after your woman and boy."

It seemed too good to be true, but Anderson was still skeptical. "When would I get to see them again?"

"After the first bomb has gone off."

Anderson was overjoyed. It was unlikely the terrorist would go back on his word if the second nuke hadn't been detonated. He glanced at his loved ones, mulling over what to do.

Tufayli exploited his prisoner's hesitation. "Think about it. She will be safe here. Once I am satisfied that you haven't tricked us, you will be back together with her again."

"What do you want in return?"

"Only for you to work twice as hard as you have been. I will push my men to do the same, so that by tomorrow morning we can be ready to leave."

"You have a deal," Anderson said.

"I'll be back in a short while to get you," Tufayli said.

The two men Hassan Nidal had sent to check out the area didn't return for another five minutes. They reported to Nidal first, who transmitted the information to Tufayli. "There was nothing out of the ordinary, just an old woman walking her dog and some children playing a few yards down."

"What about parked vehicles?" Tufayli asked.

"There were only two, and they were both on the other side of the block. This is a quiet residential neighborhood, and surveillance teams would stick out."

"Federal agents like to disguise themselves as utility workers and street repairmen," Tufayli reminded his lieutenant.

"None was seen. Our men checked everything carefully."

"Good. We will stay the night, then." Tufayli went in search of Nasrallah and found the young man busy in the kitchen, preparing a meal.

"I need to talk to you," he said.

"Your will is mine," the younger terrorist said formally.

"We are leaving in the morning," Tufayli revealed, "all of us except you."

Nasrallah slammed down the carving knife he held. "Why? I have every right to go with Hassan. I will not be deprived of this glorious chance to strike at the heart of the Great Satan.''

"Nor would I think of denying you the opportunity," Tufayli said calmly. "Instead of going with Hassan, you will help me set off the second nuke.''

"Then why—" Nasrallah began.

Tufayli explained about the soldier's request, adding, "I must play along with the American until he has served his purpose, so you will stay here with the woman and the child.''

"I am not a baby-sitter!" Nasrallah spit.

"Have more faith in me than that." Tufayli wrapped an arm around the man's shoulders. "After the first bomb has gone off, I will call you. In the meantime, feel free to have your way with the woman, if you want, then dispose of them both. Make examples of them for the American authorities. Make their deaths something they will take notice of.''

Nasrallah beamed like a child who'd just been given the present he'd always longed for. "You can count on me, brother.''

Tufayli patted the man's shoulder. "I knew that I could.''

CHAPTER TWELVE

The Executioner reconnoitered the block before he attempted to enter the house.

It was a peaceful residential neighborhood, similar to the one he'd been in two days earlier in New Orleans. This one was located in Norristown, Pennsylvania, a town of thirty thousand inhabitants, located fifteen miles northwest of Philadelphia.

According to the list of properties Brognola's team had found in Mehmet Akbar's residence in New Orleans, Akbar owned this house, too. The Golden Jihad had been wise to choose it as a safehouse. It was an old Gothic-style home situated in the middle of an acre lot. The walls were high and thick, and would hold up well to a direct assault. Open ground on all four sides allowed a clear field of fire for the defenders. A row of lilac bushes bordered the sidewalk, effectively screening the house from a frontal view. Maple trees grew on both sides, and at the rear was a shoulder-high picket fence.

The place seemed deserted, but it was hard to tell for sure, as all the blinds had been lowered.

An asphalt drive led from the street to a garage large enough to hold three or four vehicles. The door was closed, so Bolan had no way of knowing if it held any cars.

Although dressed in casual clothes so as not to attract undue attention, Bolan was armed to the teeth. As always, a Beretta was snug in his shoulder rig. A Desert Eagle rode in a holster attached to his wide leather belt. On either side of the pistol were a half dozen pouches crammed with the lethal tools of his trade.

Bolan made a complete circuit of the block. As he reached the driveway a second time, he nonchalantly turned into it and walked right up to the garage. He half expected a window to be smashed out of the house and an SMG to fling lead his way, but the only sound he heard was the chattering of a gray squirrel in a maple tree.

Square windows framed the top of the garage door. Rising onto his toes, Bolan peered. A single car sat on the left-hand side, a Volkswagen bug, barely big enough for four people to ride in comfortably, let alone all the members of the Golden Jihad.

Bolan began to wonder if the Feds had missed the mark this time. Perhaps none of the properties on Akbar's list referred to safehouses for terrorists.

Brognola had marshaled an army of blacksuits and kept the communications people hopping throughout the night. Properties in and around New Orleans had been quickly checked, with no result. Teams had been sent to check on those in other states. Brognola had held Bolan in reserve for when they turned up a solid lead.

It came in the small hours of the morning. Federal agents going through Akbar's records found communications to the effect that Akbar had recently arranged to have the telephone line at the house in Norristown activated and the utility service restored after a long period. A map of Pennsylvania had also been discovered in Akbar's den, marked with the shortest route from New Orleans to Norristown.

That had been enough for Brognola. He'd had Bolan winging from Stony Man before daylight. The Feds had a car waiting in Norristown for Bolan, but thanks to rush hour traffic, the drive had taken more than two hours.

Now Bolan slipped a hand under his windbreaker and rested his palm on the Beretta. Sidling to the corner of the garage, he scanned the house. Not a single curtain moved.

A latticework arbor fringed a side door. The soldier stepped toward it, his eyes roving over the windows and the roof. It seemed so unlikely that the Golden Jihad wouldn't have taken security precautions, that he'd about concluded his first impression had been right and the place was indeed empty. This lead was turning out to be worthless.

Bolan twisted the knob. The door was locked. Curtains prevented him from seeing inside. He stepped back from the arbor to seek another means of entry.

At that instant, from deep inside the house, he heard a woman scream.

It had to be Azadeh Anderson.

Bolan drew back his right leg and smashed his foot against the inner frame of the door, below the lock. It held. Stepping farther back, he lowered his shoulder, tensed, then hurled himself at the barrier.

He knew it was probably a mistake to burst in the way he was, making enough noise to alert everyone inside, but he didn't care. All that mattered was that a woman's life was in jeopardy.

He hit the door with the force of a steam engine. The frame cracked and the door buckled, but it still didn't open wide enough to permit him entry. A dead bolt attached to a thick chain was responsible. Bolan drew back and launched himself at the door again, with the same disheartening result.

The screaming had stopped, and he could guess the reason why. Whoever had been torturing the woman was coming to investigate the source of the noise.

Backpedaling, the soldier ran past the arbor toward the rear of the house. The windows there, too, were covered by blinds, which would make trying to crash through one of them risky. Blinds were like a net, snagging anyone trying to get through them, and in trying to get untangled, a man could cut himself to ribbons on the jagged edges of shattered glass.

Bolan raced around the corner to the back door. It was also covered by a curtain, and was, if anything, sturdier than the side door had been. There was bound to be another dead bolt.

Drawing the Beretta, he smashed out a glass pane in the door and slipped his left hand inside. Groping above the knob, he found a bolt and threw it open. Lowering his arm as far as he could, he unlocked the knob itself. Then, stepping back, he kicked.

The door reverberated but didn't open. Bolan tried again, but he managed only to crack a lower panel.

Every second counted. He didn't know how many Jihad members were inside, but they were bound to converge on the rear of the house at any moment. He had to get in before they did.

Bolan flashed a hand to one of the pouches on his belt and pulled a preshaped charge of C-4 plastic explosive. It resembled a flattened hot dog, with adhesive on one side. He applied it to the door next to the knob. A second charge went at the top, just below the transom. A third was pressed against the bottom.

Another pouch yielded a roll of wafer-thin detonation cord. In under twenty seconds he had expertly wired the three charges. He extracted a palm-sized detonator from a third pouch. He attached the wire leads to the detonator, then hastily retreated as far as the length of the cord would allow. Crouching and placing an arm over his head for protection from possible flying debris, Bolan set off the C-4.

There was a concussive crump and the door caved inward.

Bolan was in motion before the last pieces fell. Barging through a cloud of smoke, he flattened himself against the right-hand wall of a narrow hallway. Nothing moved farther in, so he jogged to a doorway.

A kitchen smelling of cooking food separated him from a wider corridor. Footsteps drummed somewhere beyond, then they fell silent.

In a combat crouch Bolan worked his way along to a refrigerator, then to a small table. A whisper of movement told him that someone wasn't far off.

Four doors opened off the corridor. A terrorist might be lurking in any one of those rooms, waiting for him to show himself.

Bolan's dash to the doorway wasn't greeted by gunfire. He held the 9-mm pistol in a Weaver stance and swung the barrel from side to side, seeking target acquisition. No one appeared. He had to remind himself that the members of the Golden Jihad were the cream of the terrorist crop. They were skilled in guerrilla tactics, weapons use and combat psychology. They wouldn't be as easy to eliminate as the amateur gunners working for Mehmet Akbar had been.

Taking a breath, Bolan crept down the corridor. He passed the first doorway, then the second. Beyond that was a junction. A shadow flitted across it.

Bolan went prone as the snout of a subgun appeared. It erupted in a roar of 9 mm rounds that ripped into the walls on either side of him. He sighted down the Beretta, but there was no one to shoot at. The shooter raked the hall from top to bottom firing until the magazine clicked empty. A few slugs tore into the floor an inch from Bolan's elbow.

A head poked out, and the Executioner squeezed off a shot, the cough of the suppressor a whisper compared to the roar of the SMG. He missed by a fraction, the bullet chewing a furrow near the terrorist's head. The man jerked back. Feet pattered, moving away.

The glimpse he'd gotten of the gunner told Bolan he was up against someone a lot younger than he was. That was good in one respect—experience and skill were on his side, but the downside was that younger killers were often unpredictable and took risks no seasoned pro ever would.

All this went through the Executioner's mind as he jogged to the junction. A check revealed the next hallway was empty. He'd seen only the one man, but there could be more. The Feds believed there were still ten Jihad members unaccounted for.

Bolan hadn't been able to tell the direction of the gunner's flight, so relying on gut instinct, he went right, his back brushing the wall, Beretta extended, finger curled on the trigger. A room appeared on the left, but other than a chair and an empty bookshelf, it was vacant.

Suddenly the soldier stopped. Something felt wrong. He scanned the hallway for alcoves or overhead trapdoors, but none was evident. About to go on, something caught his eye down at ankle level. It was a trip wire, strung across the hall just past the doorway.

Bolan didn't have time to see what it tripped. Gingerly stepping over it, he hoped the Jihad hadn't installed a pressure plate under the floorboards on the other side, or he'd be blown to bits. The boards creaked under his weight, but there was no explosion.

The Executioner advanced until he reached the corner. There was a closed door in front of him. To the left, a corridor led into a living room. To the right was a flight of stairs going to the upper floors.

Bolan crouched and listened. It was as quiet as a tomb. Sooner or later, though, the terrorists were bound to make a noise and give themselves away.

Suddenly a low sound reached Bolan's ears. It wasn't the scrape of a foot or the creak of a floorboard, but a low groan that was abruptly cut off, as though someone had jammed a hand over the person's mouth. It came from behind the door directly in front of him.

Bolan eased onto his stomach and snaked across the hall. Putting a hand to the crack at the bottom of the door, he felt a puff of cool air on his fingertips. He lowered his nose and quietly sniffed. The air smelled dank, like air rising from a basement.

The soldier didn't recall seeing any windows outside the house at ground level, so probably the only way out of the basement was through that door.

Rising to squat to the right of the door, Bolan gently tried the knob. It turned easily. He started to pull the door open, a fraction at a time. The next instant an SMG chattered, and lead chewed the top panel, sending splinters flying. Bolan ducked back, shielding his eyes.

The fire went on until the magazine apparently went dry. A loud smack told the Executioner that a new magazine had been rammed home.

Bolan straightened and exchanged the Beretta for the Desert Eagle. Stopping power had become more important than stealth, and for sheer jolting impact, few handguns were its equal.

The door hung open an inch or so. Bolan hooked it with his foot and pushed, flinging it wide. Leveling the big .44, he ducked his head beneath the jamb and made a lightning survey. He took in the stairs, railing and concrete floor, as well as the young terrorist holding the muzzle of a Madsen M-53 submachine gun against a woman in tattered clothes. Her features mirrored total shock.

It was Azadeh Anderson. Bolan recognized her from photographs Brognola had shown him, but it was hard to believe the pathetic creature below was the same one as the stunning beauty in the photos.

"Stay where you are, American!" the terrorist shouted. His English was so thickly accented, it was hard to understand him. "Come closer and the slut dies!"

Bolan drew back. "Give it up," he responded. "There's no way out. Put down your weapon and come up with your arms raised. I promise no harm will come to you."

"You think I am stupid enough to believe you, bastard?" Nayif Nasrallah said. His pulse was racing. His heart beat so loudly, he found it hard to think straight.

It had shocked Nasrallah to hear someone trying to break in. He had unfastened his pants and been about to indulge himself with the woman, when he'd heard a crash upstairs. It had taken him a minute to put his clothes in order, gather his SMG and fly to the first floor.

He'd ducked into the room nearest the side door and waited for the authorities to barge through so he could mow them down. Yet they never appeared. Then the rear door had been blown in and he'd realized they'd tricked him, drawing him to one entrance while they came in by another.

It had surprised the terrorist to see only the one big American, but he'd guessed that the others had waited outside, ready for their cue to rush in.

He was going to outfox them all. He was going to march right out of there without a hand being laid on him. "I mean it about the woman!" he said. "Throw down *your* pistol and show yourself!"

The big American didn't answer.

"Did you hear me, pig?" Nasrallah yelled. "I swear by everything holy that I will kill her!"

The continued silence from upstairs seemed to mock him. He peered around his human shield, but saw no trace of his enemy. "Why do you not answer? Do you not care if this woman lives or dies?"

Evidently the American didn't. Nasrallah shoved Azadeh toward the foot of the stairs. "We are coming up! Do not try anything, or I will kill her!"

Bending low behind the Kuwaiti, he climbed to the landing. The woman stumbled several times, and he had to keep pushing her to reach the top.

He clamped an arm around Azadeh's neck and propelled her through the door. Still the big man didn't show himself. "Where are you, American?" he roared. "What game are you playing with me?"

Azadeh moaned. Fearing she would try to break free, Nasrallah squeezed her neck harder. In Arabic, he snarled, "Do as I want, whore, or die that much sooner!"

The young terrorist shoved her into the hallway. It, too, was clear. He began to feel alarmed. There had been a certain quality about the American that disturbed him. He had met many hard, deadly men in his line of work, including some of the most successful terrorists in the world. Yet few had affected him at first glance as much as the big man; he was a killer.

Swallowing to relieve his dry throat, Nasrallah moved out into the corridor. Molding his body to the woman's so he couldn't be shot without the bullets going through her first, he made for the junction. A right turn there would take him to the front door. Once on the porch, he would demand a vehicle and make his escape with the woman at his side. He felt confident that the weak American authorities would give in and do as he demanded.

All he had to do was get past the big one with the hard eyes.

Nasrallah slowed, remembering the trip wire. He saw it and jerked the woman to a stop before she blundered and killed them both. "Look down," he said. "Lift your leg over the wire."

Azadeh numbly stood there, not moving.

"Did you hear me, cow?" he said. "Look down at your feet!" Angrily he shook her. At last, she lowered her head, mumbling something he couldn't hear. "Step over it, damn you!"

With agonizing slowness, the woman did so. She tottered as she set down her foot, and he grabbed her arm to steady her. "Be more careful!" he growled. "You might not care if you die, but I do!"

He exhaled with relief when she raised her other leg and they were in the clear. Applying pressure to her spine, he herded her to the junction and looked both ways. The hallway to the front door was empty, as were the corridor to the kitchen and the kitchen itself.

He tried a bluff. He had no intention of slaying his hostage yet, but he rammed the muzzle of his gun against her skull and called out, "I am tired of your stupidity, American! Show yourself to me right now or the whore loses her head!"

As before, there was no reply.

The terrorist's skin began to crawl. This American was even more different than he'd imagined.

He really didn't seem to care about the woman's welfare. Perhaps the devil wanted him to carry out his threat. With the woman lying dead at his feet, the American probably thought he would have a clear shot at him.

Nasrallah chuckled. "I know what you are up to, American! It will not work!"

Azadeh began to head for the front door without being urged. Nasrallah didn't try to curb her, since it would get them out of the house that much sooner. He had an overwhelming urge to begin putting some distance between himself and the big American.

Only two small rooms had to be passed to reach the main entrance, and they were both empty.

Smirking at how he'd outwitted his adversary, Nasrallah stopped the woman at the oak door, reaching around her to work the lock and bolt and fling it wide.

The only thing on the wooden porch was a rocking chair. Beyond it, bright morning sunshine bathed the green grass.

The terrorist moved the Kuwaiti out to the middle of the porch. Dumbfounded, he surveyed the yard. No one else was out front. No uniformed figures moved among the lilac bushes or the maples. No police cars or military vehicles were parked in the driveway or out in the street. Incredible as it seemed, the big man was operating alone.

Nasrallah laughed. He steered Azadeh to the edge of the porch. She stepped off and stood meekly, waiting for his orders.

"I beat him," he said, giving the house a last glance over his shoulder. The hallway was still empty. Laughing louder, he faced front just as his adversary swooped down from the top of the porch, swinging by both hands from the lip of the roof. In the blink of an eye, the American was upon him.

CHAPTER THIRTEEN

The Executioner had decided to try to take the young terrorist alive.

When Bolan had glanced down into the basement and confirmed he was up against one man, he had promptly changed tactics. Instead of coring the terrorist's brain with a lead-jacketed slug, as he could easily have done, he had retreated up the hallway.

The Feds needed more intel if they were to track down the Golden Jihad. If Mehmet Akbar had known which cities the Jihad were going to hit, he'd taken the information with him to his grave. The young fanatic was the last hope the Feds had of averting the single greatest terrorist act in U.S. history.

So Bolan had backed off.

He put himself in the young terrorist's shoes. There was always a chance that the man would slay the woman, then commit suicide. But the soldier rated that a slim prospect. Most fanatics liked to go out in a blaze of glory. It had seemed more likely that the terrorist would try to escape. Simple logic dictated the man would use Azadeh Anderson as a shield.

Acting on those assumptions, Bolan had looked for the ideal spot to jump his prey. The corridors had been out of the question, since he couldn't possibly get close enough without being seen. The rooms were mostly too small and contained few hiding places. By process of elimination, he'd narrowed it down to one of the three doors out of the house.

Picking the right one hadn't been very hard. Bolan had doubted the terrorist would go out the side door, where the arbor limited his field of fire. He didn't believe the man would go out the back, where there was no cover at all. That left the front.

It had taken but a moment for Bolan to scale a post and lie on top of the porch roof.

He'd heard the terrorist's threats to kill the woman, but the stakes were too high for him to put the welfare of an individual before all else. Although it went against everything he stood for, he had done nothing.

Then the terrorist's shouts had gotten louder, and Bolan knew they were close. He gripped the edge of the roof and coiled. The squeak of the screen door and the tread of steps on the old porch let him gauge exactly where the fanatic and the woman were. When she appeared on the short steps below, Bolan knew his moment had arrived.

With a whipcord flip, the soldier swept his legs out in front of him. The soles of his shoes slammed into the terrorist's chest.

Nasrallah was flung backward into the doorjamb. His spine cracked hard enough to jar his teeth to their roots, and bright points of light pinwheeled in front of his eyes. In sheer reflex, his finger tightened on the trigger of his Madsen. He was holding the SMG with just one hand, so the recoil whipped his arm to the right, the slugs gouging into the porch.

Bolan let go of the overhang and dropped lightly onto the balls of his feet. He hurled himself at the young terrorist as the man, straightening, attempted to bring the subgun to bear.

Nasrallah wasn't aware he stood framed in the doorway. He had eyes only for the big American, who was on him before he could aim and fire. The American's speed was incredible. The terrorist had never seen anyone move so fast.

The Executioner sprang. His right arm hooked his foe's chest even as his momentum sent them both hurtling through the entrance and into the hallway. The Madsen snagged on the doorframe and was torn from the terrorist's grasp. They hit the floor with a thud.

Bolan was on his side and he drew back a fist to end the fight, but a knee connected with his inner thigh, narrowly missing his groin. For just a moment he lost his hold.

It was all Nasrallah needed. He no longer had the SMG, but he did have a nasty surprise strapped to his right ankle: a Black Cobra dagger, a ten-inch beauty with a tapered blade and a red jewel mounted on either side of the stylized hilt.

Quick as a striking tiger, Nasrallah withdrew the dagger and thrust at the big American's chest. He fully expected the steel to slide in between the man's ribs. Yet, somehow, the man countered with a forearm block, then drove an elbow into the terrorist's jaw. The younger man scrambled backward, shaking his head to clear it.

Bolan was unhappy with his performance. He should've taken the fanatic down in the first few seconds. Now the man had a dagger, forcing the Executioner to produce his Ka-bar fighting knife. He parried a wild stab as he rose. Pivoting, he aimed at the man's chest, striving to maim rather than kill, but the young terrorist skillfully countered.

Nasrallah was no novice at knife fighting. In the back alleys of his native land he had acquired something of a reputation as a wizard with a blade. He knew many sly moves, many feints and thrusts that could dispose of a man in the time it took to blink. He applied them now, closing in on the big American with a fury born of grim desperation. The American was all that stood between him and freedom. His adversary had to die.

A determined enemy was always formidable. Bolan realized in the opening seconds that he couldn't end the combat swiftly, not if he wanted to take the fanatic alive. So he settled for defending himself, for countering a series of moves that would've disposed of anyone with less experience. He backed up a few steps, then halted.

Sunlight spilling through the doorway glittered off their flashing blades. Nasrallah was horrified to learn the American was his equal. Try as he might, he couldn't pierce the other's guard. Even worse, when their blades briefly locked and they strained against each other, the American flung him back against the wall as if he were a feather. The man had the strength of a bull.

Many times the terrorist had listened to Ahmed Tufayli say that luxury had made mush of the American will to win, and laziness had turned their bodies into flab. Tufayli had been wrong. Some Americans were made of steel every bit as tempered as his dagger.

Tiring, Nasrallah slowed for a fraction of an instant. It was enough for Bolan to slide his dagger arm, elbow to wrist.

Nasrallah yelped as blood spurted from the wound. In moments, his sleeve was soaked red, but he could still wield the dagger. He shifted on his left foot, driving the tip at his enemy's throat. It exposed his own chest, but he knew that he'd soon be weakened by the loss of so much blood. He had to strike while he could.

The Executioner jerked aside as the blade speared at his neck and slammed a fist to the man's chin.

Rocked onto his heels, Nasrallah tottered. He began to fall backward. He clutched at empty air for support. In flinging his arms about, he failed to keep track of the dagger. He thought that it was pointed away from his body.

Bolan saw otherwise. He managed to catch hold of the man's shirt, but he couldn't prevent the inevitable. The slender blade sheared into the man's side, sinking into the hilt. The terrorist stiffened, gasped and went limp.

Moving quickly, the soldier rolled him onto his side to pull out the dagger. Blood spewed onto the floor around them, splattering their clothes. With every drop, Bolan's chances of learning where the

Golden Jihad terrorists were going to strike grew less and less.

Nasrallah was surprised at how rapidly he weakened. He stared up at the big American, saw the look of disappointment on his face and grinned. "Your kind will never win, bastard!" he spit in Arabic, and died.

Bolan had tried his best. He let the limp body drop and hurried over to the woman.

Anderson's wife had collapsed on the edge of the porch. Her limbs askew, eyes unfocused, she gaped at the sky. She didn't react when Bolan gently raised her so she could sit propped against a post.

"Mrs. Anderson?" he said softly. He let her go, and she started to slide back down again. He tried to sit her up once more, with the same result.

Sliding an arm under her legs, Bolan picked her up and carried her to a patch of shade on the same side of the house as the garage. She still hadn't uttered a word. He tried to brace her with her back against the house, but she slumped over, just like before. When he lifted her arm, it plopped onto the grass. She was as lifeless as a marionette.

Bolan had seen similar cases before. The woman was in a state of profound shock. He could tell by her torn clothes that she'd been abused, but he suspected her shock stemmed from something even worse.

"Mrs. Anderson," Bolan repeated quietly, "do you know where your husband is?"

It was as if he were addressing a stone. She continued to stare upward, her face as vacant as the cloudless sky.

"Do you know where the terrorists have gone?"

Azadeh said nothing.

Bolan remembered the third family member. "Your son, Mrs. Anderson, what happened to him? Is he all right?"

Finally there was a reaction. The woman's eyelids quivered. Her lower lip trembled. For a moment it appeared as if she were going to speak. Instead, she exhaled, then began to shake violently.

"Did you hear me?" Bolan persisted. "Is your son still in the house?" He knew he should be getting on the telephone to Brognola, but he had to see about the child first.

Azadeh Anderson groaned. The sound started from deep inside of her and emerged as a wail of pure anguish.

"I'll get him for you if you'll tell me where he is," Bolan said. "Did the Jihad take him with them?"

At long last, the woman spoke. Her voice was a cracked whisper, the word barely loud enough to hear. "No."

"Is Thomas inside?"

She had to try several times before she could utter another sound. "The basement," she said. "He's in the basement."

Bolan stood. "I'll be right back." Sprinting to the front entrance, he hastened inside. He kept his fingers crossed that the sight of her son would snap the woman out of her stupor so she could tell him where the Jihad had gone.

At the top of the basement stairs, Bolan paused. There'd been one trip wire, and there could be more. He descended slowly. There were no windows, so most of the basement was shrouded in shadow. He hadn't brought a flashlight, and he couldn't see more than a few feet in front of him.

"Thomas?" Bolan called, hoping the sound of his voice would cause the child to make some noise so he could locate him. Almost at the bottom, he craned his neck to the left to probe the gloom behind the stairs. At first, he saw nothing. Then, as his eyes adjusted, he made out a small form, and above it, on the wall, an inky smear darker than the surrounding shadows.

Mack Bolan wasn't a man who swore often, but he did so now. He stared at the tiny, motionless body and had to choke back a tidal wave of fury directed at the deviates who could commit such a horrendous crime.

Stripping off his jacket, Bolan went over and covered the body.

He dealt in violence daily. He'd seen death claim countless victims, old and young alike, but this one touched him more deeply than most.

Maybe it was the victim's tender age. Maybe it was an image of the broken woman upstairs who'd never be the same again.

Whatever the case, Bolan vowed that the Golden Jihad was going to pay, and pay dearly.

MONTGOMERY HOSPITAL in Norristown, Pennsylvania, hadn't seen so much activity since a pileup on the interstate, and it was all over one patient.

The Feds whisked into the hospital like a whirlwind. Several rooms on the third floor were commandeered. Guards were posted. Staff was instructed to keep out. Only the few who were issued special passes were allowed anywhere near the patient.

Hal Brognola would much rather have taken Azadeh Anderson to a federal facility, but Montgomery Hospital was nearest and he needed to have her treated right away. At government expense, he whisked in a trio of the top people in the country.

It was shortly after eight o'clock that evening when Brognola ended a meeting with them and took the elevator to the ground floor. Earlier, on his arrival, he'd noticed a small grassy area out front. He headed there now, angling toward a bench beside a pine. In the dark, he didn't realize the bench was occupied until he was almost on top of it. He was about to move to one farther off, when the person's profile registered.

"Striker?" he said. "So this is where you got to."

"You wanted me close by," Bolan reminded him.

"That I did, but it's been hours since I saw you last. I almost forgot you were here."

"I've been spending some time alone."

In Brognola's opinion his friend spent too much time alone as it was, but he'd never say as much. Bolan was a private person who kept his feelings to himself, and the big Fed respected that. "Are you all right?"

Bolan nodded.

Brognola had his doubts, though. His friend had been unusually withdrawn since rescuing Azadeh Anderson.

"What brings you out here?" Bolan asked.

"I just had a long talk with Dr. Chivington and the other two experts. They say there's one chance in a million that they can get Azadeh Anderson to talk."

"With the shape she's in, it'll take a miracle to get through to her," Bolan pointed out.

"Or one of the most potent drugs known to man."

"Is that safe?"

The big Fed wearily rubbed his eyes. "No, it's not. Chivington says there's a chance the procedure will kill her, but we have to try. She's our last hope."

"There've been no more leads on the Akbar end?" Bolan inquired.

"My people came up with a short list of front properties, but we've no idea whether they are more safehouses, places where he stored arms, or tax write-offs. They're checking now." He stared glumly at Bolan. "By the time they learn anything of value, it could be too late. I authorized Dr. Chivington to proceed."

Bolan didn't make any comment. They both knew there'd been no choice. "How soon before we can expect to hear anything?"

"At least another hour, maybe two," Brognola said. "They have to take it slowly and administer the drugs in stages, or it could kill her outright. As

things stand, even if she lives, she might wind up
brain dead." He kicked at a pine cone and said,
half to himself, "The poor woman has already
suffered so much, and now I'm putting her
through more."

"Think of the lives that'll be lost if we don't
stop the Golden Jihad."

"I know," Brognola conceded, "but it's small
consolation."

They sat in silence for a while, until Brognola
stood. "I came out here thinking that I didn't
want to be any part of it, but I was wrong. It was
my decision. I should see it through to the end."

"I think I'll tag along," Bolan said.

AZADEH ANDERSON WAS hooked up to a battery of
monitors and life-support machines. Dr. Chivington paced by her bedside, requesting stats now and
again. He took her pulse twice by hand, as if he
didn't trust what he was being told.

Bolan and Brognola stood in a corner, out of
the way, until the specialist beckoned them forward. The woman was as pale as the sheet that
covered her. Her breathing was deep but erratic.

"We're ready," Chivington said. A short man,
with a neatly trimmed salt-and-pepper beard, he
adjusted his glasses and bent over an intravenous
tube. "I've given her as much as I think she can

stand. You have to keep in mind that the barbiturate we're using is three times as powerful as thiopental sodium. That means the risks are correspondingly as high."

Brognola pulled up a chair. Straddling it, he studied the woman. "I can ask her anything and she'll answer?"

Dr. Chivington tapped the IV tube a few times. "That's the general idea, but there are no guarantees."

Bolan moved closer.

"Mrs. Anderson," Brognola began, "can you hear me?"

No one else made a sound. All eyes were either on the woman or on various monitors. Azadeh stirred feebly, but she didn't reply.

"If you can hear my voice, please answer," Brognola pressed her. "Just a simple yes will do."

Her silence dragged on. Chivington, shaking his head, increased the IV rate slightly. "It's not a good sign, this early," he commented.

Brognola asked his question a third time.

The woman moved her lips but no sounds came out. Her features contorted, showing she was in pain, hinting at an inner struggle. "Yes," she finally whispered, "I can hear you."

The big Fed got right to the point. "I need to ask you about the Golden Jihad. You know what they intend to do. Did they tell you where they were going to strike?''

"No," Azadeh said.

Bolan sighed. There it was. The home team was on the five-yard line with no more time-outs, and they had fumbled the ball.

Into the hush that greeted her first response, Azadeh said, "They told my husband."

Brognola half rose. "Surely he must have told you."

Azadeh gave no reply.

Dr. Chivington moved to a monitor. "I must remind you, Mr. Brognola, that she will only react to direct questions. And I strongly advise you speed this along. Her pulse rate has increased dramatically. In her severely weakened state..." The physician didn't finish the statement.

Brognola tried again. "Did your husband reveal their plans to you?"

"Yes."

"Where are they going to strike, Mrs. Anderson?"

"New York City."

"Where in New York?" the big Fed pressed. "We need to narrow it down or we won't have a prayer. Did they tell your husband their specific target?"

"No."

Brognola's face fell. He glanced at Bolan, then back at her. "They didn't give you a clue? You didn't overhear any pertinent remarks?"

"Just one."

"What one, Mrs. Anderson? What did they say?"

Azadeh was breathing heavily, sucking in air in great gulps.

"She can't take much more," Dr. Chivington warned.

Brognola leaned over her. "What did they say? Please, we need to know."

"They joked about the big gorilla being grateful."

"The big gorilla?" Brognola repeated.

Suddenly a monitor beeped, and went on beeping. Dr. Chivington yelled and his team went into action, working feverishly to stabilize their patient. He administered a hypodermic.

Bolan and Brognola were relegated to the role of helpless onlookers. The big Fed clenched his fists tight in frustration and said, "She has to pull through!"

At that moment, Azadeh Anderson's heartbeat flatlined.

CHAPTER FOURTEEN

It was a long shot. Everyone agreed on that, from the Executioner and Hal Brognola, down to the FBI agents who were called in to serve on surveillance and stakeout teams. But it was the only lead they had.

The irony didn't escape Mack Bolan. The concerted effort of the entire federal government to foil fanatics, armed with the most destructive devices ever created, hinged on a monster movie decades ago.

Bolan stepped to the edge of the curb on Fifth Avenue and craned his head to see as far up the building as he could. During a predawn briefing for the FBI agents, one of Brognola's people had mentioned that the structure included well over six thousand windows. At that moment, all those on the upper stories shimmered with the golden light of the rising sun. It was a spectacular sight.

The Empire State Building was no longer the tallest skyscraper in the world, but it was still an impressive structure. It had been from the top of this building that King Kong toppled at the end of the 1933 classic film of the same name. The story of the fifty-foot-tall gorilla from Skull Island and its clash with civilization was one of the most famous movies ever made. It had been shown in practically every country in the world at one time or another.

American films were routinely exported overseas. Current hits, old favorites, they all made the rounds of cinema houses. In some Middle Eastern countries, where television sets were so expensive that only one in four families owned one, going to the movies was a weekly habit.

So it was more than likely that some, if not all, of the Golden Jihad terrorists were familiar with King Kong's tale. So it made perfect sense for one of them to joke about the gigantic gorilla being grateful for the building's destruction.

It was a warped joke. But then, any mind capable of plotting mass destruction of innocents was warped to begin with.

At that moment, teams of FBI and Justice Department agents were scouring the lower levels of the building. So far, they'd turned up nothing unusual.

A federal net had also been thrown around the area surrounding the building. Agents posing as street workers were busy near a manhole on the corner. Other agents had set up a magazine stand.

On a scaffold above the main entrance were two more, acting as window washers.

A florist delivery van was illegally parked on the avenue. Inside was a quartet of highly trained experts in electronic surveillance, manning state-of-the-art equipment.

In the lobby, there were two more clerks than usual behind the front desk. A pair of helpful elevator operators were on duty, the bulges under their coats barely noticeable. A hefty man was busy mopping the floor. If anyone had looked at him closely, they might have noticed a tiny earphone in his right ear that was clipped to a radio at the back of his belt.

Bolan also had a radio. He'd checked in with Brognola once since sunrise, but there'd been nothing new to relay. Making a circuit of the building, he smoothed his lightweight jacket over the device.

Brognola had left Bolan free to roam where he wanted, to sniff into anything that caught his interest. Other agents were doing the same.

It was a typical weekday in the Big Apple. The streets were congested with morning rush-hour traffic, the sidewalks packed with bustling pedestrians. On the one hand, the crowds made it easier for Bolan and the Feds to blend in, but on the other, so many people coming and going made it harder to notice anyone behaving suspiciously.

Inside the building, the situation was just as bad, if not worse. Few Americans realized that the Empire State Building had more than ten thousand tenants, or that more than twenty thousand business people worked in the offices.

Most people did know about the two famous observatories, however, one on the eighty-sixth floor, the other on the one hundred and second. Both were off-limits to the general public until further notice. An electrical glitch was being blamed.

Bolan reached the two FBI agents hawking magazines. One agent glanced sharply at him. The soldier stopped, casually picked up a magazine, then flipped the collar of his jacket to flash the ID Brognola had given him. "Relax," he said. "I'm one of the good guys."

"I saw you with Mr. Brognola earlier," the agent said. He scanned the street. "I hope to hell these bozos show up soon. I don't know how much of this my nerves can take."

"Stay calm," Bolan advised,

"Being nuked isn't exactly how I want to buy the farm, if you know what I mean," the agent replied.

Bolan put back the magazine and entered the building. He went straight to the bank of elevators and took one to the twentieth floor. Repairs were under way there. Weeks earlier, a water line had ruptured, damaging several offices. To be safe, a number of them had been relocated temporarily, leaving the floor pretty much deserted except for the workmen. Bolan had been meaning to check it out ever since he'd gone over the floor plans with Brognola.

Someone had beaten him to it. A pair of young Feds were coming down the corridor when Bolan stepped off the elevator. He didn't know their names, but he recognized their faces.

Hal Brognola had a small army of blacksuits under him. Many worked at Stony Man Farm. Others operated out of Brognola's office at the Justice Department. Still others were field operatives, on call twenty-four hours a day, ready to deal with crisis situations as they arose.

Bolan had worked with some of them before, or seen them around at Stony Man. They were good people, dedicated professionals. Normally they kept a low profile. Most hardly said two words to him.

But that didn't apply to the dark-haired agent who smiled at him as he faced the pair. "Good morning, Mr. Belasko, sir," he said smoothly. "May we be of assistance?"

Belasko was a cover name used by Bolan on occasion. Only someone intimately familiar with Brognola's operation would know it. Bolan studied the young Fed. "And you are?"

"Agent Blake, sir."

His partner, a petite brunette, cleared her throat. "Agent Sanders, sir."

"Enough with the 'sir' stuff," Bolan said. "We're supposed to keep a low profile, remember?"

"Sorry, si—" Blake began, then caught himself.

"Does this floor check out?" Bolan asked.

"All clear," Sanders said. "We were just on our way to check out the sixty-first floor."

"What's there?"

Sanders pointed to several workmen down the hall. "One of them just told us that it's being renovated. Hardly anyone goes there, other than the work crews."

Blake pressed the button for the elevator. They had to wait more than a minute for a car to arrive. Bolan stepped in after the Feds. He intended to pay Brognola a visit in the makeshift command center that had been set up on a lower floor, but as the elevator door hissed shut, his radio flared to life.

"All agents! All agents! Suspects sighted on the ninety-sixth floor! Repeat, ninety-sixth floor! Converge and apprehend!"

"All right!" Blake declared. "We've nailed the scumbags!"

"Not yet, we haven't," Bolan said, and stabbed the button for the lobby.

"What did you do that for, sir?" Blake asked. "Didn't you hear? The suspects are on the ninety-sixth. We should be going up."

"That's what every other agent in the building is doing right this second," Bolan pointed out, holding the radio close to his ear. All he heard was static and a low hum. "But what happens if the terrorists get past them?"

Blake didn't look very pleased to be missing out on the action. Sanders, though, nodded and watched the floor indicator lights blink on and off.

Suddenly, faintly in the distance, all three of them heard the muffled crump of an explosion.

"That came from high up somewhere," Blake said. "Are those terrorists crazy? They could bring the whole building crashing down on top of their own heads."

Bolan just looked at him.

It was Agent Sanders who said, "Do you really think they care? The Golden Jihad isn't about to go down without a fight. They'll take as many of us with them as they can."

A distorted jumble of words came over the radio. Bolan adjusted the tuning and gain control, but the voice didn't come in any clearer. He figured that all the metal in the elevator shaft was interfering with the reception.

A second blast rocked the structure. This one was louder and much stronger. The car swayed slightly, enough to cause the lights to go out momentarily.

"Sweet Jesus!" Blake blurted. "I hope those bastards don't sever the cables. We're still fifteen stories up."

Yet another thunderous boom rocked them. Bolan kept his balance, but Blake fell to one knee and Sanders had to clutch at a wall for support.

Bolan's radio squawked gibberish. Sanders whipped out hers and switched it on, but all she could pick up was the same garbled nonsense.

The lights flickered a few times. Blake paled and punched the button for the lobby, as if that would hurry the car's descent. "Come on! Come on!" he said. "Get us down, you bucket of bolts!"

Without warning the elevator ground to a halt. A metallic creak resounded. To Bolan, it sounded as if the cable were under enormous stress.

"I sure as hell don't like being cooped up in here," Blake said.

For once, Bolan agreed. He pressed the emergency button, but nothing happened. Stepping to stand under the trapdoor in the suspended ceiling, he rose on his toes and managed to get it open. He jumped, locking his elbows on the rim, then pulled himself up and climbed onto the top of the car.

Gloom shrouded the shaft. The cable quivered as if it were being shaken. From above, the creaking sound grew steadily louder. There was no sign of the counterweight.

Bolan moved to the right. He could just distinguish the cable for the next car, but he didn't see the car itself. Poking his head through the trapdoor, he told the Feds, "I'm going down on the next cable. I'll let the maintenance people know that you're stuck in here."

"Hold on, sir," Blake said. "I'd like to come with you, if you don't mind."

The Executioner didn't mince his words. "It's a long drop. One slip, and you could wind up a smear at the bottom of the shaft."

Sanders stood directly below him and held up her arms. "The same thing'll happen if this car falls. I'd rather take my chances in the open."

There was no disputing her logic. Bolan helped her up, and together they hauled her partner onto the roof. As they moved to the edge, distant screams and shouts wafted to their ears.

"It sounds like a madhouse up there," Blake said. "What the hell did those terrorists do?"

Bolan gauged the distance. He backed up three strides and tensed to hurl himself into the void. Just as he started to move, the cable lurched. The elevator dropped like a rock for a dozen feet, then drew up short. It happened so abruptly that Bolan lost his footing and sprawled onto his stomach. He heard Blake swear and Sanders gasp.

Glancing around, Bolan saw the female agent was also on her stomach. But unlike him, she was perched precariously on the rear lip, about to plunge into the shaft. Her flailing hands scrambled for purchase. Drawing his knees up under him, Bolan dived. He caught hold of her wrist as she started to go over the side.

Although petite, Sanders still weighed over a hundred and ten pounds. Bolan's wrist bore every ounce as she struggled to climb to safety. His muscles strained, and it felt as though every ligament in his arm was being ripped apart. He gritted his teeth and hung on.

For seconds the outcome remained in the balance. Just when Bolan thought she was going to slip from his grasp, she snagged the edge and heaved herself up beside him. Inhaling deeply, she rolled onto her back.

"Thank you," the woman breathed. "That was much too close for comfort."

Bolan nodded and rose. It would have helped if her partner had lent a hand, but Blake was on his hands and knees, peering over the left-hand rim. Bolan went over. "What do you see?" he asked.

"I was looking for an open door lower down, but I don't think there is one."

The car gave another convulsive heave, threatening to pitch all three of them from their perch. This time it was Blake who nearly took the plunge. Yelping in alarm, he scrabbled backward, barely in time.

Bolan didn't think the car would stay suspended much longer. Whatever the Golden Jihad had done up above, it had damaged the cable system, perhaps partially severing the hoist cable that held up the counterweight. They had to get out of there, and quickly.

Setting himself, Bolan focused on the cable to the next car over. The car itself was nowhere in sight, which was cause for concern. If it caught them off-guard and started to move while they were clinging to the cable, it would be disastrous.

Despite the danger, Bolan flung himself over the brink. For a few harrowing seconds he had the illusion of falling through an inky void, then the cable loomed in front of him. He seized it with both hands and swung in an arc to slow himself. His left palm slipped. Had he not wrapped his legs around the cable at just that moment, he would have lost his hold and plummeted.

He leaned back to see above him. The cable seemed more secure than the one holding their elevator. It wasn't shaking, and it didn't lurch when he tugged on it with all his strength. "I think it's safe," he announced.

"You *think?*" Blake asked.

Sanders motioned for him to move out of her way. She watched Bolan slide a few yards lower, then she duplicated his move, springing lithely into the air and snatching the thick cable before she overshot it.

The cable quivered but held steady. Bolan went down even lower to make room for the third Fed, and Sanders followed.

Blake's face betrayed his nervousness. He stepped to the edge, looked down, stepped back again, made as if to run and jump, then apparently thought better of it and moved to the edge one more time.

"You can make it, partner," Sanders said. "I did."

Blake didn't share her confidence. "You were a gymnast in high school. I wasn't."

"Would you rather stand up there until the cable snaps?" she asked.

Bolan was thinking of the terrorists. There'd been no more explosions, but the acrid smell of smoke was drifting down. Another bad sign was that the shouting and screaming had grown much louder. "We don't have all day," he told Blake.

The agent wiped his palms on his trousers. Moving to the far side of the car, he spun, bellowed and burst across the roof. Like an ungainly bird he flew toward the cable. His outflung hands gripped it, but he was going much too fast.

The jolt nearly tore Bolan off the cable. He saw Blake clutch frantically at their lifeline, then begin to slide. Sanders cried out, but Blake was unable to stop himself. He slammed down on top of her, and both of them slid toward the Executioner. Bolan clamped his legs and arms to the cable for all he was worth and tucked his chin into his chest.

Sanders piled down on top of him, causing him to slide down a few feet. He arrested his descent, just in time to be battered from above again when Blake collided with Sanders and both of them slid down onto his shoulders. The impact came close to tearing him from the cable.

Holding fast, Bolan shifted to get Sanders's foot off of his face. The two Feds were quick to recover. He waited until they had set themselves, then ventured lower, going hand over hand with his legs curled around the cable.

It was slow going. The line was slippery enough, and sweat made it more so.

Bolan came to the next floor. The closed door was just out of reach, even when he leaned as far as he could toward it. A narrow rim at the bottom, no more than a few inches wide, offered the only footing.

"No one can stand on that little strip and pry the door open at the same time," Sanders remarked. "It would be suicide to try."

"No more suicidal than hanging here the rest of our lives," Bolan said. He tried to swing the cable a few inches inward, but there was little enough slack, and the added weight of the Feds hampered movement even more.

Bolan extended his right arm. He was about to attempt a jump when the cable suddenly cranked downward at an alarming rate. He glimpsed the cable in the next shaft over doing the same.

Shooting a look over his shoulder, he confirmed that the car they'd been in was also dropping.

"What if we don't stop until we reach the bottom?" Blake cried. "We'll be crushed to a pulp!"

One thing was for sure. They were picking up speed. The next floor appeared and was gone a moment later. Like lead sinkers being played out at the end of a fishing line, they whizzed past another door, then one more.

Bolan couldn't see the bottom of the shaft yet, but by tilting to one side, he spotted the bottom of an elevator perhaps fifty feet above them. If they continued to descend at the speed they were going, they would be stunned on impact, unable to get out of the way before the heavy car smashed down on top of them.

A reprieve came in the form of a sudden, jarring halt. Their cable was the only one that stopped, leaving them hanging between floors. The elevator they'd vacated swept on past them.

Bolan began to move down hand over hand. "We have to get to the next door before the cable moves again," he called out. "It's our only hope." He didn't linger to confirm the Feds had taken his cue. Self-preservation would see to that.

All the while, the smoky odor had grown steadily stronger. There could be no doubt a fire had broken out, or that the terrorists had caused it.

The faint outline of a door appeared. Bolan stopped when he drew even with it. He didn't waste a precious second in thought. Pulling his entire body inward to gain a few extra inches of reach, he pushed off from the cable. His fingers closed on the outer edge of the doorframe, and his toes found the narrow ledge.

Now all Bolan had to do was open the door. He felt along the groove it fit into, seeking a grip, a notch, an opening of any kind he could use for leverage. A hollow boom from far below made him pause.

"What the hell was that?" Blake cried.

"The elevator we were in," Bolan said, working faster. The car above them still hung motionless, but for how long? If it should fall like the other one, the two agents would be stuck on the cable. And he would be knocked from his perch to perform the highest swan dive in human history.

The groove was seamless, as smooth as glass. Bolan couldn't find anything to hold on to, let alone pry at. He stretched as high as he could. At last his questing fingertips found a niche of some sort. He gripped the outer edge of the door, then tugged.

The door didn't budge. Bolan pushed harder. His effort was rewarded by the door sliding a quarter of an inch on its recessed track, but there it stopped.

"For the love of God, hurry!" Blake urged.

Locking both hands onto the door, Bolan exerted every sinew in his body. The door moved. It fought him every inch of the way, but it slid open bit by bit, until it was wide enough for him to slip through. He did, instantly whirling to help the Feds. Sanders reached toward him.

Bolan leaned out to seize her arm. As he did, a grinding rasp filled the shaft and the cable streaked downward.

CHAPTER FIFTEEN

Sanders leaped just as the cable resumed its headlong descent. Bolan, leaning out as far as he dared, snagged her wrist in his steely grip. Heaving backward, he yanked her through the opening so hard that she slammed into him and they both went down, her feet inches from the shaft.

Hardly a heartbeat later there was a thud. Blake had also jumped. He'd managed to snare the narrow rim at the bottom of the door. Terror lit his eyes as he scrambled madly to get through the opening before the elevator reached him.

Sanders, facing away from the door, hadn't noticed her partner's desperate plight, but Bolan did. He shoved her aside, twisted and propelled himself at the gap, arm outstretched. Blake had clawed partway up over the rim, and he flung his arm toward Bolan. Their fingers brushed. Blake opened his mouth to say something.

He never got the chance. Like an out of control express train, the hurtling car crashed onto the agent, ripping him from his perch. One moment the man was there, the next he wasn't. All that remained was a bloody smear at the base of the door.

Sanders saw what happened. *"No!"* she wailed, throwing herself at the opening.

Bolan stopped her and held on when she struggled to break free. "He's gone!" he said more gruffly than he normally would have, trying to shock her into dealing with the situation. "There's nothing we can do for him. Our job now is to get those who are responsible."

Tears gathered in the agent's eyes. Numbly she nodded, then gave herself a shake and blinked to clear her vision. "I know," she said. "I'm sorry. It's just that—"

"I understand, but right now we don't have time." As much as he'd have liked to spend a few moments comforting her, they couldn't afford any further delay. Down the hall a sign indicated the stairs. Bolan led the way.

Now that they were clear of the elevator shaft, the shouts from above had reached a piercing crescendo. A steady drumming added a rhythmic beat to the cacophony.

The din grew louder still once they gained the stairwell. It was now a virtual roar, echoing off the walls. Bolan cast a fleeting glance up the stairs as he started down, and caught sight of figures about two floors higher up.

"My God!" Sanders said.

Bolan took the steps three at a time, spinning around the landings to cover the distance faster.

They passed the fourth floor, then the third. As they crossed the next landing and started down the last flight of stairs, Bolan thought he heard the ratchet chatter of an SMG below, but he couldn't be certain for all the noise in the stairwell. Nevertheless, he flipped his collar to expose his ID and drew the Beretta.

He hit the last door on the fly. Spilling through into the lobby, he saw at least half a dozen bodies on the floor and another sprawled over the reception counter.

The only people alive were three men, one near the counter, the other two standing closer to the entrance. All three wore bright red, white and blue uniforms with the words Manhattan Messenger Service printed on them. All three had swarthy, bearded features. And one of them carried a large blue backpack. Bolan knew them for who they truly were. He had found three members of the Golden Jihad. More important, he had found one of the nukes.

Automatically Bolan snapped a shot at the terrorist by the counter at the same moment all three opened up on him. He dived for cover as Sanders came through the doorway, took in what was going down in a single glance and cut to the right, her pistol blossoming in her hands.

The three Jihad members retreated toward the front door. They laid down an effective suppressing fire to keep the Executioner and the Fed pinned long enough for them to make good their escape.

Bolan snaked to a potted plant and rose onto his knees to shoot. Just as he did, the uproar in the stairwell rose to a deafening pitch.

The door burst open, spewing terrified men and women into the lobby. In a blind panic, they raced toward the street, heedless of the three terrorists with leveled weapons. One of the terrorists opened up, mowing down those in the front. But there were too many, and he'd be unable to kill them all. Those to the rear pushed against those in front, forcing the few who noticed the gunners to keep on going whether they wanted to or not.

It was a tidal wave of panic-stricken fugitives from the explosions and fire on the upper levels. One urge had to be uppermost in all their minds— to survive at any cost. They weren't about to stop until they reached safety.

Bolan jumped up and sighted on the terrorist with the backpack. Before he could squeeze the trigger, he was engulfed in the frenzied mob and swept along with them. He lost sight of the Jihad members, but he did see Sanders swallowed by the throng.

Resisting was useless. The soldier could no more have held his ground against that swirling mass than he could have withstood a tornado. He was almost battered off his feet as they propelled him toward the entrance.

Many tripped over bodies or on slick puddles of blood. Yet that didn't slow the rest. They gushed out onto the sidewalk, breaking to the right and left, many fleeing into the street. Traffic was brought to a screeching halt.

Bolan was funneled into the sunlight. Frantically he tried to break away, but he was borne to the left.

At last, near the corner, the horde slowed. It began to break apart as exhausted individuals shuffled to a halt. Bolan tore free and stepped off the curb. He searched urgently for the terrorists, but spotting them among that multitude seemed impossible.

Then he spied a bright red, white and blue uniform out of one eye. He turned toward the corner and saw a bearded figure vanish into the crowd. Sliding the Beretta under his jacket so as not to attract attention, he gave chase. He plowed through the milling legion, roughly forcing his way through.

He reached the corner. For a few seconds he couldn't see his quarry, and he feared that the Golden Jihad had lucked out again. Then, halfway down the block, the figure appeared, moving briskly, heading deeper into Manhattan. Bolan pushed and shoved until he broke clear of the pack and could run freely.

The phony messenger had reached the next corner. Swiveling, he looked back.

The Executioner wasn't caught napping. He'd stopped, waiting to see what the terrorist would do. As the man turned, Bolan did, too, to stare at the Empire State Building, just as so many others were doing. Only then did he see the thick smoke curling from shattered windows high up.

Nearby, a man holding a transistor radio to his ear called out, "I just caught a news report! They say that a bunch of terrorists set off grenades up there! Two floors are on fire, and the sprinklers aren't working like they should."

This set off a confusing babble from the onlookers, most of them talking at the same time. Paying them no heed, Bolan backed to the curb where he could view the terrorist more clearly. He wasn't one of the men from the mug shots and photos Brognola had shown him.

The fanatic was the only person on the block who was smiling.

Then he took off again. Bolan trailed him at a safe distance. The Jihad had a hideout somewhere in the Big Apple, and Bolan intended to locate it.

Sirens rent the air as police and fire vehicles sped toward the building from all over Manhattan. Ambulances soon appeared. As they'd done when the World Trade Center was bombed, the city's emergency crews were responding superbly to the crisis.

The terrorist's distinctive jacket made him easier to tail. Every now and then he would look over a shoulder, and once when he did, he exposed an autopistol in a shoulder rig.

Thanks to hordes of curious citizens flocking toward the Empire State Building, Bolan was able to keep a low profile. The sidewalks became jammed with those trying to get a good look at the damage.

Bolan stayed close to the curb where the going was easier. Several times he tried his radio, but all it picked up was static. He was on his own, without any hope of backup should he get into a tight situation.

About fifteen minutes had passed when the terrorist unexpectedly turned and entered a restaurant. Bolan slowed, shoved his hands into his pockets and strolled past the brick building. He saw the terrorist at a pay phone, probably talking to another Jihad member. The man had his back to the front window, so he didn't notice Bolan duck into the doorway of a tenement.

The terrorist spoke for quite a while, gesturing excitedly. Finally he hung up, looked around and exited. He walked right past Bolan, who had blended into the shadows. When the man had gone half a block, the soldier stepped out of hiding.

The terrorist seemed convinced he was safe because he hardly looked back from then on. Bolan was able to keep the man in sight with no problem.

It helped that Manhattan was one of the world's most densely populated places, with more people crammed into the twenty-two square miles between the Hudson and East rivers than were found in whole states. The sidewalks bustled with activity, so Bolan wasn't worried about being spotted. But he never took anything for granted, and since it was possible the terrorist had noticed his blue jacket at one time or another, he stopped when he came to an alley and saw one of New York's many homeless leaning against a wall.

It was an elderly man, his clothes patched and faded, his worldly possessions piled in a battered shopping cart. What interested Bolan was the brown jacket the man wore. It was in fair condition and large enough to fit him.

Pulling out a wad of bills, Bolan peeled off a hundred and approached the man. "I'd like to buy your jacket," he said.

The homeless man was bent over, muttering to himself. Stiffening, he peered suspiciously at the Executioner. "It's mine. I found it fair and square."

Bolan waved the bill in front of the man's nose. "For your jacket, friend. This second. No fuss."

The man gaped at the C-note as if it were the Holy Grail. "You sure you know what you're doing?"

"This second," Bolan stressed. The old man nodded. Bolan removed his own jacket, then held it out. "For you. No charge."

Snickering, the man squinted at Bolan. "You're crazy, mister. You could buy all the new jackets you want. Why take mine?"

"I like the color," Bolan said, and got out of there before he lost sight of the terrorist.

For several more blocks the Jihad member went almost due north. At a side street he turned east. Using the crosswalk, he paused before he reached the corner of the first building to check if he was being tailed.

Bolan stopped next to a pair of women who were window-shopping. He kept his fingers crossed that the fanatic would think he was with them. The ruse had to have worked because the man didn't give him a second glance, and went on.

On coming to the junction, Bolan was careful not to stare up the side street in case the man was looking his way. He blended into a knot of pedestrians entering the crosswalk. He'd covered about thirty feet when, scanning ahead, he discovered that his quarry was nowhere to be seen.

Bolan wasn't prone to panic. His nature and training had molded him to where he almost always held his emotions in check. But in that awful instant when he believed he'd lost the terrorist, and with it any hope of stopping the Golden Jihad from detonating the backpack nukes, he came as close to panic as he ever had.

He hastened up the street, peering into every window and doorway. He passed a number of stores and was almost past a small bakery when he spotted the terrorist at the counter, buying a loaf of bread.

The terrorist was about to leave. Bolan had to avoid being spotted. A cab was parked at the curb a dozen feet farther along. The overhead light wasn't on, but Bolan ran to the vehicle and slid into the back seat. He startled the cabbie, who was cramming a sandwich into his mouth.

"What the—" the man said. "Can't you see, bozo? This cab ain't in service."

Bolan peeled off a ten-dollar bill and held it out.

The cabbie arched an eyebrow. "What's that for? I just told you I'm not taking you anywhere."

"I don't want you to," Bolan said, placing the money on the front seat. "All I want to do is sit here for a minute."

"What for? You don't look sick." The cabbie looked at the Executioner much as the homeless man in the alley had. "You must be some kind of weirdo. Get the hell out of my cab."

"Just one minute," Bolan stressed. The terrorist had already gone by and was nearing the next corner, the bread tucked under his arm.

The cabdriver hesitated, but not for long. Snatching the bill, he said, "I swear, the people in this city get nuttier every day. Okay, pal, you just bought yourself a minute, but you've only got forty seconds left."

That was more than enough. Once the Jihad member reached the other side of the street, Bolan intended to resume shadowing him. But to the soldier's surprise, the man made no attempt to cross the road. Instead, he stepped to the curb and gazed in both directions.

"Thirty seconds," the cabbie warned.

The terrorist was waiting for someone, Bolan realized, and who else would it be other than his comrades in the Golden Jihad?

"Twenty seconds."

Bolan shut the cabbie out. He wasn't going anywhere until the terrorist did. He saw the man smile and visibly relax, as a white van appeared down the block. The Executioner could see that the driver was wearing the same Manhattan Messenger Service uniform.

This man Bolan identified. He'd seen the killer's picture a dozen times, always in connection with an atrocity. It was Hassan Nidal, second-in-command of the Golden Jihad. In the passenger seat sat the third disguised fanatic.

"Fifteen seconds, pal," the cabbie said, his mouth full of food.

Bolan knew he couldn't chase a van on foot, and he doubted the cabbie would oblige him by following it. Just then the van slowed and angled toward the curb.

At that exact second, a police car rounded the corner. The cop behind the wheel took one look at the man standing on the corner, flicked on his flashing lights and bore down on the waiting terrorist without even noticing the other vehicle.

But Hassan Nidal had noticed the police. Bolan saw the man bark an order to his passenger. The snout of a subgun jutted out the van's window, trained on the unsuspecting patrolmen.

They had to be warned. Bolan gripped the taxi's door handle and pumped it. He knew that it was probably too late, that he couldn't attract their attention before the gunner made his play, but he had to try.

The soldier figured that an APB had been issued for suspects answering to the descriptions of the three Jihad men who'd taken part in the attack. If they'd been smart, the terrorists would've gotten rid of their colorful uniforms as soon as they'd left the scene. Even in the middle of bustling Manhattan, those red, white and blue outfits made them stand out like walking flags.

The police car screeched to a stop. The terrorist on the sidewalk unlimbered his subgun and stitched the vehicle's windshield with a short burst.

Both cops saved their lives by barreling out their doors. The patrolman who'd been behind the wheel knew his business. He came up with his service revolver leveled and, at a range of eight feet, put a slug into the terrorist's shoulder. The man crumpled, dropping the bread.

The cops moved in to cuff him. It was then that the van hurtled into play, Nidal spinning the wheel. The van's grille slammed into the nearest officer, smashing him against his own patrol car.

It all happened so swiftly that the first cop was down before Bolan jumped from the taxi. The cabbie gawked at the tableau, unable to believe his eyes, as were the many passersby.

The officer who'd shot the terrorist on the corner swung toward the van, his revolver lifted. Unfortunately he wasn't fast enough. The gunner punctured him from sternum to crotch, firing even after the cop had fallen and was convulsing wildly.

Nidal leaped from the van. He dashed to his fallen comrade and got the man on his feet. Linked at the shoulders, they scurried for the open van door, covered by the third terrorist.

Bolan didn't know if the backpack nuke was in the van, and he didn't have the luxury of making sure before he committed himself. Whipping out the Beretta, he aimed at the shooter on the passenger side and stroked the trigger.

The gunner was hammered back against the bucket seat. He sagged but didn't go down. Spying the Executioner, he got off a short burst, firing with one hand.

The spray of lead went wild, but it forced Bolan down beside the cab. Anxious to drop Nidal before the terrorists fled, he rose as high as the hood. Nidal had beaten him to the punch and was shoving the wounded man into the back of the van. Bolan aimed, then had to duck again when the SMG spewed lead.

The van's engine revved, and its tires screamed as Nidal trod on the gas pedal.

Sprinting into the open, Bolan tracked the van's front tires. A single shot blew out the one on the front passenger side. Nidal didn't stop. Looping into the street, he narrowly missed hitting a sedan whose elderly driver honked at him.

For several seconds Bolan had a clear shot at the tires on the driver's side. He'd just taken aim when a dumbfounded pedestrian blundered into his sights, causing him to hold his fire.

The terrorists were getting away. Nidal accelerated, then swerved sharply when a car sped into the intersection. Spinning out of control, the van crashed into a parked pickup. Its headlights shattered and the grille buckled, but there wasn't enough damage to cripple it.

Bolan ran, seeking to intercept the killers before they made their getaway. A pair of shots at Nidal's window had no effect. He was almost to the corner when the van bounced onto the sidewalk, skirting a streetlight and a mailbox. Bolan's shot splintered the rear window as he tried to nail Nidal in the back of the head.

Then the van careered into the flow of traffic. Bolan had to race out into the street in order to fire. As he adopted a two-handed grip, Nidal passed a garbage truck and took a right turn into an alley.

The Executioner was left with the bitter taste of failure in his mouth. The Golden Jihad was still free to carry out its vile scheme. And the next time, the terrorists just might succeed.

CHAPTER SIXTEEN

It wasn't in Bolan's nature to accept defeat. Since he couldn't catch the terrorists on foot, he would find another way.

Pivoting, he looked for a vehicle to commandeer. As his gaze fell on the taxi, the cabdriver shifted into Reverse and took off down the street like a rocket. Bolan turned toward the intersection and debated whether to take the police car, even though it was damaged and there'd be hell to pay if the police caught him.

Just then, he noticed one of the many horrified bystanders, a youth in his late teens wearing a helmet and knee pads, and a T-shirt that advertised the name of the company he worked for.

It was a bicycle messenger firm.

New York is not only one of the biggest cities in the world, it is also one of the most congested. There is a constant need for a means of speeding certain business and personal information from one part of the city to another, and bicycle messengers offer an ideal way to go. Able to weave in and out of sluggish traffic with ease, to take shortcuts no car or truck ever could, these cyclists whisk envelopes and small packages to their destinations, nine times out of ten faster than if delivered by anyone else.

The youth, who was staring in petrified fascination at the dead policeman, sat astride a ten-speed racing bicycle. He recoiled when the Executioner ran up to him, and he made as if to pedal off.

"Hold on!" Bolan said, grabbing the handlebars with one hand. He pulled his wad of expense money from his pocket. "I need your bike."

The youth, too frightened to speak, shook his head and tried to pull away.

Bolan didn't have any time to waste. Seizing the youth's wrist, he jammed the bills into his hand. "There's over eight hundred dollars. It's all yours if you'll let me have your bike."

"Eight hundred?" the youth finally found his voice.

The ten-speed was worth only about half that, but Bolan didn't mind paying so much extra, especially when so much was at stake. All he wanted was to get after the white van. He leaned toward the youth and said quietly but urgently, "Look, I don't have time to explain. You saw what those men did to the two officers. I'm out to stop them and I need your bike to do it. So will you let me have it or not?''

The appeal worked. The youth glanced at the downed cops, then at his bicycle, then at the bills. "It's yours, mister," he said, stepping aside. "I hope you make those guys pay."

"I will," Bolan vowed.

Sirens wailed in the distance as the Executioner straddled the seat and shoved off. It had been a long time since he'd ridden a bicycle, but it was like riding a horse—once a person learned how, he never forgot. Pedaling furiously, he zipped through the intersection. At the alley he turned so sharply that he nearly tipped over. Promptly correcting the angle, he was off again like a shot.

In all, less than forty-five seconds had gone by since the van had disappeared. Given the snail's pace of traffic and the van's condition, Bolan was confident he would overtake the terrorists within a couple of minutes, at the most.

It turned out to be a lot sooner.

He came to where the alley joined a street and braked, searching in both directions. There was no sign of Nidal and company.

To Bolan's left, across the street, was another alley. He sped toward it, earning a horn blast from an irate driver. Slowing at the mouth of the alley, he spied the van parked in deep shadows halfway down, just past a green trash container. Bolan approached cautiously, keeping the garbage bin between him and the vehicle.

The van's engine wasn't running. There were no sounds from within, nor was any movement apparent.

Getting off the bicycle, Bolan leaned it against the garbage bin and drew the Beretta. Gliding up to the van's shattered rear window, he peeked in. It was as empty as it appeared, except for three red, white and blue outfits scattered over the floor and seats. Two of the shirts bore bright scarlet stains.

The terrorists had changed clothes and fled on foot.

Bolan quickly reclaimed the bicycle. Riding past the van, he came to another street. The sidewalks were quieter than the previous ones had been. He eased out of the alley, rose on the pedals to see farther ahead and bore east once again.

Nidal and his two comrades were a block and a half away. They now wore jeans and jackets so they wouldn't stand out in a crowd. The men who'd been shot were walking unassisted, indicating their wounds weren't as severe as the Executioner had hoped.

Then the man Bolan had winged stumbled and nearly fell. Nidal caught hold of him and said something. The man shook his head, straightened and was able to go on, but much more slowly than before.

Bolan hung back, pedaling slowly. He saw no need to discard the ten-speed. The last thing the terrorists would expect was for someone to chase them on a bicycle. It was the perfect cover, provided he kept his head down.

Nidal had the nuke. It was apparently fully assembled, snug in its huge bright blue backpack.

For the better part of an hour Bolan kept his distance. The terrorists then seemed to act lost. At an intersection, Nidal and the man shot by the police officer appeared to dispute which way to go. Nidal pulled out a map and after consulting it they hiked north, then west, then east again, sometimes doubling back on themselves to catch anyone trailing them.

Each time Bolan hid and waited for them to go on. There was a slim chance that the rest of the Jihad, and the second nuke, were also in the Big Apple. His hope was that they would lead him to it.

The constant change of direction puzzled the Executioner. They either had no set destination in mind or they were stalling for time.

IT WAS the latter.

Hassan Nidal checked his watch again. They had several hours before they could put Ahmed Tufayli's backup plan into effect. Nidal was sure they'd eluded the police and federal authorities, but he was still extremely upset at how badly the day had gone.

It had started well enough. The five of them had risen before dawn and eaten a light breakfast. Nidal had passed out the uniforms to Nabih and Hashemi and put on one himself.

Stealing them from a branch of the Manhattan Messenger Service had been Nidal's idea, not Tufayli's. Their leader had simply wanted them to slip into the Empire State Building, set the nuclear device and leave.

In keeping with Nidal's policy of never leaving anything to chance, he'd decided they should go in disguise.

Despite what other members of the Golden Jihad believed, Nidal knew the Americans weren't fools. They knew the Jihad would strike soon, and Nidal had thought it likely that they even suspected one of the targets would be New York City. It made sense that the American authorities had staked out every prominent landmark in the city.

Nidal had left two men at the safehouse—a precaution in case he was captured. The pair was to get him out, even if they had to give their own lives in the attempt.

The ride to the Empire State Building had been uneventful. Nidal had parked several blocks away. No one had paid much attention to them on their way to the skyscraper. Their disguises had worked perfectly. Or so he'd thought.

Tufayli's plan had called for them to go up to the observatory on the one hundred and second floor and place the nuke in a maintenance closet. But as they'd waited for the elevator, cars had squealed up to the curb out front and dozens of grim-faced men and women in suits had piled out.

Federal agents. Thankfully the elevator came then, and they'd stepped in before they were spotted.

Nabih and Hashemi had wanted to go through with the original plan, until Nidal had pointed out that the observatories would be one of the first places the Americans would search. He'd told them it would be wiser to plant the nuke somewhere else.

They'd gotten off two floors below the top observatory and worked their way down, using the stairs. They had to have covered more than twenty floors before they found one that was largely deserted.

A utility closet had offered a perfect spot to hide the nuke. While Nabih and Hashemi stood guard outside, Nidal had opened the backpack and was about to begin the arming sequence when a pair of men in suits had come down the hall.

Nidal had heard them ask what his friends were doing there. Nabih spoke a little English, and he'd answered that they were delivering a package. When one of the Americans had demanded to see it, Hashemi had cut both of them down.

Things had rapidly gone from bad to worse. Nidal had elected to get out of there since he wouldn't have time to arm the device before more federal agents showed up. They'd jogged to the elevators, getting there just as one had opened to disgorge more agents.

A firefight had broken out. Nabih had thrown a grenade into the elevator. They'd retreated to the stairs and descended. More Americans had tried to stop them, and more grenades had to be used.

Somehow, they'd made it to the ground floor, only to find more enemies barring their path. They'd killed them, too, and were on the verge of making good their escape when two more agents had spilled out of the stairwell.

By a sheer stroke of luck, a terror-stricken torrent of humanity had streamed into the lobby, allowing them to slip away in all the confusion.

Nabih, however, had became separated from them.

Nidal had cruised the streets for half an hour, looking for him. He'd then telephoned their safehouse and learned that Nabih had already called in and would be waiting for him near a bakery they knew of.

The pickup should have gone smoothly. Who could have foreseen cops showing up? Who could have predicted some American would have tried to be a hero?

Nidal hadn't gotten a good look at the man who'd shot Hashemi. The quick glimpse he'd had, of a big man in a loose-fitting jacket, led him to think the man was a plainclothes policeman, not a federal agent.

All of this went through the terrorist's mind as he trudged the grimy streets of New York City. Convinced they'd shaken any tail, he headed toward their safehouse, a brownstone provided by the Golden Jihad's benefactor, Mehmet Akbar.

Hashemi began to lag. He'd taken a slug in the right side of his chest, and from the way he wheezed and puffed, Nidal knew a lung had been punctured. Nabih had been hit high on the shoulder, faring much better, the bullet missing any major arteries.

They were still several blocks from the brownstone when Hashemi groaned, then pitched forward. Nidal was at his side and arrested his fall. "Can you hold out a little longer, brother?" he asked. "We don't have far to go."

"I can make it," Hashemi said.

Nabih stepped in close. "People are watching us," he whispered.

A middle-aged couple on the porch of a nearby house was staring. Nidal smiled at them, tipped a hand to his mouth as if taking a drink and winked. The man grinned and winked back. The woman turned up her nose.

Nidal couldn't get into the brownstone fast enough. The two men who'd stayed behind helped ease Hashemi onto a sofa. Nabih sat in a chair.

While they were being tended to, Nidal placed a telephone call, using a fake calling card Mehmet Akbar had provided. He had to hand it to the arms dealer—the man thought of everything.

Ahmed Tufayli answered on the fifth ring, as he was supposed to. "Hello?" he said in clipped English.

Nidal spoke in Arabic. "It is I, my brother. The war isn't going well. We were barely able to get away with our lives."

"I've seen the newscasts," Tufayli said. "What went wrong?"

Briefly Nidal gave him an account of the bungled attempt. "As you have instructed, we leave for the secondary target in a couple of hours."

"How badly hurt are Nabih and Hashemi?" Tufayli wanted to know.

"Nabih will pull through," Nidal replied. "As for Hashemi..." He didn't complete the sentence.

"That is most unfortunate. He is a good man." Tufayli paused for a long time. "I have more bad news. We have lost others important to the success of our Holy War."

"Who?" Nidal asked. It worried him that the day just kept getting worse and worse, and it was far from over yet.

"Mehmet Akbar and his sons."

A knot formed in the pit of Nidal's gut. "*All* of them? Are you sure?"

"My source is a man who was in Mehmet's organization. The Americans are keeping it quiet, perhaps for fear that if we found out, we would go into hiding and they would never recover their precious nukes."

"Can someone step in to take Akbar's place?"

"In time, yes. For now, though, we are on our own. I have a list of places where we can hide out, and we'll still have some funds left."

Nidal had a disturbing thought. "Is it safe for us to rely on Akbar's list?"

"He assured me that no one knew of the many properties he had. They haven't raided the one you are in, have they now?"

Tufayli had a point, Nidal conceded.

The Jihad leader went on. "I am afraid that something has happened to Nayif Nasrallah. He was to have joined me in Washington, D.C., this morning, but he did not show up. When I called the house in Norristown, a recording told me that the number has been disconnected."

That knot in Nidal's stomach became a melon-sized rock. "Perhaps the Americans have found out about the house in Norristown, and they might know of the other ones we are using," he said. "I think we should get out of here and hide elsewhere. You should do the same."

"What will you do? Roam the streets? With Hashemi and Nabih in the shape they are in?" Tufayli said. "Do as you want, but if it was me, I would stay there until shortly before Mass begins. The less time you spend out in the open, the safer you'll be."

Nidal had one more question. "Is the soldier behaving himself?"

"So far, but only because he is afraid for the woman and their brat. I plan to keep him alive until your device has detonated."

"Do you still want me to set the timer for a ten-hour countdown?"

Tufayli was silent for a moment. "No. In light of all that has happened, set the nuke to go off four hours after you arm it. That will allow us enough of a safety margin, unless you plan to walk to Atlanta."

Nidal managed a chuckle. Atlanta was where they would regroup after Tufayli's team planted its bomb in the American capital. Passage had already been arranged on a ship that would take them to England. From there, they would work their way to their haven in Iran.

"I guess that is all for now," Tufayli said. "Death to all Americans!"

"May they burn in torment forever!" Nidal added, and hung up. Someone prodded him from behind. He turned to find one of the men who'd remained in the house.

"Hashemi just died. There was nothing we could do."

Nidal cursed. How much more could go wrong before this terrible day was done?

"What do you want us to do with the body?"

"Leave it where it is. Six hours from now it will be vaporized, along with everything else in this vicinity."

MACK BOLAN RODE around the block twice, fifteen minutes apart. The layout suggested a way to gain entry to the brownstone without being observed.

A frame house flanked it on the right, a smaller brownstone on the left. All three were bordered by an alley at the rear. All three also had tiny backyards, but only the yard behind the terrorists' hideout boasted a high fence.

When he cut through the alley on his second circuit, Bolan discovered that the neighbors in the frame house—a couple seated on their front porch—had several trash cans lined up next to the fence. They would make it simple for him to scale the fence.

When to do it was the big question. Bolan had no way of knowing what Nidal had in mind. The terrorists might stay in the house indefinitely, or they might try to flee the city. A third possibility, one he had to prevent at all costs, was that they would venture out to plant the nuke.

Bolan braked at the end of the alley. Across the street, in a playground, a boy of about twelve, dressed in worn clothes, was shooting hoops by himself. Bolan crossed to the wire fence that ringed the playground, kicked the bicycle's stand into place and called out, "Hey, kid, do you want a bike?"

The boy stopped playing. He stared a Bolan but didn't answer.

"It's yours if you want it, and no, it's not hot," Bolan said answering the youth's unspoken question.

He didn't look back until he reached the corner. The kid was beside the ten-speed, running his hands over the bicycle as if to prove that it wasn't a figment of his imagination.

Rather than pass by the brownstone a third time, Bolan went straight. He took up a post at the corner of the first building on the opposite corner. It gave him an unobstructed view of the entire block.

Moments later, a man came out of the brownstone. He hurried down the steps and turned toward the corner. That was when Bolan recognized Hassan Nidal. The terrorist didn't have the blue backpack with him.

The Executioner ducked out of sight, descending part way down a flight of stairs leading to a store.

Nidal clearly had a purpose. He strode briskly past the corner and kept on going.

Bolan let the man get out of sight before following him. Three blocks later, Nidal went into a pharmacy. Bolan guessed that the wounded men needed medication, men who were alone at the safehouse with the nuke.

It was a golden opportunity, made to order for Bolan. He retraced his steps at twice the speed, turning into the side street that brought him to the alley.

Bolan assumed a casual air in case one of the terrorists happened to be at a back window. On reaching the high fence, he ducked and hastened to the trash cans.

The Executioner hiked a leg to step up. As he did, a woman's voice knifed through him from the screen door of the frame house.

"Just what in the hell do you think you're doing, mister?"

The woman from the porch had her hands on her broad hips and a scowl on her fleshy face. Bolan lowered his leg. Unless he did some fast talking, she would call the police.

"I didn't mean to bother you," he said politely. "I just wanted to go through your trash for scraps of food."

"Out of work and down on your luck, are you?" the woman said. Before Bolan could reply, she moved away from the door, saying, "Stay right there. I think I have something here you'll like better than garbage scraps.''

She returned bearing a thick piece of apple pie on a paper plate. ''Thank you,'' he said.

''Think nothing of it.'' The woman started back in. ''You'd best get along before my Henry catches you. He's not very fond of bums.''

Bolan didn't delay another instant. Still holding the pie, he sprang onto the trash can, gripped the top of the fence with one hand and vaulted up and over. Soft grass cushioned him as he landed upright and turned toward the brownstone. Then he froze.

Just inside the glass-paneled back door, facing him, was a man with a swarthy complexion. It had to be a terrorist, one who hadn't been in on the attack at the Empire State Building and who wasn't weak from being wounded, a terrorist who bellowed while clawing at an autopistol wedged under his belt.

CHAPTER SEVENTEEN

Any professional soldier or mercenary knew that one of the keys to surviving in combat was being able to adapt to the flow of battle. A man might have no control over the events around him, but he could control how he reacted. Adjusting to the demands of a situation meant not only using the terrain to advantage, but also every little thing around.

The Executioner, caught flat-footed, did just that. He couldn't possibly draw the Beretta before the terrorist unlimbered his pistol, not when he held a piece of pie in his right hand. So he adjusted. He did the only thing he could do to gain him the few precious seconds he needed to draw the 9 mm pistol. He used the pie as a weapon.

As the man at the door went for his gun, Bolan hurled the slice of pie at him. It hit the pane of glass in front of the man's face with a loud splat. Naturally it did no harm, not even cracking the pane. But it did cause the terrorist to instinctively recoil, delaying his draw for the fraction of time

Bolan needed to throw himself to the right and grab for the Beretta.

The terrorist fired a heartbeat ahead of the Executioner. His autopistol wasn't fitted with a suppressor. It boomed three times, the slugs gouging the turf a hand's width from Bolan's cheek.

The soldier squeezed off two shots. He saw the terrorist jerk at the second one, but he knew he'd only winged the man. The fanatic ducked out of sight and began to shout an alarm. Elsewhere in the house footsteps pounded.

A frown creased Bolan's forehead. So much for the element of surprise. From the sound of things, there were at least two gunners in there he hadn't known about, plus the wounded pair. Four to one, and they had the nuke.

There was a very real chance they might set it off, believing as they did that if they went out in a blaze of glory, dying in battle for God and their beliefs, they would spend eternity in Paradise.

Bolan had to get in there, fast. He chugged two rounds at the door to keep the terrorist pinned down and rose to dart to the corner of the house. Suddenly a window directly in front of him crashed outward as an SMG poked through.

If the terrorist hadn't rushed his first burst, Bolan's head would have been taken off at the neck. As it was, a swarm of leaden killers buzzed over his head as he dived again, onto his stomach. Rolling onto his side, he sent three slugs in the shooter's direction, even though the terrorist had dodged out of sight.

Bolan crawled to the corner. Once there, he rose into a crouch and raced toward the front of the brownstone.

It wouldn't do him any good to go in the front way. The Jihad was bound to have all the doors covered. So that left the windows. Bolan passed under several of them, then stopped next to one at his feet.

It was a way into the basement. Small and square, it looked barely big enough for him to squeeze through. He raised the Beretta, aiming not at the basement window but at one on the first floor he'd just passed. He kicked out as he fired, so that as each slug smashed into the first-floor window, his foot connected with the basement window.

There was a purpose to his tactic. Bolan hoped that by shooting out the first floor-window, the Jihad would think he was coming in that way, plus it covered the sound of the basement window breaking.

The Beretta cycled empty. Bolan ejected the magazine and rammed home a new one. Stooping, he knocked a few slivers of glass from the basement windowframe, then went through, headfirst. His right shoulder snagged. Wriggling, he freed himself, his jacket ripping in the process.

The basement had been converted into a family room. Clearly nobody had been down there in a while, as a layer of dust covered everything. There was a carpet on the floor, which softened Bolan's landing. Broken bits of glass nicked his shoulder as he rolled and rose. Above him, the patter of feet let him know that at least one of the terrorists had rushed to the window he'd shot out. An excited exchange of words in Arabic floated down.

Bolan hurried toward a flight of steps. He went up swiftly and was almost to the top when one of the stairs creaked loudly. Stopping dead, he listened, but there was nothing to indicate it had been heard up above.

The doorknob turned easily. Bolan cracked the door and put his left eye to the opening. All he could see was part of a narrow hallway and several doors.

Then the terrorist with the SMG stepped into view. The subgun was an old Czech-made M-26, an obsolete model that had been sold in large numbers to Syria and Cuba before the Czechs stopped manufacturing them. It had a 32-round detachable box-type magazine, which could empty at a rate of six-hundred rounds a minute.

The terrorist was smirking. He knew exactly where Bolan was. His trigger finger tightened.

The smirk gave Bolan a nanosecond of warning, enough for him to fling himself backward as the upper panel was riveted by 7.62-mm slugs. The firing stopped in seconds. Before he could get to the door and return fire, he heard the smack of a new magazine being inserted.

Bolan went back down the stairs. He'd boxed himself in, and unless he could come up with a brainstorm, and quickly, he was in big trouble. At the bottom he swung to the left and squatted to cover the door.

He heard more voices, urgent whispers followed by someone running to a front room and back again. The man had gone after something. But what?

Bolan found out what it was a few moments later, when the door was jerked open. He sighted down the Beretta, but the only thing that appeared was a hand holding a grenade.

The terrorist flung it.

The soldier started to back up, then realized he'd be caught in the blast radius no matter where he took cover. In a twinkling he identified the olive green bomb as a V-40 fragmentation grenade made in Holland.

The V-40 had the distinction of being the smallest hand grenade in the world, yet it was extremely lethal at close range. Thanks to powerful Composition B explosive, five hundred fragments could be propelled over a kill zone of some seventy-five feet.

It had one drawback, though. Because of its small size, the fragments lost velocity dramatically after covering a mere fifteen feet.

Standard fuse delay was four seconds.

Bolan saw the grenade hit a step and bounce toward another. He was on his feet while it was in midair, snatching it as it arced down. The door was flung wide, and the terrorist with the M-26 took aim. For a moment their eyes locked. Then Bolan hurled the grenade, whirled and flung himself behind a sofa.

The terrorist yelped. He backpedaled frantically, vacating the doorway almost as the V-40 went off.

In the confines of the family room, the concussive force was tremendous. Fragments chewed part of the stairs to bits, tore chunks out of the wall, ripped into the floor and furniture. The couch behind which Bolan lay was blistered, the cushions shredded. Two chairs were blown apart. A table crashed to the floor.

The Executioner, though, was spared. He was on his feet before the sound died, dashing through a swirling cloud of dust to the base of the steps. Upstairs a man roared as if in pain, and swore lustily. Another man was shouting.

Bolan raced upward, stopping when he came to a wide gap where three steps had been. The next step above the gap was badly cracked. He doubted it was strong enough to support his weight, but he couldn't stay where he was. He had to take the fight to the Jihad before they threw down another grenade.

Coiling, Bolan leaped. He cleared the hole, but as he landed on the cracked step, it buckled, threatening to spill him backward. A bounding stride took him out of danger. He paused at the top, leaning against the shattered doorjamb.

He peered into the hallway. There was a hole in the hall floor and many smaller ones in the opposite wall. Of special interest to Bolan were several smears of blood, and a trail of crimson drops that led around a corner. From beyond it came grunts and a shuffling sound.

Bolan looked the other way. The hall ended at a closed door. He took a gamble that no one lurked behind it and darted toward the corner, just as the terrorist with the autopistol appeared. They fired at the same time. A slug missed Bolan by a whisker, while his round sliced into the terrorist, catching him high on the right side of his torso.

The man broke and ran.

The soldier reached the corner in four steps. Playing it safe, he peered around it. The M-26 chattered, and rounds thudded into the wall so close to his eyes that slivers of wood stung them. Pulling back, he blinked to clear his vision.

To his right was the kitchen, which was empty. He dropped down and risked a quick look around the corner again. The hall into the front room was clear, but he saw a terrorist lying on a sofa in that room. It was the man he'd shot in the van. He went to fire, then realized the man was dead.

So now there were only three Jihad members in the house, and all three of them were hurting.

Bolan had yet to spot the backpack nuke. He studied the hallway, certain the gunners were waiting for him somewhere along it. As soon as he showed himself they would probably cut loose. Well, let them, he mused. He had to peg where they were if he was to take the fight to them.

Hopping into the open, Bolan squeezed off two random shots, then sprang back. He barely beat the SMG and the autopistol, which joined in a lethal chorus. It was a stalemate. He couldn't get at them, and they couldn't get away.

Bolan knew that Nidal was the wild card in the deck, the joker who could turn the tide against him. Somehow, the soldier had to dispose of the others before their lieutenant came back.

Snapping off four rounds, he raced into the kitchen and scanned it for anything useful.

A towel hung from a hook on the wall. Snatching it, Bolan turned to the stove and cranked a front burner onto its highest setting. Keeping alert for any members of the Jihad, he held his hand over the rings as they quickly grew hotter. When they glowed red, he touched the bottom of the towel to the burner.

The cloth burst into flame. Spinning, Bolan moved to the corner, checked to make sure the coast was clear, then hurled the burning towel as far up the hall as it would go.

Only the SMG opened up this time, again too late. Bolan darted to the sink. Someone had conveniently left a dirty pot in the basin. A moment was required to fill it with cold water. Returning to the corner, he verified the towel was by this time fully ablaze.

The flames wouldn't last long. Bolan had to act. In an overhand toss, he flung the water down the hall. Not enough struck the towel to put out the flames, but more than enough to produce a cloud of smoke. Within seconds, it choked the hall from ceiling to floor.

The terrorists, suspecting that the intruder was going to rush them under cover of the smoke screen, blasted away.

Little did they know that Bolan had a different idea. While they peppered the smoke screen with their bullets, Bolan ran to the back door, opened it quietly and was outside without them being the wiser. He sprinted to the front of the house, stopping shy of the street to replace the magazine in the Beretta with his last spare. He would need a full clip for his next move.

The blaze of gunfire and muffled blasts had drawn the attention of the neighbors, and they watched from the safety of their homes.

Bolan knew it wouldn't be long before the police arrived.

He was under the gun in more ways than one. He went up the steps in a rush. As he reached the porch, a terrorist appeared, backing out the front door toward him. It was the man who'd been shot by the cop, and he held a Glock. Sinking to one knee, Bolan steadied the Beretta.

The terrorist started to turn. Spying the Executioner, he stepped to one side while bringing the Glock to bear.

There already was a wide red stain below the man's right shoulder. Bolan added two more to the man's body, his slugs hitting him squarely in the sternum.

As the man did a slow downward spin, another figure materialized in the doorway. This time it was the terrorist with the M-26, sporting a half-dozen small wounds in his chest and arms from the frag grenade. His face was twisted in a mask of pure hatred. Pointing the subgun, he vented that hatred in a torrent of firepower.

The soldier was a split second ahead of him. The moment the terrorist had appeared, Bolan had taken another header, this time off the porch, his shoulders taking the impact. He flipped to the right just as the spot in which he'd just stood became peppered with holes.

He knew that if he stopped or stood, he'd be chopped to ribbons. So he kept on rolling, the ground around him erupting in tiny geysers. He was almost to the corner of the brownstone when he heard the SMG click empty.

Lying on his back, Bolan had to sit up to see the terrorist silhouetted above him. The man had pulled out the spent magazine and was fumbling in a pocket for another.

Grinning wickedly, the terrorist found the box magazine and began to insert it into the subgun.

He was still grinning when a 9-mm bullet slammed into his ribs, still grinning when another penetrated the tip of his jaw. It tore through his mouth, sheared off his tongue and exited at the back of his skull.

That left one terrorist unaccounted for, the man Bolan had winged in the shoulder at the back door. Vaulting onto the porch, he skirted the two bodies. All was silent from inside the house.

The same couldn't be said of the street, as several people began to scream and yell back and forth.

"Hey, you!" a man yelled before Bolan could enter the house. "I've called the police! They'll be here any minute! If you know what's good for you, you'll get out of our neighborhood, now!"

Bolan would've liked nothing better, but he had a mission to complete. Pulling on the screen door, he went in fast and low, the Beretta up and ready.

A whisper of movement on the upper floor took Bolan to the stairs. He'd climbed four of them, when a sudden crash and the tinkle of falling glass were followed by a loud thump. The man had busted out a window and jumped.

Speeding to the front door, Bolan cut to the left and crossed the porch. He was almost to the corner of the house when he noticed the lady who'd given him the pie, and her husband, staring in wide-eyed amazement.

Bolan studied the area between the two homes. The terrorist was probably running down the alley, taking the nuke with him.

"Who the hell are you, mister?" the woman asked.

Since he needed to hurry to catch the last gunman, Bolan couldn't say what made him linger long enough to answer. Maybe it was her earlier kindness. "I work for the government. These men are responsible for the fire at the Empire State Building today." He started to run off.

"They are? One took off a minute ago wearing a backpack!"

Bolan drew up short. "A backpack?"

The woman nodded. "A blue one. He showed up while all the shooting was going on. I don't think he was inside more than thirty seconds when out he came again." She pointed to the corner. "He went that way."

So did Bolan. The other terrorist no longer mattered. He had to stop Nidal and recover the Gun nuke.

Apparently Ahmed Tufayli had split the Golden Jihad into two cells. Nidal's five-man unit had come to New York from Norristown, while Tufayli's cell was either already in Washington, D.C., or on its way there.

The soldier doubted Nidal would flee the city even though his cell had been virtually wiped out. Bolan would lay a bet that the terrorist was going to plant the nuke somewhere else to get revenge. The man's psychological profile hadn't described him as a "pathological killer with delusions of personal grandeur," for nothing.

Police sirens howled at various points as Bolan swept around the corner. Almost three blocks away, a figure with a blue backpack jogged rapidly into the distance.

Bolan already had the Beretta holstered. He weaved in and out of the pedestrian traffic, drawing more than a few stares and a harsh word or two. At the next street he didn't bother to wait for the light to change. He bolted across, forcing a car to brake hard to avoid running him down.

Block after block fell behind him. Bolan jumped into the air every half block or so to see above the heads of those who blocked his view of Nidal. The next time he did so, he saw the man turn left.

By then the terrorist was only two blocks ahead. Bolan figured that if he turned left one block sooner and poured on the speed, he could narrow his adversary's lead by a wide margin. The side street was less congested, allowing him to go flat out. At the end of the street he turned right.

Nidal didn't appear at the intersection ahead. Bolan placed a hand on the Beretta and moved closer to the curb. Slowing to a walk, he stepped past the last building.

His quarry was nowhere to be seen.

Bolan moved to a streetlight and shimmied up several feet for a bird's-eye view. He scrutinized every person in sight. He swung around to scan the street ahead in case the terrorist had already gone by. He looked down the side street. Incredible as it seemed, the terrorist had vanished.

Bolan slid down and hurried toward the corner where Nidal had turned. A few shops lined the sidewalk, but Nidal wasn't in any of them.

With a rising sense of urgency, the soldier stopped at the corner and pondered his next course of action. His best bet was to work the surrounding blocks in a grid pattern, overlapping as little as possible in order to cover a larger area more swiftly.

Bolan's body protested. He'd been on the go for days with very little rest. He'd pushed himself to the limit time and again, been severely beaten and suffered the concussion of two powerful blasts.

He pushed on. It was getting late in the afternoon. Soon the rush hour would begin, flooding the city with vehicles and pedestrians. The hunt for Nidal would be that much harder.

He covered block after block. Anyone wearing blue rated closer scrutiny. Once, he thought he'd hit pay dirt. Glimpsing a man about Nidal's size wearing a blue backpack, he closed in. The man was about to enter a store when Bolan caught up to him, grabbed him by the elbow and spun him. Too late, he saw that the backpack was much too small.

"Hey, what's your problem?" the man demanded.

"I thought you were someone I knew," Bolan apologized, letting go.

"Oh, really? Do you go around breaking the arms of all your friends?"

Bolan walked off. He spent another forty-five minutes in fruitless searching. At last he stopped in the shadow of a brick building and leaned against the wall. It was no use. Hassan Nidal had made good his escape. The Executioner had no idea where to look.

That was when church bells began to chime calling the faithful to service. Bolan looked up to see the twin spires of St. Patrick's Cathedral looming half a block away. People were flocking up the steps to Mass.

One person, though, was coming down them. He stood out because he was bucking the tide, and because he was laughing his head off, as if at a great private joke.

Bolan's pulse quickened. He'd found Hassan Nidal.

CHAPTER EIGHTEEN

At last something had gone the way Hassan Nidal wanted. As he left the infidels' house of worship, he reflected on how quickly the tides of fortune could shift.

He'd been close to the brownstone, after buying painkillers for Nabih, when he'd heard the sound of gunfire. Racing to the house, he'd burst inside to find his three companions fighting for their lives against a lone American. From their description, it had been the same man who'd shot Hashemi.

Nidal had wanted nothing more than to help his companions, but their Holy War came first. Since it would only have been a matter of time before more federal agents or the police arrived, he'd been forced to flee. Retrieving the backpack nuke, Nidal had ordered the others to delay anyone who might follow him long enough for him to get away.

His fellow soldiers had done their job well, and he'd made it to their secondary target without incident. The priests had been busy preparing for Mass, enabling Nidal to slip inside unnoticed.

He'd been able to plant the nuke, arming it and setting the detonation time clock for four hours, as Tufayli had directed him.

Now all he had to do was get out of the city before the bomb went off. He gave some thought to going by the brownstone to check on the rest of his cell, but decided not to. The authorities were bound to have the block cordoned off. If any of his men were still alive, they would meet him at Grand Central Station in less than forty minutes.

Nidal glanced over his shoulder as he neared an alley. He couldn't help laughing. Before the day was done, the death knell of New York City would ring out from the famous church, just as its own bells now drew worshipers by the hundreds. It was too bad, he mused, that the nuke wasn't going to go off during the service. That would be true justice.

Suddenly, out of the corner of his eye, Nidal saw a tall man spring from the alley mouth. Automatically he made a stab for the pistol under his jacket, but his attacker pounced with the speed of a striking cobra. Before he knew what was happening, his arm was seized in a steely grip and the man levered him into a neatly executed shoulder throw.

Nidal slammed down hard, just inside the alley. Still able, he pushed to one knee and again went for his gun. His attacker was a blur. A foot flashed out of nowhere, connecting with his temple. It felt as if he'd been struck by a hammer.

For a second time Nidal hit the ground. Stars danced crazily before his eyes, and he felt dazed. Vaguely he was aware of those steely hands seizing him, dragging him deeper into the alley. He was propped against a wall, in the shadows. Expert fingers frisked him from top to bottom relieving him of his pistol, his stiletto and his brass knuckles.

At last Nidal's vision cleared. He took in the tall figure, the baggy brown jacket, the man's hard features, and remembered the clash on the street corner when Hashemi had been shot. "You!" he declared.

"Me," Bolan said, checking to ensure no passersby were staring in at them.

"Who are you?" the terrorist demanded. "A local cop? FBI?"

"Who I am is unimportant. What is important is that I'm free to do as I want."

"What does that matter to me?"

Tensed to wade in if the terrorist tried anything, Bolan responded, "It means I don't have to arrest you. It means I don't have to read you your rights. It means that I can do whatever I want to you if you don't tell me what I need to know, and there's nothing you can do about it."

Nidal sneered. "Are you trying to scare me, American? Save your breath. I know your kind. You are weak at heart. You will slap me around a little to make yourself feel strong and brave, but I will never talk."

"I think you will," Bolan said, and delivered a front thrust kick to the terrorist's ribs.

It was as if a two-ton girder had rammed into Nidal's side. Pain lanced through him, doubling him over. Raggedly he gasped for breath.

Bolan moved in closer. "Tell me where you put the nuke."

"Go to hell!" Nidal spit. He didn't see the big man move, but the next instant a pain worse than the first knifed through him. The world blurred. His lungs were molten fire.

"I can do this all night, if that's what you want," Bolan told him, "or you can tell me where the nuke is." He was certain that the terrorist had hidden the primed device somewhere in St. Patrick's Cathedral. Trying to locate it on his own before it went off would be hopeless. Even calling in all the Feds in New York wouldn't help. The cathedral was so immense, it would take too long to cover every square inch.

Nidal struggled to clear his head. He was beginning to believe the American meant every word he said. That shocked him. Americans were known for going by the book. They were notorious for pampering their criminals. He'd been told that most federal prisons in the United States were on a par with luxury apartments in his native country.

"I'm waiting," Bolan warned.

Nidal licked his lips. He'd always boasted that he could withstand any type of interrogation, but now a pinprick of doubt gnawed at him. It was one thing to brag about being able to take punishment, and quite another to actually do so.

The Executioner had been trained in hand-to-hand combat by the best in the business. He knew how to kill an enemy in under five seconds flat. He knew the major nerve centers, the places to strike that would cripple or disable a foe in the least amount of time. They were essential skills for a man whose life depended daily on his combat prowess.

Bolan applied that skill now, delivering three rapid blows, burying his fingers first into the side of Nidal's neck, then into his solar plexus, and finally his abdomen.

Nidal thought he would die. He could've sworn that the American had driven spikes into him. His air choked off completely, his chest seemed to collapse and his stomach tried to claw up and out his throat. He sagged onto his side, inhaling with all his might, his body shaking uncontrollably. He saw the American standing over him, with no hint of mercy or weakness in the man's eyes, and he knew that unless he did as the American wanted, he would suffer unbearably.

"It's still your choice," Bolan said, "but the longer this drags on, the less patient I'm going to be. Is that what you want?"

Nidal didn't, but he couldn't seem to get his mouth to form the words.

Bolan waited. He couldn't let the terrorist suspect that there were limits to how far he could go, that there was a line he wouldn't cross. Killing an unarmed man was one of them, no matter how much the man might deserve it.

Nidal slowly recovered. He regained control of his limbs, and he could breathe again. Careful not to make any sudden moves, he slowly sat up.

The Executioner made a wedge of one hand and stood poised to strike. "What'll it be?" he asked. Long ago he'd learned there were times when psychological warfare was just as effective as physical pain, if not more so.

Pressing back against the wall, Hassan held his hand up. "No more, American! I am thinking over what to do."

"There's nothing to think over," Bolan said. "Either tell me or you suffer. It's that simple."

Nidal tried to stall. "Let's say I do as you wish. What happens to me, then? Will you take me into custody?"

"I'll turn you over to the Feds. After that, it's up to them." Bending, Bolan gripped the front of the terrorist's shirt. "Don't try to sidetrack me. I'll count to ten, and then you had better start talking." He paused, then said crisply, to catch the terrorist off guard, "Two, four, six, eig—"

"Enough! I will talk."

Nidal hadn't survived as long as he had by being a fool. Among his peers, and the Intelligence community at large, he was widely regarded as one of the most crafty, ruthless men alive. He put that craftiness to use now by saying, "I cannot tell you where the nuke is. It would be too hard to direct you to the exact spot. But I can show you."

Bolan didn't trust Nidal as far as he could fling a bull elephant. He suspected the terrorist was up to something, but he had no choice other than to play along. "On your feet. One false move and I'll put a bullet into you where it'll hurt the most."

Nidal smiled thinly. "I believe you would, American."

Stepping back, Bolan drew the Beretta but held it under his jacket. "Lead the way to the cathedral. Take it nice and slow."

"You have my word," Nidal said, inwardly snickering. His word was as worthless as fool's gold. He had to lull the American into thinking that he'd been cowed into obeying. Then, the moment the big man let down his guard, he would make the bastard pay.

They walked to the street. Nidal acted his part to the hilt, his shoulders slumped as if in defeat. The American walked right behind him. Nidal twisted his head to look at him.

"Look straight ahead," Bolan said. He'd seen every trick in the book at one time or another, and he wasn't about to give the terrorist an opening to pull one on him. "Turn on me, and I'll shoot. Try to run, and I'll shoot. If you so much as yell to attract attention, you take a bullet."

Mass had begun. A few people stood outside the church. None of them paid attention to Bolan and the terrorist as they entered through a side door.

Bolan brought Nidal to a stop by tugging on his arm. The wide corridor in which they found themselves was bordered on their left by small rooms. Beyond the opposite wall rose the voices of the choir. Through a door the soldier saw packed pews and at their head, the high altar. "Which floor is it on?"

"The second," Nidal said. "The stairs are not far from here."

"Let's go."

An altar boy came toward them, adjusting his garments. He passed them without a second look.

Bolan walked an arm's length behind Nidal. They went by a small chapel, a baptistery and a vestry. The interior of St. Patrick's was every bit as ornate and lavish as the outside, but Nidal was unimpressed by the splendor. A cathedral, church, temple or synagogue—they were all the same to him. A mosque was the only proper place to worship, his religion the only true religion.

When they reached the spacious stairs, Nidal began to climb them slowly, deliberately dragging his heels. As they ascended, he observed the big man on the sly. The American didn't relax his guard once. The terrorist bided his time, confident his chance would come.

"Where's the nuke?" Bolan pressed.

Nidal pointed. "Down this corridor. It was the quietest spot I could find."

Bolan believed that. The hall was deserted. The rooms they passed were empty. Everyone was at

Mass, which worked in his favor, sparing him unwanted questions.

"We are almost there," Nidal said, even though they had a way to go yet. He watched the big man's eyes carefully, counting on curiosity to shift the man's gaze from him to the corridor ahead. The instant that happened, Nidal would spin and attack.

A similar trick had worked for Nidal before. There had been the time when the Israelis had caught him, and again in Paris during an aborted plane hijacking when he blundered into the clutches of the National Gendarmes Intervention Group.

But it didn't work this time. The big American never took his eyes off him, not even to blink. Nidal fought down a feeling of despair. He couldn't give up. His captor was bound to make a mistake. All he had to do was be ready for it.

Bolan sensed that the terrorist was up to something, so he dropped back another step. They were in an area of the cathedral reserved for the priests and staff. Soon Nidal stopped in front of the sacristy.

"Here?" Bolan asked.

"Yes," Nidal replied. The door was unlocked, just as it had been earlier. He pushed it partway open and quickly stepped through, hoping that the

American would promptly follow so he could slam it in his enemy's face.

Bolan saw through the ploy. "Nice try," he said, shoving the door wide even as he whipped out the Beretta and knocked Nidal over the back of the head.

The terrorist folded like a deck of cards. Rage seized him. In all his life, he'd never met anyone as formidable as this big American. No matter what he tried, the man was always one step ahead of him.

"For the last time," Bolan said, touching the suppressor to the terrorist's nape, "where is it?"

Nidal pointed to a closet in the corner.

Keeping him covered, Bolan moved wide to the left and gripped the closet knob. For a moment he hesitated, wondering whether Nidal had set a booby trap. It seemed unlikely. Nidal wouldn't risk the device getting damaged. He twisted the knob and pulled.

Vestments on hangers filled most of the closet. Underneath them was a shelf on which rested two chalices and a paten. Bolan pushed the robes aside.

Blinking digital displays were the first things he saw. Little light penetrated past the vestments, so he had to lean into the closet to see the SADM clearly. It rested on the same shelf as the chalices and plate, only back against the rear panel. The detonation time clock told him three hours and twenty-two minutes remained until the center of Manhattan went up in a nuclear fireball.

A rush of movement alerted Bolan to a more immediate danger. He jerked back and whirled, realizing he hadn't kept his eyes on Nidal. The man was on him before he could fire, slamming a shoulder into his chest and bowling him over. His legs became entangled in a chair, which broke under him as he fell.

Nidal jumped on top of Bolan, fighting like a man possessed. He knew this was the only chance he'd have, and he intended to make the most of it. Locking his hands on the American's gun wrist, he smashed it against a jagged piece of broken chair.

Involuntarily Bolan let go of the Beretta. He boxed the terrorist on the ear, splitting the lobe. When Nidal jerked back his head to keep from being hit there again, the Executioner whipped his left forearm in an elbow smash to the jaw that nearly knocked Nidal to one side.

The terrorist managed to hold on with one hand, though, while his other drove at the soldier's face.

Bolan spared himself the brunt of the blow by twisting aside, but it still clipped him on the cheek. Arcing a knee into Nidal's groin at the same instant as he flipped to the left, he succeeded in rolling the man off him.

Still locked together, they grappled, neither able to gain a decisive edge. In unarmed combat they were almost evenly matched. What Nidal lacked in formal training, he more than made up for by having learned every dirty infighting trick in the book. He knew as many ways to kill a person with his bare hands as Bolan did, and his catlike reflexes lent him exceptional speed.

Bolan tried to end it in those opening seconds. He went for a throat smash, and when that failed, a paralyzing hit to the solar plexus. Nidal managed to elude them. He was like a human eel, able to slip past blows that would have crippled most others.

They rolled against the closet in which the nuke had been hidden, then away again. Nidal's eyes flickered beyond Bolan's head. Suddenly he lunged. When his hand reappeared, it clasped a short length of chair leg that tapered to a wicked point. Hissing through clenched teeth, he speared the tip at the Executioner's eye.

Bolan snapped his head to one side. Pain seared him as the point gashed his temple, and blood trickled down past his ear. Again the makeshift weapon lanced at him. The soldier gripped Nidal's wrist. For tense moments they strained, sinew against sinew. Then slowly, bit by bit, Bolan pushed his adversary's arm back.

Not to be denied, Nidal snarled and wrenched his body to the left. His purpose was to throw his enemy off-balance, and he succeeded, throwing everything he had into burying the wood in the big American's throat.

The point was less than an inch from Bolan's neck. It took every ounce of strength he possessed to hold Nidal's arms at bay, but he couldn't do so indefinitely. The terrorist had an edge. He was on top of Bolan, and so he could throw his entire weight into the effort.

But Bolan had an edge of his own. Nidal only straddled his torso, leaving his legs free. Pumping them upward, Bolan hammered the terrorist in the kidneys. Nidal stiffened and cried out. For a moment his hold weakened. A moment was all Bolan needed to heave his enemy backward even as he arched his legs upward again. His ankles forked Nidal's neck and locked.

The terrorist forgot about trying to pierce the American's neck. Tearing his arm loose from Bolan's grip, he stabbed at the Executioner's legs. Before the blow could land, he was flung backward. His head hit the floor with such force, that his ears rang. Shaking his head to try to clear it, Nidal scrambled up into a crouch.

Bolan had already done so and was closing in. He backpedaled to avoid a slash aimed at his eyes. The Beretta lay a few yards away, out of reach, but he still had the Desert Eagle. He reached toward the holster, but the terrorist waded in like a wild man, slicing repeatedly at his chest. Bolan had to forget about the big .44 pistol for the moment and concentrate on warding off the flurry of stabs and thrusts.

The soldier circled the sacristy as he retreated before the onslaught. He wound up back near the door, which had swung shut. It opened unexpectedly. In the doorway stood a startled priest in vestments, holding a silver tray.

"My Lord!" the man blurted. "What is the meaning of this? Who are you men?"

Nidal made a split-second decision. The priest was bound to yell for help or run off to notify the cops. To prevent his doing either, he whirled and sank the pointed piece of wood into the man's neck.

Bolan tried to stop him. Leaping, he caught hold of Nidal's arm, but he was a moment too late. Blood sprayed over his shoulder. Nidal spun on him, and they traded powerful punches.

The priest staggered against the doorjamb, and his tray fell with a resounding crash. Clutching at the piece of wood, he tried to pull it out, but he couldn't get a solid grip. Both the wood and his palms were slick with blood. He buckled, a look of disbelief on his face.

Bolan knew yet another innocent life was about to be lost. Unless he received immediate medical aid, the priest would die. That thought spurred Bolan into taking a gamble. He let himself be hit. He lowered his guard just enough for Nidal to catch him flush on the chin. It flung him backward, just as he intended. Falling to one knee, he glanced up at the terrorist and did the most chilling thing he could've done. He smiled.

Hassan Nidal felt an icy rapier slice down his spine. In knocking his enemy backward, he'd given the American room to maneuver. He saw the man's hand sweep under his brown jacket, before Nidal hurled himself forward.

Bolan had the Desert Eagle out and cocked before Nidal reached him. He jammed the muzzle into his adversary's chest so his body would muffle the blast. At that range, one shot from the .44 Magnum pistol was all that was needed.

The terrorist was catapulted against the wall. He then slid to the floor like a puppet whose strings had just been severed. He tipped over, his eyes locked wide, his waste of a life ended at last.

Bolan scooted over to the priest. The man had stopped twitching, and a check of his pulse confirmed he was dead. Pulling the body into the room, Bolan closed the door so he wouldn't be disturbed. Any distraction could prove fatal, not only for himself, but for many thousands besides. His next job was every bit as dangerous as tangling with Nidal had been.

He had to disarm the nuke without it going up in his face.

CHAPTER NINETEEN

The SADM devices were much more complicated than they needed to be. A simple timer clock and detonator switch would have sufficed to trigger a blast. But then practically anyone would have been able to set one off.

The designers had made the arming procedure difficult on purpose. That way, only someone specifically trained to operate a SADM could do so.

Also by design, the disarming sequence was just as hard. The Pentagon brass didn't want an enemy to stumble on a planted nuke, disarm it and use it for their own purposes. Once again, only someone especially trained in the proper technique could disarm a SADM—or activate the self-destruct mechanism.

The Executioner decided to try to disarm the device rather than blow it up. Three factors influenced him. First, there was plenty of time, over three hours until the bomb was due to blow. Second, a SADM cost many millions of dollars. Destroying one when there was no need would be a gross waste. Third, and the most important factor, was that the self-destruct sequence happened to be every bit as complicated as the disarming sequence. No matter which he did, a single mistake would have devastating consequences.

Taking the Gun nuke from the closet, Bolan carefully set it on the floor. He studied the flashing lights, the position of the master detonation rod and the arming initiation clocks. He compared the arming code controls to those on the training device Kissinger had showed him. They were identical.

Mentally Bolan reviewed Kissinger's directions. He had to get the sequence just right to avoid triggering the tamper bypass circuit. Wiping his palms on his pants, Bolan began. He worked methodically, each movement precise, pressing the controls in the exact sequence.

Throughout, Bolan kept an eye on the master detonation rod. It had started to descend when the detonation timer clocks had been activated. If it slid all the way down, central Manhattan would be transformed into a wasteland.

Beads of sweat began to form on Bolan's brow. Disarming the SADM reminded him of disarming a mine, only it was ten times the challenge.

Plus, it was plain unnerving to be so close to a device that could vaporize him in the blink of an eye.

Bolan lost track of time. He input an integer, locked the number in, then moved onto the next one and locked that in, too. After the final digits had been locked in, he pushed the master digit locking switch to the Off position and raised the master detonation lever.

Holding his breath, Bolan watched the master detonation rod. If he'd done everything correctly, the rod would return to its original position. For several tense seconds there was no change. Then the rod rose and locked in the disarmed mode.

Bolan leaned back. He'd done it. Now all he had to do was contact Brognola so the Feds could mop up.

One nuke down, one to go.

SERGEANT ANDERSON SNAPPED out of a fitful sleep and sat bolt upright. Sweat covered him from head to toe. He breathed heavily as he recalled his terrifying dream. In it, he'd been walking down a street late at night when he saw a woman and a small child approaching. As they drew nearer, he'd been overjoyed to see that it was Azadeh and little Thomas. Eager to embrace them, he rushed forward, only to recoil in horror when he saw their pale white faces, their empty eye sockets and the festering bullet wounds in their heads.

Anderson leaned against the headboard and fought for control. He couldn't shake the feeling that the dream had been an omen, that his beloved wife and son were really dead.

Without thinking, Anderson climbed off the bed and headed for the door. Two steps, and he was brought up short by the heavy chain attached to his right ankle. Kicking at it in frustration, he called out, "Tufayli! I need to talk to you!"

No one responded. Anderson called out again. When he still received no reply, he stamped on the floor.

Ahmed Tufayli burst into the bedroom. He'd been in the next room, going over his plan for the umpteenth time with those in his cell. He didn't appreciate being interrupted. "I warned you about making any noise," he said, raising a fist. "You should learn to listen!"

Anderson didn't react. "I want to talk to my wife."

"We've been through all this. You'll see her again after the two nukes have gone off, and not before."

"I'm not asking to see her," the noncom said. "Just let me talk to her on the phone."

Tufayli didn't like the look in the soldier's eyes. "It's out of the question," he said. "We made a deal. I agreed to reunite you with your family once we've achieved our goals, and not before."

Anderson refused to back down. Vivid images from his nightmare, of his wife and son shuffling along like zombies, prodded him to say, "I won't take no for an answer. You either let me speak to her, or I'll raise holy hell."

"What can you do, chained as you are?" Tufayli scoffed.

"I can do this," Anderson said, and spun. Before the leader of the Golden Jihad could stop him, he picked up the lamp on the nightstand and smashed it against the wall. It seemed a childish thing to do, but on their arrival at this house in Washington, Anderson had noted how his captors went to great lengths to avoid making any loud noise. Tufayli had personally told him to be quiet at all times, or else. It told Anderson that their new safehouse wasn't as secure as their last one had been. Maybe, if he made a lot of racket, someone would hear.

Tufayli was furious. The American swine threatened to ruin everything. He hadn't worked for so long and so hard to see his efforts go up in a puff of emotion.

In addition, he resented being told what to do by an *American*. He hated them with every fiber of his being, and he wouldn't rest until he'd brought their country to its knees. For the soldier to dictate to him was more than he could bear.

"So what's it going to be?" Anderson said. "Do I get to talk to her, or do I tear this place apart?"

"Make all the noise you want," Tufayli said. The truth was that they were in a Georgetown town house, and if Anderson acted up, the neighbors would hear and probably call the police. But he couldn't let the soldier know that.

"Do you think I'm bluffing?" Anderson snapped. Stepping to a chair, he hoisted it as high as his chest and poised to hurl it at a nearby covered window. "There was a phone in this room when we got here. I saw one of your men take it out. Bring it to me this second."

Anyone who knew Ahmed Tufayli well would have noticed right away the flinty cast that came over his features. To the noncom, however, it wasn't so apparent. "If it's a phone you want," Tufayli said calmly, "a phone you will have."

Stepping to the door, he addressed one of his men in Arabic. "Yahia, bring me the telephone that was in here." He kept his voice low and controlled.

Anderson allowed himself a slight smile. It had been easier than he'd hoped. He waited tensely, unwilling to put down the chair until he was sure the terrorists would do as he asked.

Tufayli's man returned with the telephone. He handed it over and waited for further orders.

"Here you are," Tufayli told the noncom. "Just as you wanted."

"Plug it in," Anderson said. He stayed where he was until the leader had done so. Motioning with the chair, he got Tufayli to back up. The man by the door made no move toward him. "You'd better hope that my wife is all right, or there'll be hell to pay."

"Call her," Tufayli said. "I'll give you the number."

Anderson had to jiggle the receiver a few times before he got a dial tone. "Keep your man back," he said.

"Don't worry, I will," Tufayli replied. He himself would teach the American a lesson and no one else.

"What's the number?" Anderson asked.

Tufayli made up one and rattled it off. He edged closer as the soldier leaned over the nightstand.

Anderson was desperate to put his fears to rest. His wife and son had to be alive, or his betrayal of all he held dear would've been in vain. As he punched in the last number, he turned his back on the terrorists.

Tufayli struck as savagely as a tiger. Seizing the soldier by the neck, he rammed a knee into the base of Anderson's spine, spun and shoved him into the wall. He intended to smash the soldier's face to a bloody pulp.

Tufayli forgot about Anderson's manacle, one end of which was looped around a leg of the bed. When he spun Anderson, the chain coiled around one of his own feet, so that when he shoved the noncom, the chain drew tight around his ankle.

Anderson was brought up short. He tripped, and as he fell, all the slack went out of the chain. A look showed him why. Tufayli, caught in a loop, had gone down, too.

All of Anderson's pent-up rage gushed up out of him like lava spewing from a volcano. He landed two powerful blows, causing the terrorist leader to double over and expose the back of his neck. Anderson raised his hand to deliver a karate chop.

A sound suppressor belched twice.

It was hard to say who was more surprised by the twin holes that marred Anderson's chest, him or Ahmed Tufayli. The latter grabbed the soldier to keep him from keeling over, and cried, ''No, damn it! Not yet!''

The noncom was overcome by weakness and he sagged. He felt a strange sensation in his lungs, making him want to cough. He was barely aware of being lowered onto his back.

Tufayli rose, his face livid. He stalked toward Yahia, who took a fearful step back, even though he had a pistol and Tufayli was unarmed.

"You damn spawn of a jackass!" Tufayli shouted in Arabic. "Did I tell you to kill him?"

"I was afraid he was going to kill you!" the man said in his defense.

The leader halted. There was no denying the underling's sincerity, or loyalty. Struggling to keep a hold on his simmering fury, he turned away before he did something he might later regret.

"Another second and the dog would have broken your neck," Yahia went on. "I could not reach you in time, so I did the only thing left to me."

"You did fine." Tufayli almost choked on the words. Stepping to the American, he looked down. The noncom wouldn't last much longer. Blood trickled from his mouth and his nose. "Damn it all. I needed you alive a little longer," he said.

Anderson was fading fast. "My wife?" he croaked. "My son?"

Tufayli saw no reason not to tell him the truth at this point. "They have preceded you to the gates of hell. I promised to reunite you with them, did I not?"

"You will pay," Anderson said weakly. "If there is any justice in this world, you'll get yours in the end."

"Spare me your drivel."

The sergeant was racked by a convulsion. When it ended, he found that he could no longer move. Suddenly, floating above him, he saw his wife and son. They were smiling and beckoning to him. "I'm coming," he said, then smiled.

That smile bothered Tufayli. Kicking the soldier, he demanded, "What do you find so amusing?" Anderson didn't answer, so the terrorist kicked him again.

"I think he is dead," Yahia said.

Sinking onto the bed, Tufayli mentally cursed incompetents everywhere. The two other members of his cell had been drawn by the commotion. Facing them, he said, "This is not good. I wanted the dog alive until after the first nuke detonated."

"We know the arming sequence," Emir said.

Tufayli nudged the body. "If this pig did not deceive us, we do."

"Do you believe he did?" Jibril asked.

Tufayli checked his watch. "We will soon know. If all went according to plan, the device Hassan and his men planted will go off any minute. Monitor the television and radio. Let me know if you hear anything."

Depressed at the turn of events, Tufayli leaned against the headboard and mulled over his options. Calling everything off wasn't one of them. They had gone too far to turn back now. He had to see it through, come what may.

Outside, a siren howled. Tufayli listened as it faded. Every time he heard one, he couldn't help but think that the authorities were coming for him and his men. Sirens were going off all the time in this city. The vile heart of the Great Satan pulsed with wickedness. Maybe, if he failed to destroy them, they would do the world a service and destroy themselves.

Now *that* would be justice.

THE JET CLEAVED the rarified air five thousand feet up, en route from La Guardia Airport in New York City to Washington's National Airport.

From his window seat, Mack Bolan gazed at the countryside below. He was tired, but he couldn't sleep. There was too much still to do, too much still at stake.

Hal Brognola came down the aisle and dropped into the seat beside him. The big Fed's expression was grim. "Not a damn sign of them," he reported. "My people are going over Washington with a fine-tooth comb, but so far they haven't turned up a single clue."

"Maybe the Jihad has flown the coop," Bolan said. He didn't really believe that himself. "Tufayli must know something is wrong by now."

Massaging a kink in his neck, Brognola said, "I toyed with the idea of feeding the Washington media a phony story to the effect that a nuclear bomb had gone off in Manhattan."

"You did? Why?"

"For about three seconds. I figured it might give Tufayli a false sense of security and lure him out into the open. But it would've also caused mass panic. And once word got out that it was a false alarm, there would've been hell to pay. I'd've caught so much flak, I would've had to hide out in a fallout shelter for the rest of my life."

Bolan mustered a grin. "What do you have for me to do when we get there?" He hated the thought of sitting around twiddling his thumbs in the middle of a crisis. "There must be something."

Brognola stopped massaging his neck and gave his head a few quick twists to either side. "There.

That's better." He looked at Bolan. "I know how you feel, but it doesn't make much sense having you track down vague leads. I need you ready to go when we get something definite. Leave the legwork to the blacksuits."

Brognola was right, so he didn't press the issue. "That reminds me," he said. "I met one of your people in New York. Agent Sanders. Did she make it out of the Empire State Building in one piece?"

Brognola leaned back in his seat. "As a matter of fact, she did. I've seen her report. She says that if it hadn't been for you, she would've ended up like her partner." He frowned. No matter how many times it happened, he never liked losing an agent. "They had to peel what little was left of him off the bottom of an elevator."

Bolan thought of the infant at the house in Pennsylvania. So many senseless deaths, all in the name of rabid fanaticism. When would it ever end?

"On another subject," Brognola said, "certain political bigwigs are being quietly evacuated from D.C. The President has already been whisked out. He didn't want to go, but I insisted, and the Secret Service backed me up on it. A few senators and the Speaker of the House are also being taken to safety."

"While average citizens go on about their business, none the wiser."

"I understand what you're saying, but what can we do? If we issue an alert, there'd be mass panic." He shook his head. "You saw what happened in New York. Imagine it magnified a thousand times. We'd have hordes of people trying to get out of the city all at once. Every artery would be clogged. The police would be unable to contain the mobs. In no time we'd have total anarchy on our hands.

"Besides," Brognola went on, "from what we know of Ahmed Tufayli, I wouldn't put it past him to set the nuke off if we alerted the general public. He's crazy enough to blow himself up if he thought he could take half of Washington with him."

"True," Bolan conceded.

The big Fed produced a cigar, stared at it for a few moments, then put it back in his pocket. "Our best bet is the real-estate angle. It turns out that the brownstone in Manhattan, where Hassan Nidal hid out, was bought by Mehmet Akbar years ago. Akbar apparently set up a dummy firm to make a number of such purchases. Shrewd man, that devil. He made it damned hard for anyone to trace the paper trail back to him."

The jet banked to the southwest and began its approach to the airport.

"It won't be long now," Brognola said. "Let's keep our fingers crossed that my people turn up something by the time we land."

But that hope was soon dashed.

They were met by a squad of blacksuits who had nothing new to report. Hustling them into a black limousine, they were whisked toward the Justice Department building.

As the limo raced down Constitution Avenue, Bolan looked out at the inhabitants going about their business, oblivious to the doom that hovered over their heads.

At Justice, Brognola went to confer with his top people working on the case.

Bolan was left to his own devices. Going to a lounge, he sat flipping through magazines. Inwardly he was champing at the bit, eager to get the word that would send him into the field.

About an hour after their arrival, Brognola returned. He helped himself to black coffee from a machine and took a seat next to Bolan. "Not a thing yet, I'm afraid."

"The clock's ticking. Tufayli won't wait long now that he knows Nidal failed."

"We're doing the best we can." Brognola took a sip of his coffee and grimaced.

"What about the real-estate angle?" Bolan asked.

"So far it hasn't panned out. I have two dozen of my best people combing the records. They haven't found any reference to Akbar or the dummy company he used in New York."

"Which means he probably used a different one here," Bolan concluded.

Brognola nodded. "Do you have any idea of how many real-estate transactions there've been in this city in the past fifteen years? It would be easier to find a needle in a haystack." He started to take another sip of the coffee, changed his mind and set down the cup. "Thank the Lord for computers. It shouldn't be long before the first phase of our cross-reference check is completed. It's a long shot, but it's all we've got."

Bolan placed his hands on his knees. "And if they come up empty-handed, what then?"

"Beats me," the big Fed admitted. "A door-to-door sweep of the city was discussed, but only as a last resort. Or we could blanket the capital with Tufayli's photograph and hope someone's seen him."

Just then a woman in a smart business suit hurried in, holding a manila folder. "Mr. Brognola," she said as she approached.

Brognola rose, saying for Bolan's benefit, "This is Beverly, one of my computer experts." He faced her. "What is it?"

She handed him the folder. "You wanted to know right away, sir." She grinned broadly. "We've done it! We've found where the terrorists are hiding!"

CHAPTER TWENTY

It was in Arlington. Seven years earlier an office building had been purchased by a corporation that existed only on paper. The document trail led the Feds back to New Orleans—and Mehmet Akbar.

The more the Feds learned about Akbar, the more they realized just how extensive his operation had been. The arms dealer and terrorist backer had had tentacles in practically every major city in the country and countless others abroad.

Confiscated records revealed that he'd also been a power broker, buying political influence left and right to grease the cogs of his illicit empire. Already the Feds were seeking indictments against a corrupt police official, a judge, and a state representative in Louisiana, and there were bound to be others.

Ironically, Bolan reflected, the Feds owed the Golden Jihad some thanks. Ahmed Tufayli and his bunch were responsible for exposing one of the most widespread criminal operations in the history of the United States.

Bolan was being driven in a black limo. On the floor lay his duffel bag. Beside him on the back seat rested the case containing the Knight Revolver Rifle, the weapon he'd field-tested at Stony Man Farm before the whole Jihad business began. From it, he removed the Ruger Magnum Super Redhawk revolver. He applied a small amount of gun grease to the front of the ten-inch barrel. Taking out the sound suppressor, he inserted a small index pin on its housing into a keyway slot on the barrel. Next he tightened the knurled coupling nut.

Bolan loaded the piece, which took special ammunition. Fitted into Federal .44 Magnum casings, the bullets had black-plastic front face seals. Both the propellant and the charge weights were closely guarded secrets, but the Ruger had as much stopping power as the Desert Eagle, if not a bit more.

In addition, the Knight Revolver system was quieter than Bolan's prized Beretta. Sound measurements had shown that when the hammer of the revolver fell on an empty chamber, the noise of the action alone was about 112db. Yet when loaded and fitted with the suppressor, the level only rose to 119db.

In layman's terms, that meant when Bolan fired, the blast would be no louder than a soft sneeze.

He took out the buttstock and slipped it into an inside pocket of his trench coat. Then did the same with the scope. He didn't touch the image intensifier or the bipod. After placing extra ammo into his pockets, he closed the case and set it beside the duffel bag.

The limo driver was one of Brognola's men. He glanced back and said, "We're two blocks away, sir. Say when."

"When."

Bolan slipped the Knight Revolver under his coat as the car slanted to the curb. He climbed out. Before closing the door, he said, "Find a spot nearby to park. When I need to be picked up, I'll contact you on the radio."

"Yes, sir. Good luck, sir."

The Executioner would need it. The remaining members of the Golden Jihad were bound to be much more alert than Nidal's men had been. Getting close to them could be difficult, another reason he was relying on the Knight Revolver Rifle. It boasted three times the effective range of the Desert Eagle.

The office building had four stories. The bottom three were occupied by business offices, while on the top floor were four apartments. A check of utility and telephone records had revealed that one of them was rented to a retired postal worker, another to two young sisters, a third to a school teacher.

The last apartment had apparently been vacant for years. That in itself was highly suspicious. Prime rental properties went for top dollar in the tight D.C. market. No landlord in his right mind would leave one empty for so long.

Bolan went by the building the first time on the far side of the street. Everything appeared normal, except that the draperies on the windows of the corner apartment had been drawn.

All the clues pointed to the Feds being right. The Golden Jihad had to be in there.

Two blocks down, Bolan crossed the street and returned to study the building up close. A beauty parlor was doing brisk business on the ground floor. Next to it was a law office, with a constant flow of people.

There were too many civilians to suit Bolan. A firefight that got out of control would result in dozens of casualties.

Across the street stood an apartment building. It was one story higher and offered a clear field of fire. Bolan crossed at the next corner and went around to the rear. Washington's fire code required at least two exits at ground level for a structure that size, and he found one on the far side. It opened into a narrow alley.

The door was unlocked. Bolan swiftly climbed the stairwell. A short flight of metal steps brought him to a door that offered access to the roof, but this time he struck out. The door was locked.

He didn't have time for C-4 or a pick. Stepping back, he pointed the Ruger at the point where the lock and the doorjamb met.

Two light strokes of the trigger was all it took to shatter the cheap lock. Bolan pushed the door open and stepped out into the hazy sunlight of late afternoon.

Crouching, Bolan catfooted to the edge of the roof. A two-foot-high parapet wall gave him ample cover. Sinking to his knees, he pulled the scope from his pocket and trained it on the windows with the drawn draperies.

The variable power scope, a Leupold VARI-XIII, could be adjusted from a magnification factor of 1x to 5x. Bolan rotated the knob to the highest setting. Right away he spied movement. The draperies fluttered, as if someone had passed close by them. Then a face appeared at the window.

A bearded man peered at the street below. His features were hard to peg, and it was difficult to tell whether he was Middle Eastern.

Bolan shifted the scope to see behind the man. A vague form passed through his field of vision. A pair of hands with painted pink fingernails appeared. They rested on the man's shoulders, and his face disappeared from the window.

The Executioner lowered the scope. As far as he knew, every member of the Golden Jihad was male. The woman was either a local contact or a prostitute. Whatever the case, it spelled trouble.

It was comforting to know the Jihad was still there, though. If they'd armed the backpack nuke, they would've been well on their way out of the country by now.

Bolan decided to stay where he was until the sun went down. He'd slip into the building under cover of darkness and take the cell by surprise. Armed with the Knight Revolver Rifle, he was confident he could snuff out the terrorists quickly and silently—provided nothing went wrong, of course.

He estimated that the sun wouldn't set for more than half an hour. He settled down to wait for nightfall, his scope fixed on the apartment across the way. Twice more the bearded man showed himself at the window, each time scanning the street. Bolan couldn't decide whether the man was expecting someone or whether he was a lookout.

Just as the sun dipped below the horizon, five city youths dressed in leather and black boots came strutting along the sidewalk. They halted in front of Akbar's building. As one, they gazed at the top floor. Seconds later the bearded man appeared again. When he saw them, he gave a thumb's-up sign. A husky youth nodded, then led his friends inside.

Bolan didn't know what to make of this new development. If he had to make a guess, he'd say the youths were gang members. But what possible link could they have to the Golden Jihad?

Twilight soon claimed the nation's capital. It was Bolan's cue to slip the scope into his trench coat and descend to street level.

The law office had closed for the day. The beauty salon was still open, but only a few customers were inside.

Bolan made as if to go past the building's entrance, but then turned into it at the last moment. A short vestibule brought him to a flight of stairs. As he started up, voices drifted down. They grew louder. He reached the first landing and leaned over the rail. A hasty look showed him the gang members and several other people were coming down.

Ducking through a door to the corridor beyond, Bolan positioned himself so that he could peer out the small window at the top of the door without being spotted. A pair of gang members came down the stairs first, followed by a tall man in a brown suit with a marked bulge under one arm. Next came the bearded man from the apartment, together with a striking woman wearing a tight green dress. By their side was the husky youth. Trailing were the last two street toughs in leather and boots.

Although it was somewhat muffled by the door, Bolan caught their conversation as they went past.

"It's a real pain, Musawi. I don't like having to leave the hood to get the deal done. You should've had the stuff handy."

The bearded man made a clucking sound. "You wanted us to keep everything in our apartment? Be serious, my young friend. Soon, Bender, you'll have all that you asked for."

"I'll believe it when I see it," Bender grumbled.

Bolan didn't stir until the last of them had gone out the front door. He was down the stairs in a flash, and saw them turn the corner. Counting to ten, he fell into step behind several shoppers burdened with bags.

Musawi and the woman, as well as Bender and some of the gang members, piled into a sedan. The rest climbed into a station wagon.

Staying between the shoppers and the wall, Bolan walked by the vehicles. As they pulled out, he slowed and unclipped the radio from his belt. "Pick me up on the west side of the building. Hurry, every second counts."

Brognola's man arrived within ten seconds, tires squealing. Bolan slid into the back seat of the limo, pointed at the two vehicles a block ahead and commanded, "Don't lose them."

"You can count on that, sir."

Bolan took the opportunity to put in a call to Brognola, giving him a rundown of the latest events.

"Frankly, Striker, I don't know what the hell to make of this. Where's Ahmed Tufayli? Who's this guy, Musawi? Where's the backpack nuke?"

"Your guess is as good as mine on all counts." The driver took a turn so tightly that Bolan was pushed against the door. "I plan to stick with them. As soon as I know something definite, I'll contact you."

"Do that," Brognola said. "In the meantime, now that it's dark, I'm having an FBI team put the Akbar building under surveillance. They'll be on-site in thirty minutes. If I haven't heard from you in an hour, I'll send them in.''

''Fair enough.'' Bolan clicked off. Now less than a block ahead, the pair of vehicles traveled toward the southwest, keeping to the speed limit. It soon became apparent they were heading for Alexandria. It only added to the mystery for Bolan. If the Golden Jihad intended to blow up a SADM in D.C., why had they holed up in Arlington, clear across the Potomac River? And now they were going even farther away from Washington.

Bolan was at a loss to explain it. He busied himself with opening the Knight Revolver case and removing the image intensifier, a night-vision device. Although it didn't magnify an image as a scope would, it did provide a whopping light amplification factor of sixty-four thousand times the ambient light. In total darkness, he could see as if it were the middle of the day. It went into his trench-coat pocket, together with the rest of the special attachments.

They took the Henry G. Shirley Memorial Parkway to King Street, and from there wound into the heart of Alexandria. Bolan saw the sedan and the station wagon wheel into a ministorage facility and make their way toward the back of the building. He had his driver go on by, then pull over between streetlights.

"Circle the block until I contact you," Bolan told him. Slipping into the cloak of night, he sprinted to the ministorage gate. The office was closed. A sign on the door read that the owner would be back from his supper in forty-five minutes.

An elderly woman was collecting cardboard boxes from a unit halfway down on the left. Bolan bore to the right and jogged past a row of closed metal doors. At the last one, he stopped. The voices he heard coming from around the corner spoke so low he was unable to hear what was being said.

Bolan could see that there was one open unit in that area, and the sedan and wagon were parked close to it. Neither of their engines were running, but their lights had been left on to illuminate the bay. Two gang members were loading a crate into the sedan's trunk, while the others stood around inside the unit.

Working rapidly, Bolan attached the buttstock to the revolver. Since bright light would override the image intensifier's ambient amplification circuit and cause it to shut down, he didn't use it. Tucking the stock into his right side, he thumbed back the hammer. As soon as the musclemen had finished loading the crate and gone back in, he crept toward the unit.

Someone was counting out loud. It sounded like the man called Musawi. "Eighty thousand. Ninety thousand. One hundred. It's all here, Bender."

"Did you think we'd try to stiff you?"

"No offense, but a man in my line of work never knows whether a buyer will turn out to be legitimate or not. It's another reason we kept the merchandise stored here, in case of a double cross."

Bender seemed to take that personally. "I've got news for you, Akbar, baby. The Crips don't go around cheating those who are up front with them. You promised enough hardware for us to take over this whole damn city, and you've delivered. So you've got nothing to worry about."

Another Akbar? Bolan stopped, trying to recall if at any time Mehmet had mentioned having another son.

"That's good to know," Musawi said. There was the sound of a briefcase being slammed shut and a pair of distinct clicks. "Thanks to you, I now have enough money to get out of this country before the Feds close in on me."

"It must really tick you off, those pigs wasting your cousin and his boys the way they did," Bender remarked. "But what else would you expect from the federal cruds? They put on a big front for the public, but we both know they like to shoot first and ask questions later."

"They are swine," Musawi agreed. "Once my wife and I are safely in Iraq, I will do everything in my power to make them pay. I will spare no expense to find out who killed Mehmet, and they will suffer."

The pieces to the puzzle fell into place for Bolan, and he couldn't help feeling bitterly disappointed. Instead of snaring the Golden Jihad, he'd stumbled onto a relative of Mehmet Akbar who was trying to flee the country before the authorities found out about him. To finance the getaway, Musawi Akbar had set up a hasty gun deal with the D.C. branch of the Crips, a notorious street gang.

"I must confess I'm amazed that your people came up with so much money on such short notice," Musawi Akbar was saying.

Bender laughed. "One hundred thousand is a drop in the bucket, baby. We make that much in drug deals in one week. You could have asked for twice the green you did, and we still would've had the cash on hand."

The Executioner was close enough to the unit to see shadows moving about inside. Suddenly one of the shadows loomed large, and a gang member stepped into the open, bearing a small crate.

He took one look at Bolan, dropped the crate and clawed for a pistol under his leather vest, while shouting, "Bender! There's a honky out here with a gun!"

Bolan stroked the trigger. At the soft phfft, the Crip was flung off his feet and tossed to the tarmac, as if by an unseen giant. Shouts broke out inside the ministorage bay.

"What the hell is this, Akbar? Are you trying to stiff us?"

"No! It must be the Feds!"

"Damn it all to hell!" Bender raged. "We didn't count on this!"

The remaining Crips spilled from the doorway. All were armed with autopistols, and they blazed away in a hailstorm of bullets. Slugs smashed into the metal doors, the wall between the doors, the ground—into anything and everything except Mack Bolan.

The soldier had moved as soon as the first Crip crumpled. Darting to the right, he ducked behind the station wagon just as the quartet charged out. Wedging the buttstock to his right shoulder, he swiveled as a gang member rushed around the front fender.

The youth had no idea Bolan was there. He was firing wildly into the darkness while reaching for the door handle. A sixth sense had to have warned him of his mistake, because he abruptly faced forward and elevated his pistol.

The Knight Revolver Rifle coughed. The crip reacted as if he'd slammed into a brick wall. His legs gave out, and he hit the ground with a thud.

His companions spied Bolan. Scattering, they slapped in new clips and blistered the night with lead. The soldier was about to down a third one, when the front window of the wagon shattered in a spray of glass. He ducked as the windshield and the side windows were given the same treatment. Rounds gouged into the vehicle, peppering the doors.

The Crips meant to keep him pinned down long enough to make their escape.

Bolan darted to the rear of the vehicle. Only one of the gang members was in sight, racing toward the far fence. The gunner looked back and snapped off a shot. The soldier sighted carefully.

Traveling at a rate of over one thousand feet per second, the round penetrated the Crip between the shoulder blades and burst out his sternum. His arms flung wide, the gang member pitched onto his face, twitched briefly and died.

Bender and the last Crip were racing for the corner of the building, weaving as they ran, crisscrossing each other.

Bolan rose and braced his elbows on the roof of the station wagon. Curling back the hammer, he tracked Bender, firing when the targets were yards from their goal.

At that instant, the gang members crisscrossed once again. The other Crip passed behind Bender and took the slug meant for his leader. Hurled forward by the impact, he plowed into him and they both went down.

Bolan tried to fix a bead on Bender, but the Crip leader, in shoving the body of his fellow gang member off him, spoiled the shot. In a flurry of speed, Bender scrambled on all fours to the corner and was around it before the Executioner could shoot.

The soldier made no attempt to give chase. It was more important to bag Musawi Akbar. He turned toward the storage unit just as the bearded Iraqi, his wife and the man with them exploded into the open. They, too, unleashed a firestorm. Instead of simple autopistols, all three were armed with subguns. And they knew how to use them.

CHAPTER TWENTY-ONE

Triggering short bursts and sweeping their sub-guns from side to side, the trio forced Bolan to dive for cover behind the station wagon. Musawi and the other man kept him pinned down while the woman darted to the sedan, yanked the door open and slid behind the wheel.

Bolan attempted to get off a shot at her, but the steady stream of lead kept him pinned to the tarmac. Another of the SMGs fell silent and he pushed up to shoot, but then rounds stitched the wagon so close to his face that he was forced to drop down again.

The trio was armed with MAT-49s out of France. Ideal for paratroopers, the MAT-49 came fitted with a telescopic steel stock and a magazine housing that swiveled forward when the weapon wasn't in use. A 9-mm powerhouse, its only drawback was a slow cyclic rate of six hundreds rounds a minute.

Still, that was more than enough firepower for a single SMG to keep Bolan down as doors slammed and the sedan squealed into reverse, angling away from him. Popping up close to the rear fender of the wagon, he sighted on a dark shape in the front seat. Suddenly the snout of a MAT-49 poked out of the sedan's side window. Bolan fired a split second before the SMG did, then hugged the earth as metal shrieked and whined above him.

Musawi's wife knew her stuff. She wheeled the car in a tight turn that brought it around to face the corner of the building, and burned rubber.

Bolan sprang up. He had time for a single shot, and he needed to make it count. Through the wagon's rear window he could see the gunner replacing the magazine in his SMG. The man glanced back at him.

The Executioner stroked the Desert Eagle's trigger. The hardman's face blotched red in the middle and collapsed in on itself as the man sank onto the seat.

In a few moments the sedan was around the corner. Bolan reached for his radio, but with all his scrambling about, it had fallen off his belt. He ran to the side of the wagon, where he'd been standing when he first hit the deck, but there was no sign of it. As he lifted his head, he discovered the keys were in the wagon's ignition.

There wasn't a moment to lose. Climbing in, Bolan set the revolver rifle on the seat beside him. He realized the station wagon might not start, with all the bulletholes in it, but he had to try. The engine growled, then sputtered. Smoke puffed from the exhaust.

Bolan twisted the ignition again and held it down. The carburetor wheezed and coughed, but then the engine caught. Backing up, he set out in pursuit.

The sedan was almost to the gate when Bolan rounded the corner. They turned right, their car slewing wildly until the woman brought it under control. As luck would have it, they almost collided with the black limo, which was making another circuit of the block. The driver braked just in time.

Bolan roared out onto the street. The wagon fought him as he tried to steer it into the proper lane, swerving toward the limo. With a spin of the steering wheel, he got it back on track. As he flashed past the limo, he motioned for the man to follow him. A check on the rearview mirror showed the Fed making a U-turn.

The woman took an intersection on two wheels. Careening off the far curb, they scattered other vehicles and pedestrians before them. Horns blared.

Bolan took the turn just as fast. He stayed in the middle of the road, thus gaining a little ground, but not enough to use the Ruger.

Through the sedan's fractured rear window, Bolan could see Musawi angrily gesturing at his wife. Then he slid over the top of the front seat.

Bolan knew what the man was up to, but that didn't slow him down. He began to twist the steering wheel, zigzagging the car from one side of the road to the other, while keeping alert for oncoming traffic.

Musawi had propped the MAT-49 on the top of the back seat and was taking deliberate aim. The muzzle swung from right to left and back again as he attempted to fix the station wagon in his sights. Bolan knew that as long as he didn't drive in a straight line for more than a dozen yards at a stretch, it would be hard for Akbar to nail him.

A muzzle-flash was all the warning the Executioner had that the man had lost patience. Bolan bent close to the wheel as the upper part of the windshield was stitched by holes. Glass slivers rained on him, stinging his hands.

The soldier cut to the left, then to the right. More rounds made a mess of the windshield, so that he could hardly see out. Grabbing the Redhawk, he smashed the buttstock against the glass. It took some doing, but he managed to batter what was left of the windshield free.

Musawi was taking more precise aim.

Bolan ducked. Slugs punched into the seat top, coming so close to his back that they plucked at his shirt. Lifting his head, he extended the Knight Revolver Rifle, rested the long sound suppressor on the bottom of the empty windshield frame, then swerved, aligning the station wagon directly behind the sedan.

It was the Iraqi's turn to drop down. Bolan fired once and knew he'd missed. Cocking the revolver, he waited for the man to pop up.

The woman took another corner. She spun the wheel so sharply that the sedan jumped the curb, rammed a mailbox and clipped a telephone pole. Musawi showed himself, but not to open up on the station wagon. Rather, he vented his rage on his wife, shaking his fist and hitting her when she twisted to respond.

The revolver spat again. This time Musawi twisted, grasped his chest and fell.

Bolan placed the weapon back on the seat. He'd dropped the Iraqi. Now all he had to do was stop his wife, and he wasn't going to treat her with kid gloves. She'd fired at him back at the ministorage facility, handling her SMG like a pro. The woman was every bit as dangerous as her husband had been.

It became apparent to Bolan that she was heading back toward the Henry G. Shirley Memorial

Parkway. Once there, she could bury the speedometer and leave the station wagon eating her dust.

Bolan pressed down on the accelerator. The wagon narrowed the gap but couldn't quite overtake the sedan. He angled to the left. The woman went into another turn much too wide, and he sliced in between her sedan and the sidewalk.

She glanced at him, her face contorted in what could only be described as hatred. She mouthed something, and even though it was impossible for Bolan to hear her words, the meaning came across loud and clear.

Bolan reached for the Redhawk. The moment he took his hand off the steering wheel, the woman spun her own wheel and slammed into him broadside. The station wagon skewed violently. The tires on his side smacked into the curb, jolting the entire vehicle. Bolan had to grab the steering wheel with both hands and hold on tight in order to return to the middle of the street.

The woman was not to be denied. A grin curling her lips, she veered again, her fender crunching against his. For a full ten seconds the two vehicles hurtled through the night, grinding, scraping and emitting sparks like two oversized firecrackers.

Bolan barely had clearance between the curb and the wagon. He locked his arms to keep his vehicle from spinning out of control.

Suddenly the woman swerved to the right, giving him breathing space. But she didn't stay there very long. Furiously churning her wheel, she slammed into him again, harder than the last time. The station wagon bounced off the curb, only to be smashed into once more.

Bolan had the bigger, heavier vehicle, but it was only a matter of time before she succeeded in causing him to crash into one of the buildings lining the street. Unless he took the fight to her. Spinning his steering wheel to the right, he did just that.

A tremendous crash rent the air. The sedan was knocked aside, then came right back again. She had to have hit him at just the right angle, because the next thing Bolan knew, the station wagon churned up over the curb and shot at the plate-glass front of a clothing store.

There were people inside. A white-haired woman near the front threw her arms up and screamed in terror.

Bolan frantically tried to straighten out the wagon. Just when a collision seemed inevitable, he succeeded. The vehicle barreled along the sidewalk, forcing pedestrians to dive out of its path.

He tried to get back onto the street, but the sedan hugged the curb, boxing him in.

They came to the end of the block. Bolan sailed off the sidewalk. The driver of a city bus leaned on the horn, barely missing him. By spinning the wheel, Bolan brought the station wagon to a lurching, sliding halt, inches from a parked van with a couple of small children inside.

The woman had gone on through the intersection and was already half a block away.

Bolan poured on the speed. The needle climbed to fifty, sixty, seventy. Just ahead, the ramp onto the parkway appeared. Once she reached it, he could kiss her goodbye.

She had to have known it, too, because she poked her arm out of the window and gave a little wave. The sedan came to the last intersection.

At the same moment, an older model Chevy roared into it from the right. The teenaged driver desperately attempted to avoid the sedan, but the Chevy's front end hit the woman's rear bumper. The sedan looped at lightning speed toward the buildings lining the street.

At the speed she was traveling, the woman couldn't effectively apply her brakes in time. She tried, though. The brake drums locked, and all four tires screeched and smoked as the vehicle zoomed erratically off the roadway. She was still doing eighty when she rammed into the front of a closed travel agency. Her front end sheared through glass and brick.

Bolan braked, too. The station wagon fish-tailed, but he brought it to a stop near the building, then leaped out. A choking cloud of dust and debris engulfed him. Hurrying to the huge jagged hole the sedan had punched in the wall, he saw the vehicle across the space, its frame buckled, its front and side panels resembling an accordion. The rear tires still spun madly.

Holding the revolver rifle at the ready, Bolan threaded past the ruined furniture and over a collapsed portion of ceiling to the driver's door. It was bent and hung half open, the bottom edge on the floor.

Bolan halted. There was no need for him to examine the woman. A beam had punctured the windshield and caught her full in the forehead. It had passed through the seat and ripped into her husband, burying itself into his body.

Having seen all he needed to, Bolan ran to the sidewalk. So many sirens were howling, it sounded as if a pack of wolves were loose in the city.

The black limo pulled up, and the front passenger door was thrown open. "Sir, get in!" the Fed said urgently. "Mr. Brognola needs to speak to you!"

As they roared up the ramp onto the parkway, Bolan leaned back to catch his breath and accepted the cellular phone the driver handed him. "Hal?"

"Bring me up to speed, Striker."

Bolan did. "We're no closer to laying our hands on the Golden Jihad than when I saw you last," he finished.

"Maybe, maybe not. My computer people have come up with another property possibly owned by Mehmet Akbar."

"Don't you think we need something more concrete? We're down to the wire on this one."

"I know, but this is the best they can do." Brognola sounded as tired as Bolan felt. "Remember that no one has ever made this extensive a search of D.C. real-estate records before. They're coming up with all sorts of leads that turn out to be dead ends."

"So what's the address?"

It was in the vicinity of Georgetown University. Bolan had reloaded the revolver rifle, attached the Leupold scope and the image intensifier by the time the federal agent cruised onto a quiet street lined with town houses and trees.

Bolan rubbed his eyes. After so many hours of being on the go with hardly any sleep, fatigue was making itself felt. He was in superb physical shape, but even his highly conditioned body had its limits.

"According to the building numbers, the one you want is the third one up on your side," the Fed said.

The Executioner looked. In a twinkling his exhaustion evaporated. Out of the town house walked four men. In their lead was a man whose every feature Bolan had committed to memory when the whole Golden Jihad business had begun.

It was Ahmed Tufayli.

THE TERRORIST LEADER was in the blackest mood. Something had gone terribly wrong, and he didn't know why. Manhattan hadn't gone up in a nuclear firecloud. There had been no word from his lieutenant, Hassan Nidal, or any of the men in Nidal's cell.

There could only be one explanation. The Americans had taken Nidal into custody, or killed him, and retrieved the other SADM device.

It seemed as if all of his carefully plotted strategy was unraveling at the seams. But he wasn't about to give up. Defeat wasn't in his vocabulary. He still had one backpack nuke. It was up to him to snatch victory from ruin, to carry out his master plan, no matter what the cost.

Yahia, Jibril and Emir flanked him, each carrying an Uzi under his jacket. Pistols and grenades were added insurance that anyone who dared interfere would pay dearly.

A black limousine drove past and turned left at the next corner. Tufayli regarded it with disgust. No other people on the globe were as fond of luxury as Americans. They wallowed in it, like pigs at a feed trough. While a third of the world went to bed hungry every night, Americans bloated their bellies on their excess. Truly, every last one deserved to be exterminated.

The night was warm. He unzipped his jacket, then adjusted the straps to the special backpack holding the nuke. The damn thing was much too heavy. It astounded him that the sergeant had been able to lug two of the devices to the rendezvous point down in South Carolina. The man had to have been as strong as a bull.

They hurried past the intersection. Tufayli looked down the side street but didn't see any sign of the limo. He felt a tiny prick of alarm. There hadn't been time for it to go very far.

Then he noticed an alley halfway down the block. He couldn't be sure, but he thought he saw the faint reddish glow of brake lights reflected on the far wall. That was strange. Why would a limo have pulled in there?

There might be a perfectly logical explanation, but Ahmed Tufayli wasn't taking any chances. Not now, when he was so close to having at least half of his master plan bear fruit. At the next corner he turned right, then stopped abruptly.

"I think someone might be after us," he announced. "Yahia, you will go on with me to the target. Emir and Jibril, you hang back to cover us. If no one suspicious appears, meet us at the site."

"And if someone does?" Emir asked.

"That is a stupid question. Kill them."

Jibril patted the Uzi under his jacket. "You can count on us."

CHAPTER TWENTY-TWO

The Executioner slid from the limo. Only then did he notice that they hadn't pulled very far into the alley. They were much too close to the street, but it was too late to do anything.

"Any orders, sir?" the driver asked.

"Contact Hal. Tell him to send in a backup team and have it stand by in case something happens to me."

"Will do." The agent paused, then said hopefully, "I could go with you, sir, if you'd like."

Bolan appreciated the offer, but in a critical situation like this one, he preferred to work alone. It reduced the odds of a fatal mistake being made. "Thanks, but no. If they spot me, they won't think much of one guy taking a stroll. Two of us might make them nervous, and we don't want that."

Quietly closing the door, Bolan slipped the Ruger Redhawk under his trench coat and moved to the mouth of the alley. The terrorists had already passed the intersection, but their shadows played over the corner building. He stayed where he was until the shadows faded, then stalked them.

Bolan knew there was no margin for error this time. He had to get close enough to drop the four terrorists in one fell swoop.

Besides, the Jihad still had the nuke with them. Strapped to Ahmed Tufayli's back was a bulging double-sized blue backpack, exactly like the one Hassan Nidal had worn in New York City.

Bolan reached the corner. The Jihad members were just going around the next one farther down. None of them looked back.

Shoving his free hand into his pocket, Bolan followed at a slow pace. Too many pedestrians were abroad to suit him. It would be better if he cornered the terrorists somewhere secluded, if possible.

When he turned right, Bolan spied vague figures a block and a half away. For some reason, they'd picked up the pace. Bolan did the same. He covered another block, getting close enough to see that there were only two terrorists up ahead, Tufayli and one other.

Instantly Bolan ducked into a doorway. He scanned the street behind him. Across the way a man was walking a dog. Much further off a woman hurried along carrying a shopping bag. The two missing terrorists were nowhere around. It was as if they had been swallowed up by the night.

But the Executioner knew better. Tufayli wouldn't split the cell without good reason, and what better reason than to have them fall back to make sure the Jihad wasn't being followed?

Bolan scoured the block. Every doorway, nook and cranny, merited attention. None revealed the two fanatics.

He realized it wasn't safe for him to venture into the open again, but he couldn't stay there indefinitely. Tufayli's lead increased with each passing second. If Bolan wasn't careful, the man would get away. Although his every instinct screamed against it, the soldier stepped to the sidewalk and kept on going. He stayed close to the buildings where the shadows were darkest. No shots rang out, but he could feel unseen eyes on him. The pair was waiting for the right moment to close in.

It soon became apparent that Tufayli was headed in the general direction of the Mall, which made sense. He would have his pick of the U.S. Capitol building, the White House, the Justice Department building and a dozen other prominent targets, or he might simply plant the nuke behind a tree somewhere. Either way, the heart of Washington—the very heart of the nation itself—would go up in a roiling, blazing mushroom cloud.

Bolan went faster. The terrorist leader and his companion were almost out of sight. He dared not lose them.

Georgetown was left behind. His adversaries angled more to the south, passing the Watergate Complex. They cut between it and the John F. Kennedy Center for the Performing Arts. Passing behind the Kennedy Center, they came to a strip of tree-lined park that bordered the Potomac.

Bolan took advantage of the trees to narrow their lead. Soon he was close enough for a clear shot. Halting behind a maple, he braced the Knight Revolver Rifle against the trunk and peered through the scope. Thanks to the image intensifier, the dark was made as bright as day.

He took deliberate aim at Ahmed Tufayli, but he found that the top of the backpack prevented him from centering the sight on Tufayli's head. He could core the other man's brain with no problem, but it was Tufayli he had to drop first. He had the nuke.

A different angle would do the trick. Lowering the weapon, Bolan angled to the left to try for a side shot. He swiftly covered twenty-five yards. Pausing at another tree, he took aim again. Through the night scope he could see a patch of skin below Tufayli's left ear. He put his finger to the trigger.

Just then the night rocked with autofire. Slugs chewed into the trunk above Bolan, sending wood slivers flying every which way. He dropped to his knees and pivoted.

At last the pair of fanatics had shown themselves. They rushed him, firing their Uzis on the fly, weaving so they would be hard to hit.

Bolan tracked the man on the right and applied his finger to the trigger. He intended it to be a chest shot, but the terrorist changed direction just as Bolan fired.

The round caught the man high on the arm, half spinning him. He hit the turf and rolled, gaining the shelter of a thick tree trunk.

At the same time, the second terrorist also sought cover. With the opposition gone to ground, Bolan ducked behind the maple. He couldn't move on until he disposed of them. It had to be done quickly or their leader would have time to plant the SADM.

Up ahead, Tufayli halted. He put a hand on Yahia's shoulder. "We are almost there. You must buy me time in case Emir and Jibril fail."

Yahia squared his shoulders. "I will not let you down. Whoever is after us will not get past me."

Nodding, Tufayli jogged off. The straps of the backpack chafed his shoulder blades, but he didn't stop to adjust it. Only one thing mattered now—arming the nuke before the Americans caught him.

Soon the green belt broadened. To Tufayli's right reared the Lincoln Memorial. Off to his left stood the Vietnam Veterans Memorial. Ignoring both, he crossed Henry Bacon Drive and reached the west end of the Reflecting Pool. To the east towered his goal. "All I need are five more minutes," he said aloud to himself, and hurried on.

Back among the trees, the Executioner was on his stomach, worming toward a different trunk. Precious seconds were ticking by. He'd lost sight of Tufayli, and unless he resumed the chase soon, posterity would remember this night forever.

The metallic chatter of an Uzi warned Bolan that the terrorists had fanned out. One was now in front of him, near the Potomac. The wounded man was to the north.

Pressing an eye to the scope, the soldier hunted for his attackers. The image intensifier made everything stand out in stark relief. At first he saw no trace of the terrorists. Then something moved, low to the ground, and he spied one of them crawling southward, almost at the river's edge. The shooter was attempting to outflank him.

Bolan steadied the revolver rifle. He fixed the cross hairs on the prone figure but held his fire, waiting for a better shot. It came when a bush barred the man's path and he rose on his hands and knees to go around it.

The Executioner went for a lung shot. At a distance of more than ninety feet he put a bullet into the man's ribs, just under his left arm.

The terrorist was flipped over by the jolting impact. Pushing up onto his knees, he looked down at himself in stunned amazement.

Bolan could guess why. There'd been no gun blast, no warning at all. He aimed at the top of the man's nose and fired just as the terrorist lurched upward. The slug ripped into the killer's mouth, blowing out a chunk of his lower jaw as well as the back of his head.

Even as the first man dropped, the other terrorist cut loose. A glint of moonlight on the image intensifier or the sound suppressor had to have given away Bolan's position because the terrorist almost drilled him. Lead death seekers made mincemeat of the earth around him and the tree next to him. He started to pull back out of sight when there were four loud pings and the Knight Revolver Rifle was wrenched from his grip.

Snagging the buttstock, Bolan pulled the weapon into his lap as he sat up with his back to the maple. He examined it. A round had sheared into the image intensifier, shattered part of the Leupold scope, dug a furrow in the suppressor and punched a hole in the polyurethane forearm.

Bolan leaned the revolver rifle against the tree and drew the Beretta. He would come back for the Ruger later, after he'd recovered the SADM.

First, he had another problem to deal with. The wounded terrorist was out there somewhere, jockeying for advantage. Without Bolan's having the night-vision device, they were on equal footing. He had to rely on his skill and wits.

Exploding into a sprint, the soldier weaved among the trees. His adversary's Uzi thundered, chipping boles and branches. Bolan's glance revealed a silhouette framed against the pale backdrop of the Kennedy Center in the distance.

Stopping and whirling, the Executioner pegged the figure dead-on with four swift shots. He was in motion before the body touched the grass.

Locking his night scope, Bolan knew it would be harder for him to locate Tufayli. There were lights on the Mall, but most were in the vicinity of the memorials and various landmarks.

Bolan crossed Henry Bacon Drive, slanting toward the Lincoln Memorial. Many tourists and locals were still around, and a knot of them, alarmed by all the gunfire, had formed close to the monument.

Nowhere among them was a man hefting a large blue backpack.

Bolan kept the Beretta out of sight. Nearing the Reflective Pool, he slowed and surveyed the Mall. North of it were the Constitution Gardens, south, the D.C. War Memorial and Independence Avenue. To the northeast, the White House was ablaze with light and activity. A function was taking place.

Where would Tufayli set the bomb? Bolan asked himself. He was running out of time in more ways than one.

Trying to predict what the fanatic would do seemed hopeless. Tufayli had a knack for picking national landmarks as his targets, but the capital was crammed with them. How in the world was Bolan to guess which one the man had chosen?

Bolan stiffened. The Washington Monument was straight ahead. As landmarks went, it had few equals. Proudly dedicated to the man known as the Father of His Country, it was safe to say that more Americans knew about it than about any other landmark.

For a madman like Ahmed Tufayli, it was perfect. Having the Monument at ground zero for the nuclear blast would send a clear message to the entire world. It would be a brilliant propaganda statement, as well as a sound tactical move.

Bolan ran, pumping his arms, no longer caring if anyone noticed the Beretta. To his right the Reflective Pool shimmered, as peaceful as the city that could at any moment suffer the worst fate known to man. He flew past a couple holding hands on a bench.

Ahead was another bench, occupied by a man who sat with his back half to the Executioner. As Bolan drew near, the man suddenly jumped up, spun and opened fire with an Uzi.

Ahmed Tufayli heard the burst. Crouched in shadows near the Washington Monument, his fingers flew as he went through the arming initiation sequence exactly as Sergeant Anderson had shown him. He shut everything else from his mind except getting the job done. If Yahia held the Americans off, so be it. If not, that was all right with him, too. In less than a minute it would be too late for them to do anything. He smiled.

Not far off, Mack Bolan had nothing to smile about. As the Uzi blistered the air, he dived, landing near the edge of the Reflective Pool. Leaden wasps stung the earth around him. Raising the Beretta, he emptied the clip.

The terrorist tottered back into the bench, momentum carrying him over it in an ungainly tumble.

People nearby began to scream and flee the vicinity.

Bolan thought he'd nailed the gunner and started to rise. When he shot someone, he usually stayed down, but not this one. The man rolled toward the Reflecting Pool, extended the Uzi under the bench and cut loose.

The soldier threw himself to the left, away from the water. Tiny geysers spouted where he'd lain. With the Beretta empty, he resorted to the Desert Eagle, unlimbering it in a flawless draw that ended with solid target acquisition and his finger pressing the trigger.

Each booming retort jerked the terrorist backward. The man took three slugs full in the chest. The third snapped him onto his back, and he lay there convulsing. With his dying breath he fired the Uzi one last time, the shots zinging wild into the sky.

Bolan shoved the Beretta into his shoulder holster as he rose. He lingered just long enough to confirm the kill, then he took off, racing past stunned people who scattered before him. He flew past the end of the Reflective Pool, skirted the pond beyond, and barreled across the street.

The Washington Monument loomed before him, all five hundred and fifty-five feet of it. The sightseers at its base broke for cover when they saw Bolan armed with his Desert Eagle. Stopping, he scanned the immediate area. Tufayli wasn't there.

Had he guessed wrong?

Tiny blinking lights north of the Monument drew Bolan like a magnet. He covered thirty feet, and there it was, fully assembled, primed and armed. As black as sin, except for the digital displays and the code controls, the SADM was counting down the minutes until detonation.

The terrorist leader had obviously taken off to save his own hide. Bolan stepped closer to read the detonation time clock. He figured that Tufayli had done the same as Hassan Nidal in New York, and there would be an hour or two, if not more, until the bomb went off. Plenty of time for him to disarm it.

Bolan glanced down, and every cell in his body seemed to turn to ice. He blinked, unwilling to believe his own eyes. The display revealed there was only one minute and fourteen seconds until the nuclear explosion took place.

He dropped to his knees, letting the Desert Eagle fall. It was impossible to disarm the Gun nuke in that amount of time. Even setting the self-destruct mechanism took at least two minutes. But he had to try. The lives of countless thousands were depending on him.

As he bent to the control panel, he heard someone bearing down on him like an express train. He whirled just as Ahmed Tufayli slammed into him, knocking him away from the backpack nuke.

Tufayli was beside himself with rage. Realizing his enemies could find the nuke before it went off if he allowed himself a margin of safety, he had decided to go out in style, to die a martyr to the cause. He'd set the detonation time clock for a mere two minutes.

Tufayli wasn't going to allow anyone or anything to stop the blast from taking place. He'd melted into the shadows to keep watch on the SADM, and it was well he had.

Now Tufayli drove an uppercut at Bolan's jaw, but the soldier, twisting, evaded it. The Executioner pivoted, drove a fist into the terrorist's gut that made Tufayli double over, then smashed an elbow into the fanatic's temple that dropped the man where he stood.

Bolan sprang to the backpack nuke. Less than forty seconds remained. Again he reached for the controls but a brawny arm looped around his throat and he was roughly hauled backward.

"No, you don't, scum!" Tufayli screamed.

The soldier grabbed Tufayli's forearm, shifted and executed a shoulder toss. The fanatic went flying. Bolan whirled. Thirty-two seconds were left. There was no way he could stop the detonation now.

Like a pouncing panther, Tufayli leaped on Bolan once more. Grappling, they moved to the right. The soldier shook the terrorist off and blocked a hand slash aimed at his throat. Tufayli stooped, seized the Executioner by the ankles and brought him crashing down. In falling, Bolan's right hand made contact with a familiar object.

Tufayli's eyes widened when he saw the Desert Eagle. A cannonball cored his chest, and he fell.

The end was near. Just how near was clear when Bolan faced the nuke. He watched the clock tick down from three seconds, to two, to one. A row of zeros appeared. Bolan braced for the last sensation he would ever feel, that of burning, searing annihilation.

Nothing happened.

Bolan studied the controls. It took a few seconds for him to understand why he was still alive, and when he did, he began to grin. It meant he'd never been in any danger of the nuke in New York going off. The terrorists had been beaten before they ever set the timers.

Behind him a weak voice called out. "American! I must know! Why hasn't the bomb gone off?"

The Executioner gazed down on the man who'd yearned to bring America to its knees. Tufayli was fading fast, a pool of blood spreading around him. "You forgot to press the detonation time clock lock."

"The what?" he said. "That dog Anderson never told us about any..." He broke off, dumbfounded, and died.

Bolan slowly straightened. Sergeant Anderson had done terribly wrong in stealing the nukes, but he'd redeemed himself in the end by proving true to his oath of allegiance.

The Executioner glanced toward the White House, sparkling with light.

It felt good to be alive.

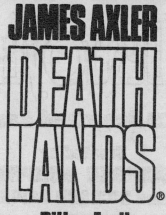

Killer rays from space threaten
to cook America's goose....

THE Destroyer

#105 Scorched Earth

Created by
WARREN MURPHY
and RICHARD SAPIR

A single superheated zap from an invisible object in space
literally vaporizes the Biobubble habitat scientists. More
sizzling attacks are followed by eyewitness sightings of
giant Cyrillic letters in the sky.

Look for it in December, wherever Gold Eagle books are sold.